Broken Prince

The Royals Series by Erin Watt

✦ ✦ ✦

Paper Princess
Broken Prince
Twisted Palace
Fallen Heir
Cracked Kingdom

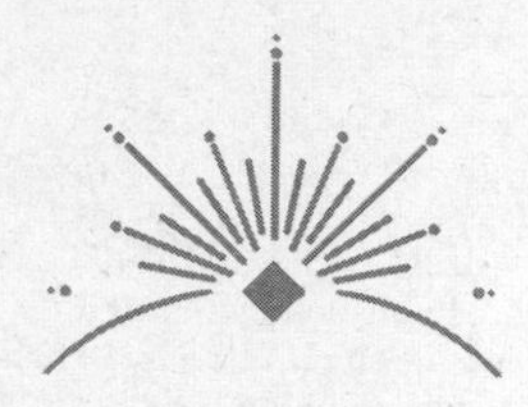

Broken Prince

ERIN WATT

Berkley Romance
New York

BERKLEY ROMANCE
Published by Berkley
An imprint of Penguin Random House LLC
penguinrandomhouse.com

Library of Congress Cataloging-in-Publication Data

Names: Watt, Erin, author.
Title: Broken prince / Erin Watt.
Description: Berkley Romance trade paperback edition. |
New York: Berkley Romance, 2023. | Series: The Royals
Identifiers: LCCN 2023025960 (print) | LCCN 2023025961 (ebook) |
ISBN 9780593642153 (trade paperback) | ISBN 9780593642160 (ebook)
Subjects: CYAC: Wealth—Fiction. | Love—Fiction. |
LCGFT: Romance fiction. | Domestic fiction. | Novels.
Classification: LCC PZ7.1.W4165 Br 2023 (print) |
LCC PZ7.1.W4165 (ebook) | DDC [Fic]—dc23
LC record available at https://lccn.loc.gov/2023025960
LC ebook record available at https://lccn.loc.gov/2023025961

Broken Prince was originally self-published, in different form, in 2016

Berkley Romance trade paperback edition / October 2023

Printed in the United States of America
1st Printing

Book design by Alison Cnockaert

To the fans who love this series as much as we do

Broken Prince

One

REED

THE HOUSE IS dark and silent when I let myself in through the mudroom off the kitchen. Nearly ten thousand square feet and no one is here. A grin splits my face. With my brothers scattered, the housekeeper gone, and my dad off who knows where, that means my girl and I have the Royal mansion all to ourselves.

Hell yeah.

I break into a light jog as I cross the kitchen and climb the back stairs. Hopefully Ella is waiting for me upstairs in her bed, looking all cute and sexy in one of my old T-shirts she's taken to sleeping in. It would be even better if that was *all* she was wearing . . . I speed up, bypassing my room, Easton's room, and Gid's old room until I'm outside Ella's door, which is disappointingly closed. A quick knock gets me no response. Frowning, I fish my phone out of my back pocket and shoot off a quick text.

Where RU, babe

She doesn't answer. I tap my phone against my leg. She's probably out with her friend Valerie tonight, which is kind of good, actually, because I could use a shower before I see her. The boys were smoking a shit ton of weed over at Wade's place tonight, and I don't want to stink up Ella's room.

New plan. Shower, shave, and then hunt my girl down. I pull off my T-shirt, wad it up in my hand, and shove open my bedroom door without bothering to turn on the light. I kick off my shoes and cross the carpet to my attached bath.

I smell her before I see her.

What the . . . ?

With the sickening scent of roses clinging to my nostrils, I swing toward the bed. "No way," I growl when I make out the shadowy figure on the mattress.

As a jolt of annoyance rips up my spine, I march back to the doorway and flick the light switch. Then I instantly regret it, because the pale yellow glow that fills the room reveals the naked curves of a woman I want nothing to do with.

"What the *hell* are you doing here?" I snap at my father's ex-girlfriend.

Brooke Davidson offers a coy smile. "I've missed you."

My jaw falls open. Is she fucking serious right now? I quickly swing my head out in the hall to make sure Ella's still gone. Then I head straight for the bed.

"Get out," I growl, grabbing one of her wrists to pull her off my bed. Shit, now I'm going to have to change the sheets, because if there's anything that stinks worse than old beer and weed, it's Brooke Davidson.

"Why? You never complained before." She licks her red lips in a way that I'm sure is supposed to look sexy, but that I find stomach turning. There're a lot of skeletons in my past that Ella doesn't know about. A lot that would make her downright sick. And the woman in front of me is one of them.

"I distinctly remember telling you that I never wanted to touch your skank ass again."

Brooke's smug smile turns thin. "And I told you not to talk to me like that."

"I'll talk to you however I want," I spit out. I cast another glance at the door. Desperation is starting to make me sweat. Brooke can't be here when Ella comes home.

How the hell would I begin to explain this? My eyes fall on Brooke's clothes strewn across my floor—the skimpy minidress, the lacy underwear, a pair of stilettos.

My shoes happened to land by hers. This all looks like a hot mess.

I grab Brooke's heels off the floor and toss them at the bed. "Whatever you're selling, I'm not buying. Get the fuck out."

She throws the shoes back. One of the heels scratches my bare chest before they fall to the floor. "Make me."

I squeeze the back of my neck. Short of forcibly picking her up and tossing her out, I'm not sure what my options are. What the hell would I say now if Ella caught me hauling Brooke out of my bedroom?

Hey, baby, don't mind me. I'm taking out the trash. See, I slept with my dad's girlfriend a couple times, and now that they've broken up, I think she wants back in my pants. That's not sick or anything, right? Cue awkward chuckle.

I clench my fists to my side. Gideon always told me I was self-destructive, but man, this is self-destruction on a whole new level. *I* did this. I let my anger toward my father drive me into bed with this woman. I told myself that after what he did to Mom, he deserved to have me screw his girlfriend behind his back.

Well, the joke's on me.

"Get your clothes on," I hiss out. "This conversation is over—" I halt at the sound of footsteps in the hall.

I hear my name called.

Brooke's head tilts. She hears it, too.

Oh fuck. Oh fuck. Oh *fuck*.

Ella's voice is right outside my door.

"Oh goodie, Ella's home," Brooke says as my blood pumps unsteadily in my ears. "I have some news I can share with both of you."

It's probably the dumbest thing I could ever do, but the only thought running through my mind is *fix this*. I need this woman *gone*.

So I drop everything and charge forward. I grab Brooke's arm to haul her off the mattress, but the bitch yanks me down. I try to avoid making contact with her naked body but end up losing my balance. She takes advantage and pushes herself up against my back. A soft laugh puffs in my ear as her store-bought tits burn against my skin.

I watch in panic as the doorknob turns.

Brooke whispers, "I'm pregnant and the baby is yours."

What?

My entire world lurches to a stop.

The door swings open. Ella's gorgeous face takes in mine. I watch her expression turn from joy to shock.

"Reed?"

I'm frozen in place, but my brain is working overtime, frantically trying to calculate the last time Brooke and I were together. It was St. Paddy's Day. Gid and I were hanging out by the pool. He got drunk. I got drunk. He was beyond upset about something. Dad, Sav, Dinah, Steve. I didn't understand it all.

I vaguely register the sound of Brooke giggling. I see Ella's face, but I'm not really seeing it. I should say something, but I don't. I'm busy. Busy panicking. Busy thinking.

St. Paddy's Day . . . I'd stumbled upstairs and crashed and woke up to wet, hot suction around my dick. I knew it wasn't Abby, because I'd already broken it off with her and she wasn't the type to creep into my bedroom anyway. And who am I to turn away a free BJ?

Ella's mouth falls open and she says something. I can't hear it. I'm caught in a tailspin of guilt and self-loathing, and I can't pull myself out of it. All I can do is stare at her. My girl. The most beautiful girl ever. I can't turn away from all that golden hair, those big blue eyes pleading at me to explain myself.

Say something, I order my uncooperative vocal cords.

My lips won't move. I feel a cold touch against my neck and flinch.

Say something, dammit. Don't let her walk away—

Too late. Ella flies out the door.

The loud slamming snaps me out of it. Sort of. I still can't move. I can barely breathe.

St. Paddy's Day . . . That was more than six months ago. I don't know much about pregnant women, but Brooke's barely got anything going on. There's no way.

No. Way.

No. Way. That. Baby. Is. Mine.

I shoot off the bed, ignoring the wild trembling of my hands as I lunge for the door.

"Really?" comes Brooke's amused voice. "You're going after her? How will you explain this to her, sweetie?"

I spin around in fury. "Swear to God, woman, if you don't get the hell out of my room, I'm throwing you out." Dad has always said that a man who raises a hand against a female lowers himself beneath her feet. So I've never hit a woman. Never had the urge to until I met Brooke Davidson.

She ignores the threat. Continues to taunt me, spelling out all my fears. "What lies will you tell her? That you never touched me? That you never wanted me? How do you think that girl will respond when she finds out you screwed your daddy's girlfriend? Do you think she'll still want you?"

I glance toward the now-empty doorway. I can hear muffled sounds coming from Ella's bedroom. I want to sprint across the hall, but I can't. Not when Brooke is still in this house. What if she runs out there, butt-ass naked, saying that she's pregnant with my kid? How do I explain that to Ella? How do I get her to believe me? Brooke needs to be gone before I face Ella.

"Get out." I turn all my frustrations on Brooke.

"Don't you want to know the sex of the baby first?"

"No. I don't." I take in her slender, naked body and see a slight mound on her belly. Bile fills my mouth. Brooke's not the type to get fat. Her looks are her only weapon. She's not lying about being pregnant.

But that kid isn't mine.

It might be my dad's, but it sure as hell is *not* mine.

I wrench the door open and run out. "Ella," I call. I don't know what I'll say to her, but it's better than saying nothing. I'm still cursing myself for freezing up like that. God, what a fuckup I am.

I skid to a stop outside her bedroom door. A quick survey nets me nothing. Then I hear it—the low, throaty sound of a sports-car engine being revved. With a burst of panic, I sprint down the front stairs, while Brooke cackles behind me like a witch on Halloween.

I lunge at the front door, forgetting it's locked, and by the time I get it open, there's no sign of Ella outside. She must've raced down the driveway going at Mach speed. Shit.

The stones under my feet remind me I'm wearing jeans and nothing else. Spinning on my heel, I take the stairs three at a time, only to grind to a halt when Brooke steps onto the landing.

"There's no way that's my baby," I snarl. If it was really mine, Brooke would've played this card a long time ago instead of holding it tight until now. "I doubt it's my dad's, either, or you wouldn't stripping down like a cheap whore in my room."

"It's whoever's I say it is," she says coldly.

"Where's your proof?"

"I don't need proof. It's my word against yours, and by the time any paternity tests arrive, I'll already have a ring on my finger."

"Good luck with that."

She grabs my arm when I try to brush past her. "I don't need luck. I have you."

"No. You never had me." I shake her grip off. "I'm leaving to find Ella. You stay here as long as you want, Brooke. I'm done playing your games."

Her frosty voice stops me before I can reach my bedroom. "If you get Callum to propose to me, I'll tell everyone the child is his. Don't help me, and everyone will believe the child is yours."

I pause in the doorway. "The DNA test will show it's not mine."

"Maybe," she chirps, "but DNA will show it belongs to a Royal. Those tests don't always differentiate between relatives, particularly fathers and sons. It'll be enough to put doubt in Ella's mind. So I'm asking you, Reed, do you want me to tell the world—tell *Ella*—that you're going to be a daddy? Because I will. Or you can agree to my terms, and no one will ever know."

I hesitate.

"Do we have a deal?"

I grit my teeth. "If I do this, if I sell this—this"—I struggle to find the right word—"idea to my dad on your behalf, you'll leave Ella alone?"

"Whatever do you mean?"

I turn slowly. "I mean, you bitch, that none of your bullshit ever touches Ella. You don't speak to her, not even to explain this—" I wave my hand at her now clothed body. "You smile, you say hi, but no heart-to-hearts."

I don't trust this woman, but if I can bargain for Ella—and, yes, for me—then I'll do it. Dad's made his rotten bed. He can roll around in that filth again.

"Deal. You work on your father, and you and Ella can have your happily ever after." Brooke laughs as she bends to pick up her shoes. "*If* you can win her back."

Two

TWO HOURS LATER, I'm freaking out. It's past midnight, and Ella isn't back.

Would she just come home and yell at me already? I need her to tell me that I'm an asshole who isn't worth her time. I need her in my face, spitting fire at me. I need her to scream at me, kick me, punch me.

I fucking need her.

✦ ✦ ✦

I CHECK MY phone. It's been hours since she left.

I punch in her number, but it rings and rings.

Another call and I'm shuttled to voicemail.

I text, Where RU

No response.

Dad's worried

I type out the lie hoping that it gets a response, but my phone remains silent. Maybe she's blocked my number? The thought stings, but it's not totally crazy, so I run inside and go up to my brother's room. Ella can't have blocked us all.

It's just past five a.m. and Easton's still sleeping, but his phone is charging on his nightstand. I flick it on and type out another message. She likes Easton. She paid off his debt. She'd answer Easton, wouldn't she?

Hey. Reed told me something happened. U OK

Nothing.

Maybe she parked down the road and is walking on the shore? I pocket my brother's phone in case she decides to contact him and hurry downstairs toward the back patio.

The shoreline is completely empty, so I jog down to the Worthington estate, a property four houses down. She's not there, either.

I look around, down the rocky shoreline, out into the ocean, and see nothing. No person. No imprints in the sand. Nothing.

Frustration gives way to panic as I race back to the house and climb into my Range Rover. Finger on the start button, I rapidly tap my fist against the dashboard. Think. Think. *Think.*

Valerie's. She must be at Valerie's.

In less than ten minutes, I'm idling outside of Val's house, but there's no sign of Ella's sporty blue convertible on the street. Leaving the Rover's engine running, I hop out and hurry up the driveway. Ella's car isn't back there, either.

I glance at my phone again. More time has elapsed than I realized but still, no messages. None on Easton's, either. The display tells me I have football practice in twenty minutes, which means Ella's expected at the bakery where she works.

We usually ride together. Even after she got her car—a gift from my dad—we rode together.

Ella said it was because she didn't like to drive. I told her it was dangerous to drive in the morning. We told each other lies. We lied to ourselves because neither of us was willing to admit the truth: we couldn't resist each other. At least that's the way it was for me. From the moment she walked in the door, all big eyes and guarded hope, I couldn't keep away.

My instincts had screamed at me that she was trouble. My instincts were wrong. She wasn't trouble. I was. Still am.

Reed the destroyer.

It'd be a cool nickname if it wasn't my life and hers that I'm taking down.

The bakery's parking lot is empty when I arrive. After five minutes of nonstop pounding on the door, the owner—Lucy, I think—appears with a frown.

"We don't open for another hour," she informs me.

"I'm Reed Royal, Ella's . . ." What am I? Her boyfriend? Her stepbrother? What? "Friend." Hell, I'm not even that. "Is she here? There's a family emergency."

"No, she hasn't shown up." Lucy's brow creases with worry. "I tried to contact her and she didn't answer. She's such a good employee, I thought maybe she was so sick she couldn't call."

My heart sinks. Ella's never missed a day at the bakery even though it requires her to get up at the ass-crack of dawn and work nearly three hours before classes start.

"Oh, okay, she must be home in bed," I mumble, backing away.

"Wait a minute," Lucy calls after me. "What's going on? Does your father know Ella is missing?"

"She's not missing, ma'am," I call back, already halfway to my car. "She's at home. Like you said, sick. In bed."

I peel out of the parking lot and call Coach. "I'm not gonna make it to practice. Family emergency," I repeat.

I shut out the shouted expletives from Coach Lewis. He winds down after a few minutes. "All right, son. But I expect your ass to be in uniform bright and early tomorrow."

"Yessir."

Back home once again, I find our housekeeper, Sandra, has arrived to make breakfast.

"You see Ella?" I ask the plump brunette.

"Can't say that I have." Sandra checks the clock. "She's usually gone by now. So are you, for that matter. What's going on? Don't you have practice?"

"Coach had a family emergency," I lie. I'm so damn good at lying. It becomes almost second nature when you hide the truth every hour of every day.

Sandra tsks. "Hope it's nothing too serious."

"Me, too," I answer. "Me, too."

Upstairs, I enter the room I should have checked before racing off. Maybe she crept in while I was trying to find her. But Ella's bedroom is dead silent. Her bed is still made. The desk is spotless.

I check her bathroom, which also looks untouched. Ditto with the closet. All her stuff is hanging on matching wooden hangers. Her shoes are lined up in a neat row on the floor. There are unopened boxes and bags still stuffed with clothes that Brooke probably picked out for her.

Forcing myself not to feel bad about invading her privacy, I dig through her nightstand—empty. I flipped her room once, back when I still didn't trust her, and she always kept a book of poetry and a man's watch in the nightstand. The watch was an exact replica of my dad's. Hers had belonged to Dad's best friend Steve, Ella's bio-dad.

I pause in the middle of the room and look around. There's nothing here to indicate her presence. Not her phone. Not her book. Not her . . . Oh hell no, her backpack is gone.

I tear out of the room and down the hall to Easton's.

"East, wake up. East!" I say sharply.

"What?" He groans. "Is it time to get up?" His eyes flicker open and he squints. "Oh shit. I'm late for practice. Why aren't you there already?"

He shoots out of bed, but I grab his arm before he can dart off. "We're not going to practice. Coach knows."

"What? Why—"

"Forget that right now. How much was your debt?"

"My what?"

"How much did you owe the bookie?"

He blinks at me. "Eight grand. Why?"

I do some quick math. "That means Ella's got about two G's left, right?"

"Ella?" He frowns. "What about her?"

"I think she ran."

"Ran where?"

"Ran away. Ran off," I growl. I shove away from the bed and stalk to the window. "Dad paid her to stay here. Gave her ten grand. Think about it, East. He had to pay this orphan who was stripping for a living ten grand to come live with us. And he was probably gonna pay that to her every month."

"Why'd she leave?" he asks in confusion, still half-asleep.

I continue to stare out the window. Once his grogginess wears off, he'll put it together.

"What did you do?"

Yep, here we go.

The floor creaks as he whips around the room. Behind me I can hear him muttering curses under his breath while he dresses.

"Doesn't matter," I say impatiently. Turning back, I give him the rundown of the places I've been. "Where do you think she is?"

"She's got enough for a plane ticket."

"But she's careful with her money. She hasn't spent hardly any of it while she's been here."

Easton nods thoughtfully. Then we lock eyes and speak in unison, almost as if we're the twins of the Royal household, instead of our brothers, Sawyer and Sebastian. "GPS."

We call the GPS service Atlantic Aviation owns and that my dad installs in every car he's ever bought. The helpful assistant tells us that the new Audi S5 is parked at the bus station.

We're out the door before she even starts to recite the address.

✦ ✦ ✦

"SHE'S SEVENTEEN. ABOUT this tall." I hold my hand beneath my chin as I describe Ella to the ticket clerk. "Blond hair. Blue eyes." Eyes like the Atlantic. Stormy gray, cool blue, fathoms deep. I got lost in that gaze more than once. "She left her phone behind." I hold up my cell. "We need to get it to her."

The ticket clerk clicks her tongue. "Oh sure. She was in such a hurry to get away. She bought a ticket to Gainesville. Her grandmother died, you know."

Both East and I nod. "What time did the bus leave?"

"Oh, hours ago. She'd be there by now." The ticket lady shakes her head in dismay. "She was crying like her heart had been broken. You don't see that anymore—kids caring about old folks like that. It was sweet. Felt terrible for her."

East clenches his fists beside me. Anger radiates off of him in waves. If we were alone, one of those fists would be in my face.

"Thanks, ma'am."

"No problem, dear." She dismisses us with a nod.

We exit the building and stop at Ella's car. I hold out my hand and Easton slaps her spare keys into my palm.

Inside, I find her key fob in the middle console, along with her poetry book and what looks like the title for the car stuck between the pages. In the glove compartment, she stashed her phone, which still shows all my unread text messages.

She left everything behind. Everything associated with the Royals.

"We gotta get to Gainesville," Easton says flatly.

"I know."

"Are we telling Dad?"

Informing Callum Royal means we could take his plane. We'd be there in an hour. Otherwise it's a six-and-a-half-hour drive.

"I don't know." The urgency to find her has lessened. I know where she is now. I can get to her. I just need to figure out what angle I should take.

"What'd you do?" my brother demands again.

I'm not ready for the wave of hatred he's going to send my way, so I stay quiet.

"Reed."

"She caught me with Brooke," I say hoarsely.

His jaw falls open. "Brooke? Dad's Brooke?"

"Yes." I force myself to face him.

"What the *hell*? How often have you been with Brooke?"

"A couple times," I admit. "Not recently, though. And definitely not last night. I didn't touch her, East."

His jaw clenches. He's dying to take a swing at me, but he won't. Not in public. He'd heard the same things from Mom. *Keep the Royal name clean, boys. It's easy to tear it down, so much harder to build it up.*

"You should be strung up by your nuts and hung out to dry." He spits at my feet. "If you don't find Ella and bring her back, I'll be first in line to see it done."

"That's fair." I try to stay calm. No point in getting upset. No point in tipping this car over. No point in roaring even though I'm dying to open my mouth and release all of my anger and self-loathing into the air.

"Fair?" He snorts with disgust. "So you don't give a shit that Ella's in some college town getting groped by drunks?"

"She's a survivor. I'm sure she's safe." The words sound so ridiculous I practically gag as they come out. Ella's a gorgeous girl, and she's all by herself. There's no telling what could happen to her. "You want to drive her car back home before we head to Gainesville?"

Easton gapes at me.

"Well?" I ask impatiently.

"Sure. Why not?" He rips the key fob from my hand. "I mean, who cares that she's a hot seventeen-year-old by herself, carrying almost two grand in cash?" My fingers curl into fists. "It's not like some junkie high on meth is gonna look at her and think, 'There's an easy mark. That five-foot-something chick who weighs less than my leg isn't gonna fight me off'"—it's becoming hard to breathe—"and I'm sure every dude she runs into has good intentions. None of them will drag her down a dark alley and run train on her until she's—"

"Shut the fuck up!" I roar.

"Finally." East throws up his hands.

"What do you mean?" I'm practically panting with rage. The pictures Easton painted with his words make me wish I could Hulk out and run to Gainesville, destroying everything in my path until I find her.

"You've been walking around like she's nothing to you. Maybe you're made of stone, but I like Ella. She . . . she was good for us." His grief is almost tangible.

"I know." The words are wrenched out of me. "I know, goddammit." My throat tightens to the point of pain. "But . . . *we* weren't good for her."

Gideon, our older brother, tried to tell me that from the beginning. *Stay the hell away from her. She doesn't need our kind of drama. Don't ruin her like I ruined—*

"What's that supposed to mean?"

"What it sounds like. We're poison, East. Every single one of us. I slept with Dad's girlfriend to get back at him for being a dick to Mom. The twins are involved in shit I don't even want to know about. Your gambling is out of control. Gideon is—" I stop. Gid's living in his own hellhole right now, but that's not something Easton needs to know about. "We're screwed in the head, man. Maybe she's better off without us."

"That's not true."

But I think it might be. We're no good for her. All Ella has ever wanted is to live a normal, regular life. She can't have that in the Royal household.

If I wasn't completely selfish, I'd walk away. I'd convince

East that the best thing for Ella is to be as far away from us as possible.

Instead, I stay quiet and think of what I'm going to say to her when we find her.

"Let's go. I have an idea." I pivot and head toward the entrance.

"I thought we were going to Gainesville," East mutters from behind me.

"This'll save us the drive."

We make a beeline for the security office, where I slip a hundred bucks to the rent-a-cop and he gives us access to the camera footage from Gainesville. The guy rewinds the tape to the moment the bus from Bayview pulls in, and my heart seizes up as I scan the passengers. Then it drops to my stomach when I realize that none of those passengers is Ella.

"What the hell," East blurts out as we leave the bus station ten minutes later. "The ticket lady said Ella was on that bus."

My jaw is so tight I can barely get a word out. "Maybe she got off at a different stop."

We trudge back to the Rover and slide in. "Now what?" he asks, his eyes narrowed menacingly at me.

I rake a hand through my hair. We could drive to every bus station on the route, but I suspect that'd be a wild-goose chase. Ella's smart, and she's used to running, used to skipping town at a moment's notice and making a new life for herself. She learned it from her mother.

Another queasy feeling twists my gut as a thought occurs to me. Is she going to get a job at another strip club? I know Ella will do whatever she needs to do to survive, but the thought of her taking her clothes off for a bunch of skeezy perverts makes my blood boil.

I have to find her. If something happened to her because I drove her away, I won't be able to live with myself.

"We go home," I announce.

My brother looks startled. "Why?"

"Dad has an investigator on retainer. He'll be able to find her a lot faster than we will."

"Dad's gonna lose his shit."

No kidding. And I'll deal with the fallout the best I can, but right now, finding Ella trumps everything.

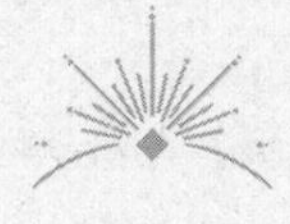

Three

AS EASTON PREDICTED, Dad is livid when we tell him Ella's missing. I haven't slept in over twenty-four hours and I'm exhausted, too exhausted to face off with him tonight.

"Why the *hell* didn't you call me earlier?" my father booms. He paces the massive living room in the mansion, his thousand-dollar wing tips slapping the gleaming hardwood floor.

"We figured we'd find her before it came down to that," I say tersely.

"I'm her legal guardian! I should have been informed." Dad's breathing grows labored. "What did you do, Reed?"

His furious gaze bores into me. He's not looking at East, or the twins, who are on the couch wearing identical looks of concern. I'm not surprised Dad's decided to lay the blame at my feet. He knows my brothers follow my lead, that the only Royal who could've driven Ella away is me.

I swallow. Shit. I don't want him to know that Ella and I got involved right under his nose. I want him to focus on finding her, not distract him with the news that his son is hooking up with his new ward.

"It wasn't Reed."

Easton's quiet confession shocks the hell out of me. I glance at my brother, but his eyes are on Dad.

"I'm the reason she's gone. We had a run-in with my bookie the other night—I owed him some cash—and Ella got spooked. This dude's not the friendliest guy, if you know what I mean."

The vein in Dad's forehead looks like it might burst. "Your *bookie*? You're mixed up in that shit again?"

"I'm sorry." Easton shrugs.

"You're sorry? You dragged Ella into one of your messes and scared her so badly that she ran away!"

Dad advances on my brother, and I immediately step into his path.

"East made a mistake," I say firmly, avoiding my brother's eyes. I'll thank him later for taking the heat. Right now, we need to calm the old man down. "But it's done, over with, all right? We should be concentrating on finding her."

Dad's shoulders drop. "You're right." He nods, his expression hardening. "I'll call my PI."

He storms out of the living room without another word, his heavy footsteps echoing in the corridor. A moment later, we hear his study door slam shut.

"East," I start.

He turns with a deadly look. "I didn't do it for you. I did it for her."

My throat tightens. "I know."

"If Dad knew about . . ." He trails off, warily glancing at the twins, who hadn't said a word during the entire exchange. "It would distract him."

"You think the PI will find Ella?" Sawyer asks.

"Yes," I answer with conviction I don't feel.

"If she uses her mom's ID, we can definitely find her," East assures our younger brother. "If she figures out how to get a fake ID . . ." His shoulders slump in defeat. "I don't know."

"She can't hide forever," Seb says helpfully.

Yeah, she can. She's the most resourceful person I've ever known. If Ella wants to stay hidden, then she will.

My phone buzzes in my pocket. I eagerly grab it, but it's not the person I want to hear from. Bile coats my throat when I see Brooke's name.

A little birdie told me your princess is missing

"Ella?" East says hopefully.

"Brooke." Her name burns my tongue.

"What does she want?"

"Nothing," I mutter, just as another message pops up.

Callum must be beside himself. Poor man. He needs someone to comfort him

I grit my teeth. She ain't subtle, that's for sure.

In our mad search for Ella, I haven't allowed myself to think about Brooke's pregnancy and the deal I struck with her last night. Now I can't ignore it, because the messages keep coming.

You have a job to do, Reed

You made a promise

Answer me, you little prick!

You want some baby mama drama? Is that it?

Jesus. I don't need this right now. I choke down my rage and force myself to respond. Relax. I'll talk to him

"What does she want?" Easton repeats angrily.

"Nothing," I say again. Then I leave him and the twins in the living room and drag myself to my father's study.

I don't want to do this. I really, really don't want to do this.

I knock on the door.

"What is it, Reed?"

"How did you know it's me?" I ask as I push the door open.

"Because with Gideon gone, you're the leader of your merry band of brothers." Dad throws back his tumbler full of Scotch while reaching for a refill. And I wonder why I can't get East off the bottle.

I heave a breath. "I think you should call Brooke."

Dad halts in the middle of stoppering the Scotch.

Yeah, you heard me, old man. And trust me, I'm as shocked as you are.

When he doesn't respond, I force myself to push forward. "When you bring Ella back, we're gonna need help. We need someone to provide a buffer." I gag on my next words. "A woman's touch, I guess. Ella was tight with her mom. Maybe if Brooke had been around more before, Ella wouldn't have left."

My father frowns at me. "I thought you hated Brooke."

"How many times do you want me to say I'm a dumbass?" I stretch a painful smile across my face.

He remains unconvinced. "She wants a ring and I'm not ready for that."

Thank God. I guess the booze hasn't erased *all* his good judgment.

"You don't have to marry her. Just . . ." I lick my lips. This is effing hard, but I press on because I made this deal. I can't have Brooke telling people that demon spawn is mine. "Just know it's cool if you bring her back. I get it. We need people to care about. Who care about us."

That much is true, at least. Ella's love made me believe that I could be a better person.

"That's generous of you," Dad says dryly. "And hell, maybe you're right." He fingers the full glass. "We'll find her, Reed."

"I hope so."

He gives me a tight smile and I back out of the room. As the door is closing, I hear him pick up the phone and say, "Brooke, it's Callum. Got a minute?"

I quickly send her a text.

It's done. Don't tell him about the baby. It'll just distract him

She sends me back a thumbs-up emoji. The thin metal casing bites into my fingers as I clench my phone, fighting back the urge to throw it at the wall.

Four

"REED." VALERIE CARRINGTON catches up to me on the back lawn, her chin-length hair blowing around in the crisp October wind. "Wait."

I reluctantly stop, turning to find a pair of dark eyes blazing up at me. Val is pixie-sized, but she's a commanding force. We could use someone with her bulldozer approach on our O-line.

"I'm late for practice," I mutter.

"I don't care." She crosses her arms. "You need to stop playing games with me. If you don't tell me what's going on with Ella, I swear to God I'm calling the police."

It's been two days since Ella took off and we still have no word from the PI. Dad's been forcing us to go to school as if everything is normal. He told the headmaster that Ella is home sick, which is the same thing I tell Val now. "She's home sick."

"Bull. *Shit.*"

"She is."

"Then why can't I see her? Why isn't she texting or returning my calls? It's not like she has cholera! It's the *flu*—there's a shot for that. And she should still be able to see her friends."

"Callum pretty much has her quarantined," I lie.

"I don't believe you," she says bluntly. "I think something's wrong, like seriously wrong, and if you don't tell me what it is, I'm going to kick you in the balls, Reed Royal."

"She's home sick," I repeat. "She's got the flu."

Valerie's jaw opens. Then closes. Then opens again to release an aggravated shriek. "You're such a liar."

She follows up on her threat, lunging forward to knee me in the balls.

Agonizing pain shoots through me. "Son of a *bitch*." My eyes water as I cup my junk.

Valerie stalks off without another word.

A loud hoot sounds from behind me. Still gripping my aching nuts, I groan as Wade Carlisle sidles up to me.

"What'd you do to deserve that?" he asks with a grin. "Turn her down?"

"Something like that."

He runs a hand through his messy blond hair. "You gonna be able to spot me, or should we go find some ice first?"

"I can spot you, asshole."

We head for the gym—I hobble and Wade cackles like an old man. The gym is reserved for the football team between three and six, which gives me three hours to work out until my body and mind completely shut down. And that's exactly what I do. I lift until my arms turn to jelly, pushing myself into a state of pure exhaustion.

Later that night, I go into Ella's room and lie on her bed. The scent of her skin grows fainter every time I enter. I know that's my fault, too. East popped his head in last night and said the room stunk of me.

The house stinks, all right. Brooke has been here every night since Ella took off, her hands on Dad and her eyes on me. From time to time, her palm lingers over her stomach as a warning that if I step out of line, she's going to bust out the pregnancy news. The baby must be Dad's, which means it's my half brother or sister, but I don't know what to do with that or how to process it other than that Brooke's here and Ella's not—and that's the perfect symbol for everything that's wrong in my world.

◆ ◆ ◆

THE NEXT DAY is more of the same.

I go through the motions, sitting in my classes without hearing a word the teachers say and then heading for the field to attend afternoon practice. Unfortunately it's just a walk-through so I don't get to hit anyone.

Tonight there's a home game against Devlin High, whose offensive line breaks apart like a cheap toy after every snap. I'll get to pummel their quarterback. I'll get to play myself numb. And when I get home, hopefully I'll be too drained to obsess over Ella.

Ella once asked me if I fought for money. I don't. I fight because I enjoy it. I like the feel of my fist in someone's face. I don't even mind the pain that blooms when someone else lands a punch. It feels real. But I never needed it. Never really needed anything before she came along. Now I'm finding it hard to breathe without her next to me.

I reach the back doors of the building just as a group of guys breeze out. One of them jostles my shoulder, then snaps, "Watch where you're going, Royal."

I tense up as I lock eyes with Daniel Delacorte, the creep who drugged Ella at a party last month.

"Nice to see you again, Delacorte," I drawl. "I'm surprised your rapist ass is still at Astor Park."

"You shouldn't be." He sneers. "After all, they let all kinds of scum in."

I don't know whether he's referring to me or Ella.

Before I can reply, a girl runs between us, her hands covering her face. Loud, choking sobs momentarily distract both Daniel and me, and we watch as she runs to a white Passat in the student lot and climbs inside.

He turns back to me with a smirk. "Isn't that the twins' girlfriend? What happened? Did they decide that they were tired of their toy?"

I swing around and take another glance at the girl, but it's definitely not Lauren Donovan. This one is blond and willowy. Lauren's a tiny redhead.

Turning back, I give Daniel a contemptuous look. "Don't know what you're talking about." The twins' relationship with Lauren is screwed up, but it's their business, and I'm not about to hand Delacorte any ammo over my brothers.

"Sure you don't." His lip curls. "You Royals are sick. The twins sharing. Easton slamming everything that moves. You and your dad dipping your wicks in the same pot. Do you and the old man compare notes about Ella? I bet you do."

I clench my fists at my side. Punching this douchebag's lights out might feel good, but his daddy is a district court judge and I suspect I'd have a harder time buying my way out of an assault charge backed by the Delacortes.

Last time I got in a fight at Astor, Dad threatened to ship the twins off to military school. We were able to smooth everything over because a few other kids were willing to swear that the other punk threw the first punch. I don't remember if he did or not. All I remember is him saying my mom was a drugged-out whore who offed herself to get away from me and my brothers. After that, all I saw was red.

"Oh, and I heard your daddy got little orphan Ella pregnant," Daniel crows, on a roll now. "Callum Royal, pedophile. Bet the board of directors of Atlantic Aviation love hearing that."

"You're gonna want to shut your trap," I warn.

I surge toward him, but Wade appears suddenly at my side and yanks me backward.

"What are you going to do, hit me?" Daniel taunts. "My dad's a judge, don't you remember? You'll be hauled into juvie so fast your head will spin."

"Your dad know that the only way you get any chicks is because you drug them?"

Wade shoves Daniel back. "Move on, Delacorte. No one wants you around."

Daniel is dumb as rocks because he doesn't listen. "You think he doesn't know? He's bought off chicks before. Your Ella won't talk, either, because her mouth is so full of Royal dick."

Wade's arm shoots out to bar my attack, and if it was only Wade, I would've been able to shrug him off. But two other guys from my team appear and grab Daniel, and even as he's dragged away, he still can't shut up. "Your control over this school is slipping, Royal! You won't be king here much longer."

As if I give a fuck about that.

"Get your head straight," Wade warns. "We've got a game tonight."

I jerk out of his hold. "That piece of shit tried to rape my girl."

Wade blinks. "Your girl . . . ? Wait, you mean your sister?" His jaw drops. "Aw man, you're dicking with your *sister*?"

"She's not my sister," I growl. "We're not even remotely related."

I push Wade off and watch with narrowed eyes as Daniel gets into his car. I guess the asshole didn't learn his lesson after Ella and a couple of her friends stripped him down and tied him up as revenge for what he did to Ella.

Next time we cross paths? He's not getting away that easy.

As Coach goes over some last-second changes with Wade, our QB, I methodically wrap one hand with tape and then the other. My pre-game ritual has been the same since I played Pop Warner ball, and usually the routine centers me, narrows my focus to only what's going down on the field.

Dress, tape, listen to some beats. Today it's Lil Uzi Vert telling me "I'm a winner, I can't lose."

Tonight, the ritual doesn't work. All I can think about is Ella. Alone. Hungry. Terrorized by men at a strip club or on the street. The scenes Easton described at the bus station keep replaying themselves over and over. Ella violated. Ella crying. Ella needing help and no one there to answer her.

"You still with us, Royal?" A sharp bark catches my attention and I look up into the annoyed face of my coach.

Across from me, East makes a winding motion with his finger. Time to finish wrapping up and go.

"Yessir."

We run down the short tunnel and onto the field behind polo-playing Gale Hardesty and his horse. It's a miracle none of us have stepped in horse shit during this circus routine.

I slap one taped fist into another. Easton joins me.

"Let's kill these motherfuckers."

"Absolutely."

We're in complete agreement. Neither of us can take out our aggression on one another, but the game here and a fight afterward? Maybe both of us can work ourselves into a livable state.

Devlin High wins the toss and elects to receive. Easton and I crack our helmets together and run out on defense.

"How much did you pay the refs tonight?" the tight end chirps as I line up across from him. He's a mouthy ass. I can't remember his name. Betme. Bettinski. Bettman? Whatever. I'll look at his jersey after I've smashed his ass into the turf on the way to his quarterback.

The ball snaps and Easton and I fly into the backfield. The tight end barely touches me, and East and I are there to greet the running back as he gets the handoff. I lower my head and drive my shoulder into his gut. The ball pops loose and the crowd releases a giant roar that extends long enough to let me know that someone from Astor Park is running it deep.

A teammate grabs me by my pads and hauls me to my feet as Easton crosses the goal line.

I look down at the running back and offer my hand. "Dude, heads up—East and I are in a piss-poor mood and we're gonna take it out on you tonight. Might want to spread the word."

The little guy's eyes widen in alarm.

Bettman shoulders his way over. "Lucky hit. Next time it'll be your ass on the turf."

I bare my teeth. "Bring it."

If I get enough hits in, maybe I'll be able to push Ella out of my mind for more than five seconds.

Wade slaps my helmet. "Nice tackle, Royal." He cheers when East comes off the field. "Going to let the offense on the field, Easton?"

"Why? We can do it all tonight. Besides, heard you might've pulled a groin muscle with a cheerleader from North High."

Wade grins. "She's a gymnast, not a cheerleader. But yeah, if you wanna score a few more times, it's good with me."

Over his shoulder I see Liam Hunter giving us the death glare. He wants as much time in the game as possible. It's his senior year and he needs the film.

Ordinarily I've got no problem with Hunter, but the way he's staring at me right now makes me want to take a swing at his square jaw. Damn. I need a fight.

I slam my helmet into my hand. On the field, Bettman keeps jawing, his mouth working when his blocks don't. I get into his face after one play, but East drags me away.

"Save it for after," he warns.

By halftime, we're up by four touchdowns—one more by the defense and the other two by the offense. Hunter got a couple of highlights for his college recruiting reel after pancaking a few D-line men. We're all supposed to be in good spirits.

Coach doesn't even give us a motivational speech. He walks around, delivers a few pats on the head, and then hides himself in his office to tinker with his fantasy lineup, smoke, or jack off.

As the guys start chattering about the post-game party and whose pussy they're going to destroy, I pull out my phone.

Fight 2nite? I text.

I glance up at East and mouth, *You in?*

He nods emphatically. I toss the phone between my hands and wait for a response.

Fight @ 11. Dock 10. E in?

E's in.

Coach comes out of his office and signals that halftime is over. After the offense scores again, we're told that this will be the last set of downs for the starting squad. Which means I have to sit for the rest of the third quarter and all of the fourth. This sucks balls.

By the time I line up across from Bettman, the trigger on my temper is about a centimeter long. I dig my hand into the artificial turf and test the bounce in my legs.

"Hear your new sister is so loose it takes two of you Royals to fill her."

I snap. Red washes over my eyes and I'm on that jackass before he can pull his hand off the ground. I rip his helmet off and swing with my right fist. The cartilage and bone on his nose give way. Bettman cries out. I punch him again. A mob of hands haul me away before I can land another hit.

The ref blows a whistle in my face and jerks his thumb over his shoulder. "You're out," he yells, face redder than a boiled lobster.

Coach screams from the sidelines. "Where's your head, Royal? Where's your fucking head!"

My head is securely on my shoulders. No one talks about Ella that way.

Back in the empty locker room, I strip down to my jock and sit my bare ass down on a towel in front of my locker. I realize my mistake within seconds. Without the action of the game to distract me, all I can do is obsess over Ella again.

I try to push thoughts of her aside by concentrating on the faint whistles and cheers from the field, but eventually images of her creep in until they flash in front of my eyes like a movie trailer.

Her arrival at the house looking sexier than any girl had a right to be.

Her coming down for Jordan's party wearing the good-girl outfit that made me want to tear all her clothes off and bend her over the banister.

Her dancing. Damn, her dancing.

I shoot to my feet and find my way to the showers. Angry, with lust pumping through my body, I wrench the cold water knob on and duck my head under the freezing stream.

But that does nothing.

The need is relentless. And hell, what's the point of fighting it?

I take myself in hand and close my eyes so I can pretend I'm back in Jordan Carrington's house watching Ella move. Her body is sinful. Long legs, tiny waist, and perfect rack. The tinny music from the television transforms into a sultry track when told through the sway of her hips and the grace in her arms.

I grip my dick tighter. The image switches from the Carrington house to her room. I remember the taste of her on my tongue. How sweet she was. How her mouth formed this perfect, fuckable O when she came for the first time.

I don't last long after that. The tension tingles at the base of my spine and I imagine her below me, her shiny, sun-colored hair against my skin, her eyes staring up at me with greedy desire.

When my body quiets, the self-loathing returns in full force. I stare at my hand wrapped around myself in the middle of the locker room. If I could sink much deeper, I'd be halfway to China.

The release leaves me hollowed out. I turn on the hot water and wash up, but I don't feel clean.

I hope the guy I fight tonight is the biggest, meanest asshole in three states and that he lays the hurt on me—the one that Ella should deliver but isn't here to get it done.

Five

EAST AND I skip the post-game party and head home to kill an hour before the fight. I'll regain some control and perspective when I'm smashing some dude's face in with my fists down at the docks.

"Need to call Claire," East mutters when we walk inside. "Wanna see if she'll come over later."

"Claire?" I wrinkle my forehead. "I didn't know you were tapping that again."

"Yeah, well, I didn't know you were screwing Brooke. Guess we're even."

He lifts his phone to his ear, dismissing me.

His actions sting. East has been icing me out ever since Ella took off.

When I get upstairs, my bedroom door is ajar, and a sick sense of déjà vu washes over me. Suddenly I'm transported back to Monday night, when I found Brooke in my bed.

I swear to God, if that bitch is playing games with me again, I'm gonna lose my shit.

But it's Gideon I find in my room. He's sprawled on my bed,

tapping on his phone. When I enter, he greets me with cloudy eyes.

"Didn't think you were coming home this weekend," I say carefully. I texted him on Tuesday to let him know Ella was gone, but every time he tried calling me this week, I pressed the ignore button. I wasn't in the mood to deal with Gid's guilt trips.

"You would've liked that, huh?"

"Don't know what you're talking about." Avoiding his gaze, I strip out of my T-shirt and replace it with a tank.

"Bullshit. You've been avoiding this conversation since Ella skipped town." Gideon pushes off the bed and advances on me. "Can't avoid it anymore, little brother."

"Look, it's not a big deal, okay? Ella and I are"—were?—"together. So what?"

"If it's not a big deal, then why'd you hide it from me? Why'd I have to find out from East? And what the hell were you thinking, hooking up with her? We don't need to drag anyone else into our mess—"

"Your mess," I interrupt, then regret it instantly, because he flinches as if I hit him.

"Right," he mutters. "*My* mess. I guess it was stupid of me to think that my brother might have my back."

"I do have your back. You know I do. But Ella has nothing to do with this." Helplessness jams in my throat. "Our relationship is—"

He cuts me off with a harsh laugh. "Your relationship? Well, lucky you. Must be nice. I used to have one of those."

I bite back an angry retort. I get that he's miserable, but I'm not the one who put him in the position he's in. He did that all by himself.

"You know what I have now? Absolutely nothing." Gideon looks ready to rip his own hair out as he paces my room.

"I'm sorry." Completely inadequate, but it's all I can say.

"You should be. You need to stay away from Ella. She's a good girl and you're messing her up."

The truth of his words burns hotter than his judgmental stare. Guilt is thick in my throat. "Maybe," I say hoarsely, "but I can't let her go."

"Can't? You mean you won't." Gideon's face turns red. "Forget Ella."

Impossible.

"You're a selfish asshole," my brother hisses when he sees the refusal in my eyes.

"Gid—"

"I had an Ella once, too. I had a girl I saw a future with and I broke her heart. Now she's so mad at the world she can't see straight. Is that what you want for Ella? You wanna be our dad? Drive someone to kill herself because she's so fucking miserable?"

"Ahem."

We both spin around to find Easton in the doorway. His wary blue eyes shift from me to Gid. "Won't even ask if I'm interrupting," he says. "'Cause I see that I am. Won't apologize, either."

Gideon's jaw tenses. "Give us a minute, East. This doesn't concern you."

Our younger brother's cheeks flush. He stalks forward and closes the door. "No way. You two aren't shutting me out. Not anymore." East jams his finger in the center of Gideon's chest. "I'm sick to death of your secrets and your whispered conversations. Let me guess, Gid. You knew that Reed was doing Brooke."

Gid shrugs.

East's bitter gaze flies to me. "What, I wasn't important enough to be in the loop?"

I clench my teeth in frustration. "There's no loop. It was a stupid mistake, okay? And since when do you need to know about every chick I hook up with? You trying to live vicariously through my dick or something?"

That gets me a fist to the solar plexus.

I stumble backward, slamming my shoulder against the edge of the dresser. But I don't strike back. East is practically foaming at the mouth. I've never seen him this pissed off before. The last time he threw a punch at me, we were kids. Arguing over a video game, I think.

"Maybe I should give Brooke a call," East fumes. "Right? Because obviously banging Dad's girlfriend is some kind of sick requirement for getting a VIP pass to the inner circle. If I drop trou for her, you'll have no choice but to let me into the loop, right?"

Gideon responds with stony silence.

I don't speak, either. There's no point, not when East is in a mood.

Running both hands through his hair, he lets out a growl of frustration. "You know what? Screw you both. Keep your secrets and take 'em to hell with you. Just don't come crawling to me when you need someone to put out the fire."

He storms out of my bedroom and slams the door so hard it rattles the doorframe. The silence he leaves in his wake is deafening. Gideon looks exhausted. Me, I'm wired. I need a fight. I need to let out the aggression before I hurt someone in this house.

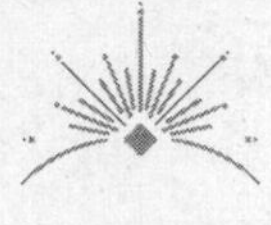

Six

I DRAG MYSELF out of bed the next morning, my entire body protesting the simple act of moving. I wasn't exactly in top form at the fight last night. Yeah, I had blinding rage on my side, but not enough endurance. I took some hits that make me wince in the light of day.

The bruise on the left side of my ribs is already purple and green. I dig around for a loose-fitting T-shirt to hide the injury and pull on a pair of track pants.

Downstairs in the kitchen, I find Brooke perched on my father's lap. It's only nine thirty and Dad's got his ever-present tumbler of Scotch next to his hand. If I was screwing Brooke, I'd be drinking twenty-four seven, too, I guess, but damn, why doesn't he see her for what she is?

"Any word from the PI?" I ask my father.

He gives a curt shake of his head. "Nothing yet."

"I'm just sick to my stomach about all this," Brooke moans. "That poor girl, all alone out there." She touches my dad's cheek. "Darling, you really need to have a talk with Easton about his gambling. Imagine how scary that bookie must have been to spook Ella like that."

Brooke meets my eyes over Dad's head and winks at me.

This is a fucking nightmare. I busy myself with breakfast. Sandra was up early and there's a pile of French toast in the oven waiting to be devoured, along with a stack of bacon. I pile my plate up and lean against the counter, unwilling to take a seat at the table while the she-devil and my dad are making nice.

Dad notices and slides Brooke onto the chair beside him. "Come and sit down, Reed. We're not animals."

I glare at him. "Using Mom's old sayings against me? That's low," I mutter, then regret it when his mouth tightens with hurt. Brooke doesn't look much happier, but that's because she likes to pretend Maria Royal never existed.

"Any French toast left?" Sebastian's voice at the door interrupts whatever Brooke is about to say.

"Yeah, I'll make you a plate," I offer. "Is Sawyer coming down?"

"Not yet. He's on the phone."

A smirk dances around the edges of Seb's mouth. Sawyer's probably sexting Lauren, the twins' girlfriend.

Daniel's taunts suddenly flit through my mind. "You being careful?" I ask in a low murmur as I hand Seb his plate.

He scowls. "What the hell do you care?"

"Word's getting around school, is all. I don't want anyone running to Dad with rumors that would get you sent to boarding school."

"Because you're so good at keeping your nose clean?" Seb mocks.

I notice Brooke watching our hushed exchange with deep interest, so I turn my back and lower my voice. "Look, I care about you guys and I don't want to see anything happen, but your little twin switches aren't fooling anyone."

"Mind your own fucking business. At least we can hang on to the girl we have instead of running her off." The shock must show on my face, because Seb chuckles. "Yeah, we know it's your fault and not East's. We're not *that* dumb. And we know about her, too." He discreetly jerks his head toward Brooke. "So keep your stupid opinions to yourself. You're just as sick as we are."

Seb grabs his plate and stomps out of the kitchen.

"What was that all about?" Dad asks from the table.

"Boys will be boys," Brooke chirps. The smile on her face is genuine. She enjoys seeing us fight. She *wants* us to fight.

I shovel down some French toast, even though my stomach feels full of lead. I don't know if this family is ever going to recover from Mom's death. The vision of her sprawled across her bed, face slack, her eyes cold and unseeing, is always at the back of my mind. With Ella, all the noise in my head quieted.

Now everything is falling apart.

◆ ◆ ◆

THE HOUSE IS quiet tonight. I don't see Seb again, or Sawyer, for that matter. I don't want to think about where Gid might be right now. And East is avoiding me—he hasn't answered any of my texts or returned my calls.

I have a feeling he might not talk to me again until Ella shows up.

Around nine, Wade messages me about a party at Deacon Mills's house. I have no desire to get drunk or be around drunks, so I decline the invite. But I do send a follow-up message.

> Lemme know if E shows up. Can't track him down.

Around eleven, Wade messages back. Ur bro's here. He's wasted.

Shit.

I shove my feet into a pair of kicks and throw on a long-sleeve shirt. The coastal air is getting chilly now that fall's set in. I wonder how Ella's doing. Is she warm enough? Is she sleeping well? Does she have food? Is she safe?

When I get to Mills's house, it's packed. The entire senior class looks like it's getting lit inside. After fifteen minutes of searching for East, I give up and shoot another text to Wade, who's also nowhere to be found.

Where is he?

Game room.

I bypass the living room, heading for the huge den that doubles as a billiards room. Wade is at the pool table, chatting with one of our teammates. He catches my eye when he sees me and nods to the left.

I follow his gaze. My brother is sprawled on the couch with a blonde in his lap. Her pale hair falls over her face like a curtain, so I can't tell who it is, but I can see that her lips are glued to East's. His hand is slowly tunneling underneath her skirt. She giggles, and I instantly freeze. I know that giggle.

She lifts her head and . . . yep, it's Abby.

"East," I boom from the doorway.

He looks over, blue eyes glazed, cheeks flushed. He's drunk out of his mind. Awesome.

"Look, Abs, it's my big bro," he slurs.

"C'mon, time to go," I order, reaching for him.

Abby stares at me with wide, guilty eyes, but I'm more concerned about East. Some demon is riding him hard if he's decided to hook up with my ex.

"What's the hurry? Abs and I are just getting started. Right, baby?"

Her cheeks turn pinker. "Reed," she starts.

I ignore her. "Get up," I snap at my brother. "We're leaving."

"Not going anywhere."

"Yeah, you are."

He doesn't move. "Just 'cause you're not getting any doesn't mean my dick should go unused, right, Abs?"

Abby makes some small noise. Could be agreement. Could be denial. Hell if I care. I just want to get Easton home before he does something he's going to regret.

"Your dick gets plenty of play."

"Maybe I want more." East grins. "And whatta you care? We both know I can do 'er better."

Abby's face is bright red now. "Easton," she says tightly.

"What? You know I'm right." His mocking gaze shifts toward her. "You're wasting your time pining over him, babe. Did he ever tell you he loved you? No, right? That's 'cause he didn't."

Abby makes a gasping, wounded sound. "Screw you, Easton. Screw both of you." Then she rushes out of the den without a backward look.

Easton watches her go, then turns to me and starts to laugh. Cold and humorless. "Made another one run, huh, brother? Ella, Abby . . ."

"You're the one who ran her off." I shake my head at him. "Leave Abby alone. She's not one of your toys, East."

"What, she's too good for a screwup like me?"

Yes. "That's not what I'm saying," I lie.

"Bull*shit*. You don't want me to taint your pure, sweet Abby. Don't want me to mess her up." East moves forward, swaying on his feet. The wave of alcohol on his breath nearly knocks me over. "Goddamn hypocrite. You're the bad apple. You're the one who ruins chicks." He comes even closer, until our faces are inches apart, and then he dips his mouth toward my ear and hisses, "You ruined Ella."

I flinch.

Everyone's eyes are on us. The Royals are in shambles, ladies and gentlemen. The twins have stopped talking to me. East's trying to screw his pain away. Gid's angry at the world. And me? I'm just drowning.

"All right. I'm done here." I sidestep him, struggling to keep myself under control. "You do what you want, buddy."

"Damn right I will," he slurs.

I catch Wade's eye and jerk my head toward the door. He wastes no time meeting me there. "Make sure East gets home all right," I mutter. "He can't drive."

Wade nods. "I'm on it. Go home. It'll all be better in the morning."

If Ella shows up, yes. If not? We're screwed.

Feeling defeated, I drive home and try not to think about how my life has gone to hell. Ella's gone. East's a mess. Brooke's back. I don't know what to do with the anger. I can't fight again. My ribs are too sore. But my hands are fine, so I duck downstairs to the weight room and take out my aggression on the punching bag.

I pretend the bag is me. I pummel it until my hands are bloody and there are red marks on my feet and up and down my legs.

It doesn't do a damn bit of good.

Afterward, I wash off my sweat and blood in the shower, throw on a pair of sweats, and climb upstairs. In the kitchen, I dig out an energy drink and am startled to realize the time. It's past one a.m. I was down in the basement for almost an hour and a half.

Exhausted, I haul my tired ass up the stairs. Maybe I can finally fucking sleep tonight. The hallway is dark and every door is closed, including East's. I wonder if he's back from the party.

As I approach my door, I hear noises. Low grunts, gasps.

What the hell?

Brooke better not be in there.

I throw open the door and the first thing I see is my brother's bare ass. He's on my bed. So is Abby, who's moaning softly as East pumps into her. Her hands clutch his shoulders, legs wrapped around his hips. Her hair is fanned out across my pillow.

"Seriously?" I growl.

Easton stops moving, but keeps one hand curled over my ex's breast. He glances over his shoulder and offers a savage smile.

"Oh man, this is your room?" he says mockingly. "Must've gotten it mixed up with mine. Sorry, brother."

I slam the door and stumble back into the hall.

✦ ✦ ✦

I SLEEP IN Ella's room. Or more accurately, I lie on Ella's bed and brood all night. In the morning, I run into East in the kitchen.

"Abby tasted good last night." He smirks and takes a bite of an apple.

Idly I wonder how he'd feel if I took that apple and shoved

the whole thing down his throat. He'd probably laugh and say he wanted another one just to show me. Show me what, though? That he hates my guts?

"Didn't realize we were sharing like the twins." I grab the pitcher of water with more force than I intend and the filtered water spills over my hand.

East forces a laugh out. "Why not? Maybe if I was the one boning Ella, she wouldn't have left."

Blood washes over my eyes. "You touch her and I'll—"

"She's not even here for me to touch, you asshole." He hurls the half-bitten apple and it explodes against the side of the cabinet just inches from my head. "I wish that was a fucking brick and it smashed your head in."

Yeah, we're doing really well here in the Royal household.

I avoid East for the rest of the day.

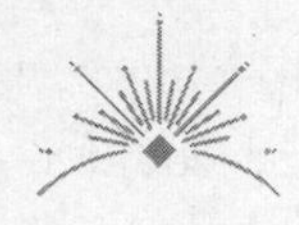

Seven

ANOTHER WEEK PASSES. Ella's still gone and my brothers still aren't talking to me. Life sucks, and I have no idea how to make it better, so I stop trying. I just give in to the misery and shut out the world and spend every night wondering what Ella is doing. If she's safe. If she misses me . . . But of course she doesn't. If she missed me, she'd have come home already.

On Monday, I get up and go to practice. It's obvious to everyone that East and I are feuding. He stands on one end of the sidelines and I stand on the other. The distance between us is larger than a stadium. Hell, the entire Atlantic could probably be dumped in the chasm that's growing between us.

After practice, Val stops me in the hall. I check the urge to cup my balls.

"Just tell me she's okay," she begs.

"She's fine."

"Is she mad at me? Did I do something?" Val's voice cracks.

Dammit. Can't anyone keep their shit together? Irritation makes me snap, "What am I? Your couples therapist? I don't know why she's not calling you."

Val's face crumples. "That's a shitty thing to say, Reed. She's my friend, too. You have no right to keep her from me."

"If Ella wanted to hear from you, she'd call."

That's the worst thing I could say, but the words fall out anyway. Before I can take them back, Val runs off.

If Ella didn't hate me before, she will when she gets back and sees the mess I've made of everything.

Pissed and frustrated, I turn and slam my foot into the locker. The metal door crumples under the impact and a corresponding jolt zips up my leg. It doesn't feel good.

Down the hall, I hear laughter. I turn to see Easton holding out his hand. Dominic Brunfeld slaps something into East's palm. A few other guys from the team pull out bills and hand them over.

"Never thought I'd see you torn up over a chick," Dom says as he walks past me. "You're letting us all down."

I flip him off and wait for East to reach me. "Want to explain what's going on?"

East fans his money in my face. "Easiest cash I've ever earned. You're unhinged, bro. Everyone in school knows it. It was just a matter of time before you'd lose your cool. It's why Ella ran."

I breathe heavily out of my nose. "She's coming back."

"Oh, did you magically find her in the middle of the night?" He spreads his arms out wide and twists around. "Because she's not here. You see her? Dom, you see Ella?" Dom shifts his gaze from me to East and back again. "No, he doesn't see her. What about you, Wade? You see her? She join you in the bathroom?"

"Shut up, East."

Pain shines in his eyes as he makes a zipping motion across his lips. "Shutting up, Master Reed. You know what's best for the Royals, right? You do all the right things. Get all the good grades. Play ball smart. Screw all the right girls. Except when you don't. And when you fuck up, you affect us all." His hand wraps around the back of my neck and drags me forward until our heads are pressed together. "So why don't *you* shut up, Reed? Ella's not coming back. She's dead, just like Mommy Dearest. Only this time, it's not my fault. It's yours."

Shame swamps me, a murky, ugly substance that glues itself to my bones and weighs me down. I can't escape the truth. East is right. I helped kill Mom, and if Ella's dead, I helped killed her, too.

I wrench myself away from his grasp and stalk back into the locker room. I've never fought in public with my brothers before. It's always been all for one, one for all.

Mom hated when we fought at home, but didn't tolerate it when we were out. If we even so much as sniped at each other, she pretended we weren't hers.

Maria Royal's boys don't ever embarrass her or themselves in public. One disapproving look from her had us straightening our clothes, throwing our arms around each other like it was opening day at the ballpark and we were happy to be alive—despite being seconds away from thrashing each other within an inch of our lives.

The door to the locker room creaks open. I don't look up to see who it is. I know it's not East. When he gets mad, he keeps to himself.

"Last Friday"—it's Wade—"before the game, one of the Pastels took scissors to some freshman and cut off her hair. Chick ran out of here bawling her eyes out."

I tense. Shit. That must've been the girl Delacorte and I saw streaking out of the building and into the VW. "Blond, skinny? Drives a white Passat?"

He nods and the bench creaks as he takes a seat next to me. "Day before that, Dev Khan torched June Chen's science project."

"Isn't June a scholarship student?"

"Yup."

"Huh." I force myself to sit up. "Any other pretty stories you want to tell?"

"Those are the two big ones. I've heard rumors about other shit, but haven't confirmed them. Jordan spit on some girl during health. Goody Bellingham is offering fifty grand to anyone who's willing to run train on the homecoming court."

I rub a tired hand over my jaw. This stupid school. "It's barely been two weeks."

"And in those two weeks, your brothers stopped talking to you, you got into it with Delacorte, smashed a locker. Oh, and before Ella left, apparently you decided you didn't like the look of Scott Gastonburg and tried to rearrange his face."

"He was talking smack." The guy insulted Ella. I didn't hear it, but I knew by the smug look on his face when we were at the club that he'd thought he'd gotten away with something. Not on my watch.

"Probably. Nothing that comes out of Gasty's mouth is ever worth listening to. You did us all a favor getting it wired shut, but the rest of the school's falling apart. You need to man up."

"I don't care what happens to Astor."

"Maybe you don't. But without the Royals running things, the school's going to shit." Wade shifts on the hard metal surface. "People are talking about Ella, too."

"Whatever. Let them talk."

"You say that now, but how's it gonna be for her when she gets back? She's already gotten into a catfight with Jordan. I mean, yeah, it was hot as hell. But then there was the Daniel thing and now she's disappeared. Everyone says she's off getting an abortion or recovering from an STD. If you're hiding her, now's the time to trot her out, make a show of force."

I remain silent.

Wade sighs. "I know you don't like being in charge, but guess what, dude—you are and have been since Gid graduated. If you let things continue to slide, by the time Halloween comes it'll be a horror show here. There'll be intestines and brain matter splattered on the school walls. Someone will have gone full-on *Carrie* on Jordan by then."

Jordan. That chick is nothing but trouble. "Why don't you take care of it?" I mutter. "Your family's got enough money to buy Jordan's." Wade comes from old money. I think some of it is still stored in gold bullion in their basement.

"It's not money. It's the Royals. You make people listen. Probably 'cause there're so many of you."

He's right. The Royals have ruled this school since Gid was a sophomore. I don't know what happened, but one day we woke up and everyone looked to Gid. If a kid stepped out of line, Gid was there to set him straight. The rules were simple. Pick on someone your own size.

Size being a metaphorical thing. Size being social status, bank account, intelligence. Jordan going after one of the Pastels would've been fine. Jordan going after a scholarship student? Not so good.

Ella had fallen into a gap. She wasn't a scholarship student. She wasn't a rich kid, either. And I'd thought that she was sleeping with my dad. That he'd brought home a whore from a high-class brothel. He and Steve liked to frequent those places on business trips. Yeah, Dad's a real class act.

I'd stood back and waited, and everyone waited with me. Except Jordan. Because Jordan immediately saw what I did. That Ella was made of something stronger than we'd seen before at Astor Park. Jordan hated it. I was drawn to it.

"I don't want that kind of control," Wade is saying. "I just wanna get laid, play a little football, annoy my mom's boyfriends, and get wasted. I can do all that stuff even if Jordan's terrorizing every pretty girl that breathes the wrong way. But you? You've got a conscience, man. But with all this shit . . . with Daniel still walking around the halls like he didn't try to rape Ella . . . well, silence is kind of considered approval." He gets to his feet. "Everyone leans on you. It's a burden, I get it, but if you don't stand up, it's gonna be a massacre."

I get up, too, and head for the door. "Let the school burn," I mutter. "It's not my job to put out the flames."

"Bro."

I pause in the doorframe. "What?"

"At least let me know which way things are gonna go. I don't care. I just wanna know if I need to start wearing a hazmat suit."

Shrugging, I glance at him over my shoulder. "Things can go to hell for all I care."

I hear a sigh of defeat behind me, but I don't stick around for another second. As long as Ella's MIA, I refuse to concentrate on anything other than finding her. If everyone around me is miserable, then fine. We can all be miserable together.

I keep my head down as I trudge down the hall. I almost make it all the way to class without talking to a single person, until a familiar voice calls out to me.

"What's the matter, Royal? You moping 'cause nobody wants to play with you?"

I stop walking. The barking laughter of Daniel Delacorte has me slowly swiveling to face him.

"Sorry, I didn't quite hear you," I say coldly. "Wanna repeat that? To my fist this time?"

He stumbles over his own feet, because the menace in my voice is unmistakable. The hallway is crowded with kids getting out of their after-class electives. Music students, debate team, the cheer squad, the science club.

I advance with purpose, adrenaline spiking in my veins. I got in one punch with this jerkwad before, but only one. My brothers dragged me away before I could do any more damage.

Today, no one is stopping me. The pack of animals that makes up the student body of Astor Park smells the blood in the air.

Delacorte shifts to the side, not fully facing me, but wary of having his back to me. *I'm not the kind of guy to stab someone in the back*, I want to tell him. *That's your deal.*

But Delacorte thinks differently. He's screwed up in the head, preys on people he thinks are weaker than him.

Anger radiates off his lean frame. He doesn't like to be confronted with his cowardice. Daddy gets him off, after all. That's fine, but Daddy's not here right now, is he?

"Is everything about violence for you, Royal? You think your fists can solve your problems?"

I smirk. "At least I don't use drugs to solve my problems. Chicks don't want you, so you drug 'em. That's your MO, right?"

"Ella wanted it."

"I don't like her name coming out of your mouth." I step forward. "You should forget her name."

"Or what? Are we dueling to the death?" He spreads his arms out in invitation for the audience to laugh with him, but either they hate him or they're afraid of me, because there's not so much as a titter in response.

"No. I think you're a waste of space. You're taking up oxygen that could be better spent coming out of someone's ass. I can't kill you—stupid legal reasons and all—but I can hurt you. I can make every waking moment of your life miserable," I say matter-of-factly. "You should leave school, dude. No one wants you here."

His breath comes in shallow pants. "It's you no one wants," he jeers.

He looks to the crowd again for support, but their bright-eyed interest is in potential bloodshed. They move closer, pushing Daniel forward.

The coward inside of him snaps. He throws his phone at me, the plastic casing striking my forehead. The students gasp. Something warm and coppery trickles down, clouding my vision, coating my lips.

I could punch him. That'd be easy. But I want him to really hurt. I want us both to hurt. So I grab him by the shoulders and slam my forehead against his.

My blood paints his face, and I grin with satisfaction. "Your face looks prettier already. Let's see what other magic I can make for you." Then I slap him, hard.

He flushes with anger, more at the disdain in my touch than the actual pain. A slap is a girl's weapon, not a blow exchanged between guys. My open palm makes a smacking sound when I slap him again. Daniel backs away, but he can't get far from me—his retreat is halted by the lockers.

Grinning, I step in and slap him again. He blocks me with his hand, leaving his entire left side open. I deliver two strikes to the left side of his face before backing away.

"Hit me," he screams. "Hit me. Use your fist!"

My smile widens. "You don't deserve my fists. I use fists on men."

I smack him again and this time it's hard enough that his skin splits. Blood pools around the wound, but that doesn't satisfy my lust for revenge. I clap a hand against one ear and then the other. Weakly, he tries to defend himself.

Daniel purses his lips, gathering up saliva. I feint to the left to avoid the stream of spittle that spills out. Disgusted, I grab his hair and shove his face into the locker. "When Ella gets back, she's not gonna want to see trash like you around, so either leave or start practicing your invisibility skills because I don't want to see or hear from you again."

I don't wait for an answer—I slam his forehead into the metal locker and let go.

He tips over, one hundred and seventy pounds of trash collapsing on the floor like a discarded toy.

I turn to find Wade standing there behind me. "Thought you didn't care," he murmurs.

The grin I give him must be feral because everyone but Wade and his stoic shadow, Hunter, takes a step back.

Leaning down, I swipe Daniel's phone off the floor, then roll him over and pick up his limp hand. I press the thumb against the home button and then key in my dad's number.

"Callum Royal," he answers impatiently.

"Hey, Dad. You're gonna need to come to school."

"Reed? What number are you calling from?" he demands.

"Daniel Delacorte's phone. Judge Delacorte's son. You should bring your checkbook. I beat him up pretty good. He asked for it, though, literally," I say cheerfully.

I hang up and swipe a hand across my face as the blood

from the cut drips down into my eye. Stepping over Daniel's body, I drawl, "Later, Wade. Hunter." I give the big, silent lineman a nod.

He returns the gesture with his own chin jerk, and I head outside to get some air.

✦ ✦ ✦

DAD IS FROTHING at the mouth when he appears in the waiting area outside Headmaster Beringer's office. He doesn't comment on my bloody forehead. He just yanks me up by the lapels of my blazer and brings his face close to mine.

"This needs to stop," he hisses.

I shrug out of his grasp. "Chill out. I haven't been in a fight in over a year," I remind him.

"You want a medal for that? A pat on the back? Jesus, Reed, how many times do we have to go through this routine? How many goddamn checks do I need to write before you smarten up?"

I look him square in the eye. "Daniel Delacorte drugged Ella at a party and tried to rape her."

Dad sucks in a sharp breath.

"Mr. Royal."

We turn to see Beringer's secretary standing in the headmaster's open doorway.

"Mr. Beringer will see you now," she says primly.

Dad stalks past me, tossing over his shoulder, "Stay here. I'll deal with this."

I try to hide my pleasure. I get to kick it out here while Dad cleans up my mess? Sweet. Not that I consider it a "mess." Delacorte had it coming. He's deserved a total beating since the night he tried to hurt Ella, but I got sidetracked from delivering retribution because I was too busy falling in love with her.

I plant my ass back in the plush waiting room chair, studiously avoiding the disapproving frowns that Beringer's secretary keeps flashing my way.

Dad's meeting with Beringer lasts less than ten minutes. Seven, if the clock over the door is accurate. When he strides out of the office, his eyes contain that triumphant gleam he usually has after he closes a lucrative business deal.

"All taken care of," he tells me, then gestures for me to follow him. "Go back to class, but make sure you come straight home after school. Your brothers, too. No unnecessary stops. I need all of you at home."

I instantly tense up. "Why? What's going on?"

"I was going to wait until after school to tell you, but . . . since I'm already here . . ." Dad pauses in the middle of the huge, wood-paneled lobby. "The PI found Ella."

Before I can even begin to process that bombshell, my father stalks out the front entrance, leaving me staring after him in shock.

Eight

ELLA

THE BUS ROLLS into Bayview much, much too soon. I'm not ready. But I know I'll never be ready. Reed's betrayal lives inside of me now. It slinks through my veins like black tar, attacking what's left of my heart like a fast-acting cancer.

Reed broke me. He *tricked* me. He made me believe that something good could exist in this awful, screwed-up world. That someone could actually give a damn about me.

I should have known better. I've spent my entire life in the gutter, frantically trying to crawl my way out of it. I loved my mother, but I wanted so much more than the life she gave us. I wanted more than seedy apartments and moldy leftovers and a desperate struggle to make ends meet.

Callum Royal gave me what Mom couldn't: money, an education, a fancy mansion to live in. A family. A—

An illusion, a bitter voice mutters in my head.

Yeah, I guess it was. And the sad thing is, Callum doesn't even know it. He doesn't even realize he's living in a house of lies.

Or maybe he does. Maybe he's fully aware that his son is sleeping with—

No. I refuse to think about what I saw in Reed's bedroom the night I skipped town.

But the images are already bubbling to the surface of my mind.

Reed and Brooke on his bed.

Brooke naked.

Brooke touching him.

A gagging noise flies out of my mouth, causing the elderly woman across the aisle to glance over in concern.

"Are you all right, sweetie?" she asks.

I swallow the ball of nausea. "Fine," I say weakly. "I have a bit of a stomachache."

"Sit tight," the woman says with a reassuring smile. "They're opening the doors now. We'll be out of here in a jiffy."

God. No. A jiffy is too soon. I don't ever want to get off this bus. I don't want the cash that Callum forced on me back in Nashville. I don't want to go back to the Royal mansion and pretend that my heart hasn't been shattered into a million pieces. I don't want to see Reed or hear his apologies. If he even has any.

He didn't say a word when I walked in on him and his father's girlfriend. Not one word. For all I know, I'll walk through the door and discover that Reed is back to his old cruel self. Maybe I'd prefer that, actually, and then I can forget I ever loved him.

I stumble off the bus, holding my backpack strap tight to my shoulder. The sun has already set, but the station is all lit up. People bustle around me as the driver unloads everyone's luggage from the belly of the vehicle. I don't have any bags, only my backpack.

The night I ran, I didn't take any of the fancy clothes Brooke had bought me, and now they're all waiting for me at the mansion. I wish I could burn every scrap of fabric. I don't want to wear those clothes or live in that house.

Why couldn't Callum leave me alone? I could have started a new life in Nashville. I could have been *happy*. Eventually, anyway.

Instead, I'm in Royal clutches again, after Callum used every threat in the book to bring me back. I can't believe the lengths he went to in order to find me. Turns out the bills from the original ten grand he gave me had sequential serial numbers—all he had to do was wait until I used one, and then he was able to pinpoint my location.

I don't even want to know how many laws he broke to trace the serial number of a hundred-dollar bill in this country. But I guess men like Callum are above the law.

A car honks, and I stiffen when a black town car pulls up to the curb. The one that followed the bus from Nashville to Bayview. The driver gets out—it's Durand, Callum's chauffeur-slash-bodyguard, who's as big as a mountain and just as forbidding.

"How was the ride?" he asks gruffly. "Are you hungry? Should we stop for food?"

Since Durand is never this chatty, I wonder if Callum ordered him to be extra nice to me. I received no such order, so I'm not at all nice as I mutter, "Get in the car and drive."

His nostrils flare.

I don't feel bad. I'm sick to death of these people. From this point on, they're my enemies. They're the prison guards and I'm the inmate. They're not my friends or my family. They're nothing to me.

✦ ✦ ✦

IT SEEMS LIKE every light in the mansion is on when Durand stops the car in the circular driveway. Since the house is pretty much a sprawling rectangle of nothing but windows, all that dazzling light nearly blinds me.

The oak doors at the pillared entrance fly open and Callum appears, his dark hair perfectly styled, his tailored suit clinging to his broad frame.

I square my shoulders, prepared for another showdown, but my legal guardian smiles sadly and says, "Welcome back."

There's nothing welcoming about it. This man tracked me all the way to Nashville and threatened me. His list of dire consequences if I didn't return seemed endless.

He would have me arrested as a runaway.

He would report me to the police for using my mother's identification.

He would tell them I stole the ten grand he gave me and have me charged with theft.

None of those threats are what made me cave. No, it was his emphatic declaration that there was no place I could run that he couldn't find me. Anywhere I went, he'd be there. He'd hunt me for the rest of my life, because, as he reminded me, he owed it to my father.

My father, a man I never even met. A man who, from the sound of it, was a spoiled, selfish jerk who married a money-hungry shrew while neglecting to tell her—or anyone else, for that matter—that he knocked up a young woman when he was on shore leave eighteen years ago.

I don't owe Steve O'Halloran a thing. I don't owe Callum

Royal, either. But I also don't want to be looking over my shoulder for the rest of my life. Callum doesn't bluff. He would never stop hunting me if I ran again.

As I follow him into the mansion, I remind myself that I'm strong. I'm resilient. I can handle two years of living with the Royals. All I have to do is pretend they're not around. My focus will be on finishing high school and then I'm off to college. Once I graduate, I'll never have to step foot in this house again.

Upstairs, Callum shows me the new security system he installed on my bedroom door. It's a biometric hand scan, supposedly the kind of security he has at Atlantic Aviation. Only my handprint can grant access to the room, which means no more late-night visits from Reed. No more watching movies with Easton. This room is my cell, and that's exactly what I want.

"Ella." Callum sounds weary as he follows me into my room, which is as pink and girlish as I remember. Callum had consulted with a decorator but picked everything out himself, proving that he knows absolutely nothing about teenage girls.

"What?" I ask.

"I know why you ran off, and I wanted—"

"You know?" I cut in warily.

Callum nods. "Reed told me."

"He *told* you?" I can't contain or hide my surprise. Reed told his father about him and Brooke? And Callum didn't kick him out? Hell, Callum doesn't even look upset! Who *are* these people?

"I understand why you might've been too embarrassed to come to me yourself," Callum continues, "but I want you to know that you can always talk to me about anything. In fact, I think we should file a police report first thing tomorrow morning."

Confusion washes over me. "A police report?"

"That boy needs to be punished for what he did, Ella."

"That boy?" What the heck is going on right now? Callum wants to have his son arrested for . . . for what? Underage sex? I'm still a virgin. Can I be prosecuted for—jeez. I flush deep red.

His next words shock me. "I don't give a damn if his father is a judge. Delacorte can't get away with drugging and attempting to sexually assault a girl."

I suck in a breath. Oh gosh. Reed told Callum what Daniel tried to do to me? Why? Or rather, why *now* and not weeks ago when it happened?

But whatever Reed's reasons were, I resent him for saying something. The last thing I want to do is get the cops involved, or to find myself caught up in a long, messy court case. I can imagine exactly what would go on in that courtroom. High school stripper alleges some rich white boy tried to drug her for sex? No one is believing that.

"I'm not filing a report," I say stiffly.

"Ella—"

"It was no big deal, okay? Your sons found me before Daniel could do any real damage." Frustration floods my belly. "And that's not why I ran off, Callum. I just . . . I don't belong here, okay? I'm not cut out to be some rich princess who goes to prep school and drinks a thousand-dollar glass of champagne at dinner. That's not me. I'm not fancy or wealthy or—"

"But you are wealthy," he interrupts quietly. "You're very, very wealthy, Ella, and you need to start accepting that. Your father left you a fortune, and one of these days we'll need to sit down with Steve's lawyers to decide what you're going to do with that money. Investments, trusts, that sort of thing. In fact—" He pulls out a leather wallet and hands it to me. "Your cash for the month, per our agreement, and a credit card."

I suddenly feel light-headed. The memory of Reed and Brooke together is the only thing I've been able to concentrate on since I left. I forgot all about the inheritance from Steve.

"We can discuss it another time," I mumble.

He nods. "Are you sure you won't reconsider telling the authorities about Delacorte?"

"I won't reconsider," I say firmly.

He looks resigned. "All right. Would you like me to bring you up something to eat?"

"I ate at the last rest stop." I want him gone, and he knows it.

"Okay. Well." He edges to the door. "Why don't you turn in early? I'm sure you're exhausted after that long bus ride. We can talk more tomorrow."

Callum leaves, and I feel a pang of irritation when I notice he didn't shut the door all the way. I walk over to close it at the same time it flies open, nearly knocking me on my ass.

The next thing I know, a pair of strong arms wrap tightly around me.

At first I stiffen, because I think it's Reed, but when I realize it's Easton, I relax. He's as tall and muscular as Reed, with the same dark hair and blue eyes, but the scent of his shampoo is sweeter, and his aftershave isn't as spicy as Reed's.

"Easton—" I start, then gasp because the sound of my voice only tightens his grip.

He doesn't say a word. He hugs me as if I'm a security blanket. It's a chest-crushing, desperate embrace that makes it hard to breathe. His chin lands on my shoulder and then burrows into my neck, and although I'm supposed to be mad at every Royal in this mansion, I can't stop myself from stroking one hand through his hair. This is Easton, my self-proclaimed "big brother" even though we're the same age. He's larger than life, incorrigible, often annoying and always screwed up.

He probably knew about Reed and Brooke—there's no way Reed kept that a secret from Easton—and yet I can't bring myself to hate him. Not when he's trembling in my arms. Not when he sags backward and gazes at me with such overwhelming relief it takes my breath away.

And then I blink and he's gone, stumbling out of my room without a word. I feel a spark of concern. Where were the smart-ass remarks? Some cocky comment about how I came back because of his fine bod and animal magnetism?

Frowning, I shut the door and force myself not to dwell on Easton's strange behavior. I'm not allowing myself to get caught up in any Royal drama again, not if I want to survive my time here.

I stick the wallet into my backpack, whip my sweatshirt off, and crawl onto the bed. The silk coverlet feels like heaven against my bare arms.

In Nashville, I was staying in a cheap motel with the scratchiest bedspread known to man. The thing was also covered with stains I never, ever want to know the source of. I'd landed a job waiting tables at a diner when Callum showed up, same way he'd shown up in Kirkwood and dragged me out of the strip club.

Has my life been better or worse since Callum Royal found me?

My heart clenches as I picture Reed's face. Worse, I decide. So much worse.

As if he knew that I was thinking about him, Reed speaks from behind my closed door. "Ella. Let me in."

I ignore him.

He knocks twice. "Please. I need to talk to you."

I roll over on my side with my back to the door. His voice is killing me.

A growl comes from the other side of the door. "You really think this scanner is gonna keep me out, baby? You know better." He pauses. When I don't answer, he goes on. "Fine. I'll be back. Grabbing a toolbox."

The threat—which I know isn't an empty one—has me flying off the bed. I slap my hand on the security panel and a loud beep fills the room as the lock clicks. I throw open the door and meet the eyes of the guy who was in the process of destroying me before I left. Thank God I put a stop to that. He's never getting close enough to have any impact on me again.

"I am *not* your baby," I hiss out. "I am *nothing* to you, and you're nothing to me, you understand me? Don't call me 'baby.' Don't call me anything. Stay the hell away from me."

His blue eyes do a thorough examination of me from head to toe. Then he speaks in a gruff voice. "Are you okay?"

My breathing is so short it's a wonder I don't pass out. No oxygen is getting in. My lungs burn and my vision is red and hazy. Did he not listen to a word I just said?

"You look thinner," he says flatly. "You haven't been eating."

I move to close the door.

He just shoves a palm against it and pushes it open, stepping inside while I glare at him.

"Get out," I snap.

"No." His gaze continues to sweep over me, as if he's checking me for injuries.

He should be checking himself, because *he's* the one who looks like he got beat up. Literally—there's a purplish bruise peeking out from the collar of his T-shirt. He's been in a fight recently. Or maybe several fights, judging by the slight grimace on his face when he draws a breath, as if his rib cage can't handle the act of breathing.

Good, a vindictive part of me crows. He deserves to suffer.

"Are you okay?" he repeats, his gaze never leaving mine. "Did anyone . . . touch you? Hurt you?"

Hysterical laughter bubbles out. "Yes! Someone hurt me! *You* hurt me!"

Frustration clouds his face. "You left before I could explain."

"There's *no* explanation you could give that would make me forgive you," I spit out. "You screwed your father's girlfriend!"

"No," he says firmly. "I didn't."

"Bull."

"It's true. I didn't." He takes another breath. "Not that night. She was trying to convince me to talk to my dad on her behalf. I was trying to get rid of her."

I stare at him in disbelief. "She didn't have any clothes on!" I stop abruptly, my mind snagging on one particular thing he'd said.

Not that night?

Anger rises in my throat. "Let's pretend for a second that I believe you didn't have sex with Brooke that night"—I glare at him—"which I don't. But let's pretend I do. You still slept with her some other time, didn't you?"

Guilt, deep and unmistakable, flickers in his eyes.

"How many times?" I demand.

Reed runs a hand through his hair. "Two, maybe three."

My heart seizes. Oh my God. A part of me had expected a denial. But . . . he's actually admitting to having sex with his dad's girlfriend? More than *once*?

"Maybe?" I screech.

"I was drunk."

"You're disgusting," I whisper.

He doesn't even flinch. "I wasn't with her when you and I were together. The moment you and I hooked up for the first time, I was yours. Only yours."

"Oh, lucky me. I got Brooke's sloppy seconds. Hurray!"

This time he *does* wince. "Ella—"

"Shut. Up." I hold up my hand, so grossed out I can barely look at him. "I'm not even going to ask you why you did it, because I know exactly why you did. Reed Royal hates his daddy. Reed Royal decides to get back at his daddy. Reed Royal has sex with his daddy's girlfriend." I gag. "Do you realize how messed up that is?"

"Yeah. I do." His voice is hoarse. "But I never claimed to be a saint. I made a lot of mistakes before I met you."

"Reed." I meet his gaze head-on. "I will never forgive you for this."

A flash of determination lights his eyes. "You don't mean that."

I step toward the door. "Nothing you say or do will make me forget what I saw in your bedroom that night. Just be happy I'm keeping my mouth shut about it, because if Callum finds out, he'll lose his shit."

"I don't care about my dad." Reed advances on me. "You *left* me," he growls.

My jaw drops. "You're mad at me for leaving? Of course I left! Why would I spend another second in this awful house after what you did?"

He moves even closer, his big frame invading my personal space, his hand coming out to cup my chin. I shrink from his touch, and that makes his eyes blaze hotter.

"I missed you every second you were gone. I thought about you every goddamn second. You want to hate me for what I did? Don't bother—I was hating myself for it long before you showed up. I slept with Brooke and that's something I've gotta live with." His fingers tremble against my jaw. "But I didn't screw her that night, and I'm not letting you throw away what you and I have just because—"

"What we have? We have nothing." I feel sick again. I'm done with this conversation. "Get out of my room, Reed. I can't even look at you right now."

When he doesn't budge, I plant both hands against his torso and shove him. Hard. And I keep shoving, keep slapping at his muscular chest until I move him, inch by inch, to the doorway. The slight smirk on his face only heightens my anger. Does he find this funny? Is everything a game to this guy?

"Get *out*," I order. "I'm done with you."

He stares at my hands, which are still pressed up against him, then at my face, which I'm pretty sure is redder than a tomato.

"Sure, I'll go, if that's what you want." He cocks one eyebrow. "But we're not done, Ella. Not by a long shot."

I barely wait until he's stepped past the threshold before I slam the door in his face.

Nine

THE FIRST THING I see when I wake up is the fan over my bed. The smooth, heavy cotton sheets remind me I'm no longer in that shitty, forty-dollar-a-night hotel room anymore, but back in the Royal palace.

Everything is the same here. I even smell Reed on the pillowcases, like he slept in here every night while I was gone. I throw the pillow on the floor and make a mental note to buy new bedding.

Did I make the right decision coming back? Did I have a choice? Callum proved he could track me down anywhere. I made what demands I could. The hand-scan security lock on my bedroom door. A credit card in my name. A promise that once I was done with high school, the scrutiny would be lifted.

The question I should be asking myself is whether I'm going to let one guy ruin my life. Am I so weak that I can't handle Reed Royal? I've been in charge for years, first taking care of my mom and then myself. The hole in my heart left by Mom's death eventually healed over. The hole that Reed put there will heal, too.

Right?

Rolling over, I spot the phone that Callum gave me lying on the nightstand. I left it behind, along with the car, the clothes, and everything else I'd been gifted. But separating myself from the Royals, specifically Reed, didn't mean I stopped thinking about him. I couldn't leave that behind, and those memories haunted me every mile I traveled.

I grab the phone with purpose and force myself to face the mess I left behind. Seeing all the messages is bittersweet. Every other time I've picked up and left, no one has missed me. Mom and I never stayed in any one place for longer than a couple of years.

This time, I have more than thirty messages from Valerie, along with several from Reed. I delete those without reading them. There are a few from Easton, but I suspect those are also from Reed, so I delete them, too. The other messages are from my boss, Lucy, the owner of the French Twist, a bakery close to Astor Park Prep. Those start out with concern and end with impatience.

But it's Val's messages that bring an uncomfortable knot to my stomach. I should've said something to her. I thought about it a lot while I was gone, but I was afraid. Not just that the Royals might weasel information out of her, but also because she was a link to something I wanted to forget. I feel bad about how I treated her, though. If she up and disappeared, I'd be pissed.

> I'm sorry. I'm the shittiest friend ever. Do you still want to talk to me?

I set the phone down and stare at the ceiling. To my surprise, the phone rings immediately. Val's picture pops up.

I take a deep breath and answer it.

"Hey, Val."

"Where have you been?" she shrieks. "I've called and called!"

I open my mouth to feed her the illness excuse, but her next words stop me.

"And don't tell me that you were sick because no one is sick for two weeks and can't even make a phone call! Well, unless she's patient zero at the beginning of a zombie apocalypse."

As I listen to her concerned words, I realize that this is a test of our friendship. Even after I seemingly ducked her calls for two weeks, she's still accepting me back into her life. Yeah, she's asking questions, but ones she deserves an answer to. She's important. Important enough for an honest answer, no matter how embarrassing it is.

"I ran away," I confess.

"Oh, Ella, no." She sighs sadly. "What did those Royals do to you?"

I don't want to lie to her. "I'm . . . not ready to talk about it. But I might have overreacted."

"Why didn't you come to me?" she asks, the hurt clear in every word.

"I didn't think of it. I . . . Something happened here and I got in my car, bought a bus ticket, and left. The only thing on my mind was getting as far away from here as possible. It didn't occur to me to come to you. I'm not used to relying on people. I'm sorry."

She's silent for a moment. "I'm still pissed at you."

"You should be."

"Are you coming to school today?"

"No. I got back late last night, so Callum's giving me a day to get settled."

"Fine. Then I'm skipping school and you're coming over and telling me everything."

"I'll tell you what I can." I don't even want to think about the Brooke and Reed stuff anymore. I want to forget it happened. I want to forget that I opened my heart to Reed.

"I got shit to tell you, too," she admits. "When can you come over?"

I check the clock. "An hour? I need to shower, eat, get dressed."

"Sounds like a plan. Come to the back door; otherwise my aunt will wonder why we aren't at school."

Val lives with her aunt so she can attend Astor Park. I've only met Val's evil cousin, Jordan, and I guess the day that I play hooky isn't the best time to introduce myself to the rest of her family.

"Roger. See you soon."

I take a deep breath and call Lucy next. "Hey, Lucy. It's Ella. I'm so sorry I disappeared on you like that. Can I come in this afternoon?"

"I'm sorry, too, but I can't talk right now. It's busy." Lucy is curt, and I suddenly regret not going in the moment I woke up this morning. "If you can stop by before two today, I can chat."

"I'll be there," I promise. I have a feeling I'm not going to like what she has to say.

I drag myself out of bed, shower, and then throw on a pair of old jeans and my flannel shirt. Ironically, this is essentially the same outfit I wore the first time I arrived at the Royal mansion. My closet here is stuffed full of expensive clothes, but I'm not wearing a single stitch that was picked out by Brooke Davidson. That might be petty and stupid, but I don't care.

I open my door and stop. Reed is leaning against the wall opposite my bedroom.

"Morning."

I slam the door shut.

His strong voice easily carries beyond the door. "How long are you going to ignore me?"

Two years. No. For as long as humanly possible.

"I'm not leaving," he adds. "And eventually you're going to forgive me, so you might as well hear me out."

I walk over to the window beside my bed and look down. The drop from the second story to the ground is pretty steep and I'm not sure the whole knotted-sheet thing works in real life. With my luck, the sheets would come untied and I'd crash to the ground, breaking several bones, and be stuck in my bed for weeks.

I cross the room, throw open the door, and march past him without a word.

"I'm sorry I didn't tell you about the Brooke thing."

You can take your sorrys and choke on them.

Halfway down the stairs, he catches me by my upper arm and tugs me around to face him. "I know you still care or you wouldn't be giving me the silent treatment." He even has the nerve to flash me a smile.

Oh my God. He is *not* allowed to smile. First, because he's insanely hot when he does that. And second, because . . . argh . . . because I'm *mad* at him.

I give him a cold look and jerk out of his grasp. "I've decided that I'm not going to waste my time or energy on people who don't deserve it."

Reed waits until I'm down the steps before calling after me. "So you don't care about Easton, then?"

His mention of Easton has me turning back, because other than Val, Easton has become one of my closest friends here. "Is there something going on with him?"

Reed descends the rest of the stairs to stand next to me. "Yeah. You ran off and he's had his whole life full of women he loves abandoning him."

The guilt makes me flush hot. "I didn't abandon *him*."

I left your cheating ass behind.

Reed shrugs. "Then you'll need to convince him of that, not me. But I'm confident you'll win him over."

What an arrogant ass. I school my features into as sweet of an expression as I can manage. "Will you do me a favor?"

"Of course."

"Take your condescension, your unwanted advice, your creepy lurking outside of my door, and shove it up your ass."

I whirl around. There's no grand exit for me, though, because Reed merely follows me into the kitchen, where I find the rest of the Royal household, sans Gideon.

"Doesn't anyone have practice this morning?" I ask warily.

Easton and Reed play football. Those two should be at school by now. Callum's usually gone to his office before dawn breaks. I have no idea when the twins roll out of bed. This morning, everyone is sitting at the large glass-topped table that's situated in a nook that overlooks the pool and then the Atlantic Ocean beyond.

"Special day," Callum says over the top of his coffee mug. "Everyone is participating in this family get-together. Sandra prepared breakfast for you—it's in the refrigerator. Why don't you grab it and sit down? Reed, stop hovering and take a seat."

It's not a suggestion for either of us, and despite Callum not being my dad and despite Reed's tendency to not listen to him, we both do as Callum says.

"It's good to have you back," Sawyer says as I take my seat. At least I think it's Sawyer. The burn mark around his wrist that I once used to identify the twins has healed over, so I'm not positive.

"Yeah. It's getting cold and Reed promised you'd take us all shopping for winter clothes," Seb chimes in.

"Oh, he did, did he?"

"Yeah, we're pretty helpless without you." Reed's low voice strikes me hard in the gut.

"Don't talk to me," I snap.

"I agree," Easton says. "Don't talk to her."

I jolt up in surprise to see all three Royal boys shoot glares in Reed's direction. His mouth tightens. I tell my stupid heart that it's not allowed an ounce of sympathy for Reed. Whatever he's reaping here at the breakfast table, I know he's sown a thousand times over.

"Morning, Easton," I chirp. "Have I missed anything interesting in bio?" I want to bring up the strange hug from last night, but this isn't the place.

Still, I need to know that he's okay. Easton has a few addiction problems. I think he misses his mom and is trying to fill that gap with everything and finding that nothing works. I've been there.

"Yeah, we're dissecting pigs."

"Seriously?" I make a gagging noise. "Glad I skipped."

"Nah." He nudges me with his shoulder. "I'm kidding. You haven't missed shit. Assessments are next week, though."

"Oh crap."

"Don't worry. Callum will take care of everything, won't you, Dad?" Easton sticks his chin out.

Callum ignores Easton's challenge and nods placidly. "Yes, if you need more time, Ella, I'm sure that can be arranged."

Because in his world, money buys anything, including extra time to take standardized tests. Maybe I won't even need to take a college entrance exam. I don't know whether that makes me happy or upset. Both, I guess. Confused emotions are the standard in my head right now.

Like when Reed takes a seat next to me, my body rejoices, remembering all the pleasure he pulled out of it. And my heart flips in memory of how he filled the cracks in my heart with affection and warmth that I hadn't even realized I needed in my life. But my head reminds me that this boy was terrible to me. The one concession I can make is that he tried to warn me off, but I kept after him like a lovesick idiot, telling him that he wanted me and that he just needed to admit it. So I guess we're both to blame.

He told me to stay away.

He told me I didn't belong.

If only I'd listened to him.

"Your bagel offend you in some way?" Easton asks.

I look down to see my breakfast lying in shreds on the plate. I push it aside and pull the bowl of fresh fruit, granola, and yogurt toward me. The single greatest thing about living in the Royal house might be the amount of food in the kitchen at all times. There's no eating one meal a day or hoping that your body doesn't revolt if all you can get your hands on is a single fast-food taco.

And everything is fresh, bright, green, and healthy.

If Callum had just reminded me of the contents of the refrigerator, maybe I wouldn't have put up as big of a fight.

"Not feeling the carbs this morning," I tell Easton.

"So, baby sis, what're we gonna do today?" He rubs his hands together. "I hear we're not going to school. Well, the twins are, but that's 'cause they're too dumb. They miss one class, they'll flunk out."

Both twins give him the finger.

"I'm going over to Valerie's."

"Great," Easton says. "I like Val. Sounds like we're gonna have a good time."

"You missed the pronoun *I*."

Everyone at the table is watching our exchange.

"I didn't miss it." Easton grins sunnily, but his eyes are darting all over. "I'm conveniently ignoring it. What time are we leaving?"

I rap my fingers on the table. "Easton, pay attention." I wait until his frenetic gaze lands back on me. "You are staying here. Or you can leave, but either way you're not coming with me."

"You're saying words but they're not really making any sense. When do you want to meet at your car?"

I look around the table for help, but everyone averts their faces. Across from me, the twins are nearly shaking with suppressed laughter.

Callum peers over the top of his newspaper. "You should give in now. If you don't let him ride with you, he'll show up at the Carringtons' anyway."

Easton tries to look gracious and contrite, but triumph gleams in his eyes.

"Fine, but we're painting our nails and talking about which maxi pads are the most absorbent. There might even be scientific experiments."

His smile doesn't waver, but the twins groan. "Gross," they

say in unison and push away from the table. Sawyer—I'm going with that—taps Sebastian on the shoulder. "Ready to go?"

Seb tosses a napkin on the table and rises. "I guess. I'd rather learn about geometry than maxi pads."

"Let's leave in about fifteen?" Easton says to me before bounding out of the kitchen.

I rub my forehead as a pain starts to develop over my right eye.

"Ella . . ." Reed is so quiet I barely hear him.

I ignore him and stare out the window at the clear, still water in the pool, wishing life were as smooth and calm.

"I'll leave you two to finish breakfast." Callum folds his paper noisily. The chair legs scrape against the tiled floor when he stands. "I'm glad you're back, Ella. We missed you." He places a hand on my shoulder and then leaves the room.

"I'm done, too." I throw my spoon down next to my uneaten breakfast.

"Forget it. I'm going." Reed gets to his feet. "You need to eat and it's obvious you won't while I'm here."

I keep ignoring him.

"I'm not your enemy," he says, unhappiness coloring his voice. "I didn't tell you about my past because it was messed up and I didn't know how you'd react. I was wrong, okay? But I'm gonna make it right."

He leans down, his mouth inches away from my ear. His scent surrounds me, so I force myself not to breathe. Force myself not to let my gaze linger on his sculpted arm, which flexes as he braces one hand against the table.

"I'm not giving up," he murmurs, his warm breath tickling the side of my neck.

I finally offer a response. Low and mocking. "You should. I'd screw Daniel before I'd get back together with you."

His breath whistles between his teeth as he sucks in a breath. "We both know that's not true. But I get it. I hurt you and now you want to pay me back."

I look him in the eye. "No. I don't want payback. It's not worth the mental energy, and I don't plan on spending much time thinking about you. I don't care about you or your girls. I just want to be left alone."

His jaw hardens. "I'm willing to do almost anything for you. I'd go back in time to change things if I could." He gazes down at me with determination. "But I'm not leaving you alone."

Ten

EASTON IS SPRAWLED on my bed when I walk in. He's got a can of pop—not beer, thank goodness—cupped between his legs and my remote in his fist.

"How'd you get in here?" I demand.

"You didn't close your door all the way." He pats the empty space on the mattress. "Hop up. I'll watch ESPN while you call Val."

"I already called before I came down for breakfast." I shove a few things into my backpack and sling it over my shoulder. "You guys have a thrift store around here?"

Easton rolls off the bed and joins me in front of the closet. "No clue, but if you're tired of your clothes, you can donate them during Formal week. They have a charity drive."

Formal week? I start to ask, and then decide that I don't really want to know. I'm not attending any stupid Astor Park shit in the future.

"Of course they do," I mutter. "Callum says I have money. I guess I can access it."

"What do you want it for?"

"To buy clothes."

"You have them." He gestures toward the closet.

"And I'm going to torch these and buy new ones, okay?" Anger and impatience make me ruder than I mean to be. "I don't see why it's a big deal that I want to shop. Girls are supposed to like to shop."

Easton studies me with shiny eyes that are far more intuitive than I give him credit for. "You're not a regular girl, Ella. So yeah, it's weird, but I'm putting it together. Brooke bought these clothes. You hate Brooke. These clothes gotta go."

I cross my arms. "Did Reed tell you or have you known all along?"

"He just told me," Easton admits.

"Good news. Your balls have been saved." I push him out of the way and grab a pair of sneakers.

I'm going to build a new life, starting today. It won't include guys who sleep with their dad's girlfriends and romance their stepsister on the side. I will also cut any bitch who tries something with me.

Good thing bitch number one, Jordan, is at school today, or I might shove her into her pool with some rocks tied around her neck.

"You have a mean look on your face. It's crazy hot. Promise me you'll let me orgasm before you kill me?" Easton jokes.

"You're going to get slapped very hard by someone someday."

"I know you mean that as a threat, but honestly I can't wait. Sounds like a good time."

Whatever girl takes on Easton is going to have to hold a whip in one hand and a pistol in the other. I think he's uncontrollable, though.

I pick up the key fob to my gorgeous custom-painted convertible. I was really sad to leave that baby behind.

"You think Val will have some food for me?" Easton asks. "I'm getting hungry again."

"Go downstairs, then, because you're not coming with me."

"Then it's gonna be Reed."

I stop at my bedroom door. "What're you talking about?"

"Dad's worried you're going to skate again, so one of us is on you at all times. Good news is, you get to piss by yourself, but there's an alarm on your window."

I throw my keys on the dresser and stalk into the bathroom.

"See the red sensors here?" Easton leans forward and points out two tiny pinpoints of light in the casing of the window. "Dad'll get a text message if you open it. So who's going with you to Val's? Me or Reed?"

"This is insane." I shake my head. "Fine, let's go."

Easton obediently follows me down the stairs and out into the carport. I'm not in the mood to talk, but he has other ideas as I drive through the huge gates.

"I'm the one who should be pissed off. You ran off without a word. I was worried. You could've been killed or something."

I've already had this conversation with Reed and I'm not interested in rehashing it with Easton. I change the subject. "Seems like I'm not the only one you're mad at. What's with you and the twins glaring at Reed during breakfast?"

"He's being a dick."

"You're just now discovering this?"

Easton stares at his sneakers when he answers. "It didn't matter before."

There's no point in responding. Besides, I'm already pulling into the Carringtons' driveway. Val is waiting at the back door and she doesn't look happy.

"What's wrong?" I ask when we reach her.

She nods toward Easton. "What's he doing here?"

"Sorry, one Royal has to be with Ella at all times," he says. "Dad's orders."

Val looks at me incredulously. "For real?"

"No idea, but I promise you if I could've left Easton at home, I totally would have."

"Hey, you're hurting my feelings," he protests.

And because that might be true, I plead with Val. "He's not going to say anything."

She rolls her eyes. "Whatever. Just get in here."

"Got anything to eat?" Easton asks as we pass through the kitchen.

"Help yourself." She waves a hand toward the counter that's topped by a cornucopia of fruit and a cake underneath a glass case. "You can stay here. Ella and I need alone time."

"Aw, no. I want to come with you." Easton leans past me. "Ella told me you guys were testing the absorbency of maxi pads. I'm interested in that myself."

Val gives me a confused look.

"Easton, please. Give us just ten minutes by ourselves," I beg.

"Fine, but I'm eating this entire cake."

"Knock yourself out, champ," Val says as she drags me out onto the sunporch that runs the length of her house.

The Carrington place is a true Southern mansion with big porches, fluted columns, and a lawn that looks like it's cut by hand. I imagine years ago the ladies of the house sat on rocking chairs in big dresses and with lace-gloved hands holding painted fans, saying things like "my land." I may have watched *Gone with the Wind* one too many times.

Val collapses on one of the floral couches. "I think Tam might be cheating on me."

"No!" I suck in a shocked breath and plop down beside her. Tam and Val have been dating for over a year. He's attending college only a few hours away, and from what Val has allowed to slip out, she and Tam have a lively sex life that involves things like showing off and phone sex. I haven't even had in-person sex yet, let alone kinky sex. If any relationship could survive the long-distance thing, it would be theirs, right? "Why do you think that?"

"He was supposed to visit me last month. Remember?"

I do. She'd been so excited, but then he bailed at the last minute. "You said he couldn't come because he was slammed with homework." At her miserable expression, I guess, "That was just an excuse?"

She releases a quavery sigh. "He called last night and said we needed to talk."

"Oh no."

"So we talked on the phone and he told me that college was fun and that it made him realize how much of a child he was in high school. He hasn't cheated on me, he swears, but he thinks that the distance and the temptations are too much for him and that to be *honorable*"—she spits out the word—"he needed to make sure I was cool with him seeing other people."

"Hold up." I raise my hand. "He didn't call to break up with you, but instead he wants your permission to cheat?"

"Right?" Val gives me an angry look. "That's super shitty."

"And you told him to . . ." *I hope you told him to stick his permission down his own throat where he chokes on it,* I want to say, but I don't want to look judgmental, either. That's the last thing she needs now. Later, yes, I'll remind her how awesome she is and that she doesn't need a fuckboy like Tam sucking up her energy, but for now I'm going for supportive. "Well, I hope you told him how you felt," I finish.

"I told him he could screw all the girls he wanted but he wasn't ever getting another go at me." She sweeps her hair back in a careless gesture, but her hand is trembling and her eyes are glassy with tears.

"His loss, you know that, right?"

"I keep telling myself that, but I don't feel any better. Part of me wants to steal Jordan's car and drive up to State. I'm not sure what I'll do when I get there. Either kick him in the balls or kiss him." She shudders and then peers at me out from under her eyelashes. "I kicked Reed in the balls for you, by the way."

"You did?" A wild laugh escapes as I envision tiny Val kicking giant Reed between his legs. "What brought that on?"

"His mere existence. His smug face. His refusal to tell me where you were." Val throws herself at me and hugs me again. "I'm so glad you're back."

"Ahem."

I look up to see Easton standing there, smirking at us.

"I thought you guys wanted to talk. If there's going to be girl-on-girl action, I'm available."

"You tell that to every female from age sixteen to sixty-two," Val grumbles.

"Well, yeah." He gives a faux-offended look. "I don't want anyone to feel left out."

He pushes away from the door and waltzes in, settling on the other side of Val. "Dude trouble?"

Val drops her head into her hands. "Yeah. My boyfriend decided we need an *open* relationship."

"So he wants to eat out and still come home for dinner?"

"Yup."

"And you're not down with that."

"Um, duh. I prefer guys who are faithful. You Royals might not understand that."

"Ouch, Val. What did I ever do to you?" He rubs his chest in mock pain.

"You have a penis. Therefore you're automatically on the wrong side."

He waggles his eyebrows. "But I do great things with my penis. Ask any of the girls at Astor."

"Like Abby Kincaid?" Val challenges.

I jerk my head toward Easton in shock. "You hooked up with your brother's ex?"

He slumps into the cushions, his cheeks reddening. "So what if I did? I thought you hated Reed."

Wow. It's one thing for the Royal brothers to fight at home, but this kind of public dissension is new and . . . uncomfortable. And as mad as I am at Reed, I don't like seeing this rift between the brothers. It makes me awkwardly sympathetic toward Reed, which, dammit, he does not deserve.

I try to change the subject. "Besides assessments, what's going on at school?"

"Tomorrow's Halloween, but Beringer doesn't allow costumes in school." Val shrugs. "There's a party at the Montgomery house after the game on Friday. Everyone will be wearing their best fits then."

I make a face. "Pass."

I'm not a big fan of Halloween. My mom worked nights at the clubs, so growing up I never got to go trick-or-treating like a normal kid. And I hate dressing up. I did enough of that when *I* was working the clubs.

"What else?" I ask.

Val points an accusing finger at Easton. "Well, the Royals can't stand each other anymore and Reed can't be bothered to keep the crazies in line. And anyone else with a conscience is too lazy or afraid to say something, so Astor Park has gone to shit. Every day, it escalates. I'm actually afraid someone's going to get physically hurt."

So this morning wasn't an anomaly. I frown at Easton. "What's going on?"

"You go to school to learn, right?" he says carelessly. "Well, one of those things kids need to learn is how to take care of themselves. The world is full of bullies. They don't go away when you leave high school. Might as well learn those lessons now."

"Easton. That's terrible."

"What do you care?" he accuses. "You left everyone behind. So what if the rich little boys and girls at Astor are feeling the sting of not having a Royal in charge? Aren't you happy that the place is turning out exactly like you thought it would?"

Truthfully, I didn't spare Astor Park Prep a thought when I left, but now that I know people are getting hurt, the whole thing doesn't sit well with me. "No, that doesn't make me happy. Why would you say that?"

He turns to look at the perfect lawn while Val shifts uncomfortably between us.

"Just let it go, Ella," he says finally. "You can't change anything. The most you can do is keep your head down and survive."

Eleven

THE BAKERY IS quiet when I arrive at two. I wanted to come sooner, but Lucy would've been busy. I'd like for her to yell at me, get it out of her system, and then tell me to grab an apron and get behind the counter.

Easton wanted to come in, complaining he hadn't eaten in the last two hours. After a bit of pleading, he agreed to wait in the car.

"Is Lucy here?" I ask the barista at the register. The tall, gangly boy is new, and I have a sinking feeling he's my replacement.

"Lucy," he calls over his shoulder. "Some girl's here to see you."

Lucy sticks her head out of the back door. "Who is it?"

He jerks a thumb in my direction.

Her pretty face darkens when she spots me. "Oh, it's you, Ella. Give me a minute. Why don't you have a seat over there?"

Yup, getting fired.

The cashier gives me a sympathetic look before turning to the next customer. I grab a seat at a spare table and wait for Lucy.

She doesn't take long. After a minute or so, she bustles out of the back room with two mugs of coffee. One she sets in front of me, the other she sips from before setting it down.

"Two weeks ago, Reed Royal showed up here looking for you. The next day your guardian, Callum, called to let me know that you were very sick and would be out for an undetermined time. Fast forward and you're here, looking healthy, albeit thinner than when you left." She leans forward. "Do you need help, Ella?"

"No. I'm sorry, Lucy. I should've called, but I wasn't able to come to work." The lie doesn't sit easy on my tongue. Lucy's a super-nice lady and I love working here. I tell her so. "I love it here and I know you took a chance when you hired me."

She presses her lips together before taking another drink from her mug. She taps the sides of the cup before speaking. "I really needed someone, and when you weren't around and I couldn't get ahold of you, I had to move on. You understand, don't you?"

I nod because I do understand. I don't like it, but I get it. "I'm sorry," I repeat.

"I'm sorry, too." Her hand dips into the pocket of her flour-dusted apron. "Here, call me if you need anything."

Anything but a job, I think. "Thanks," I say, pocketing the card.

"Don't be a stranger, Ella," she says kindly as she gets to her feet. "If I have another opening, maybe we can try again."

"Thanks." My vocabulary is reduced to two words: *thanks* and *sorry.*

Lucy takes another gulp of her coffee and leaves for her kitchen while I'm left to contemplate how poorly I handled my departure. I'm not used to being the unreliable one, and even though there's a sick feeling in my stomach for having let her down, there's also a small part of me that's happy she cared. That anyone cared.

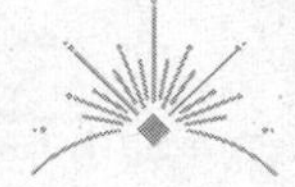

Twelve

I HEAR THE whispers the moment I step onto campus the next morning. I got a few smirks and stares when I was parking my car in the student lot, but it's much worse inside. A deafening hush, then an endless murmur of voices and smug laughter that follows me down the hall.

At my locker, I study my reflection in the little mirror on the door, wondering if there's a piece of hair sticking up or a booger in my nose. But I look fine. Just another cookie-cutter Astor Park student in my white uniform shirt and navy skirt and blazer.

My legs are bare because it's still nice enough out to not have to wear tights, but almost every girl in the hall also has bare legs, so I don't think it's my appearance that everyone is whispering about.

I don't like this. It's way too similar to my first day at Astor, when nobody said a word to me because they were waiting to see which way Reed and his brothers would swing. Hate Ella or welcome her. In the end, the student body settled for something in between. Most of the kids never really warmed up to me, but that's probably because I was purposely antisocial and hung out only with Val.

Today, almost everyone I pass eyes me with contempt. As I make my way to my first class, I can't stop fidgeting. I feel self-conscious and I hate it.

I'm jostled violently when a dark-haired girl shoves me to the side instead of walking around me. She saunters forward a few feet, then stops to look at me.

"Welcome back, Ella. How was the abortion? Did it hurt?" She smiles innocently.

My jaw opens just slightly before I force it shut. The girl in front of me is Claire something-or-other. She used to hook up with Easton before he got bored of her.

"Screw you," I mutter before brushing past her.

I reach bio class at the same time as Easton. He takes one look at my face and frowns deeply. "You okay, little sis?"

"Fine," I answer through gritted teeth.

I don't think he believes me, but he doesn't say a word as he follows me into the classroom. We settle at the table we've shared since the semester started, and I notice several smirks aimed our way.

"Nice. The Royal sex doll is back, huh, Easton?" a guy drawls from the back of the room. "Bet you and Reed are thrilled."

Easton twists around in his chair. I can't see his face, but whatever his expression is, it silences the heckler in a heartbeat.

There's a cough followed by sounds of notebooks opening and clothes rustling.

"Ignore 'em," Easton advises.

Easier said than done.

My morning only gets worse. Easton's in most of my classes and he plants his ass beside me in each one. My cheeks burn as I overhear two girls whispering about how I'm sleeping with two of my stepbrothers.

"She's definitely doing Gid, too," one of them says, not even bothering to lower her voice anymore. "It was probably his baby she got vacuumed out."

Easton does his turn-around-and-glare-bloody-murder thing again, but although it quiets the catty bitches, it doesn't silence the uneasy voice in my head.

Val warned me there were rumors floating around about me, but is this what people actually think? That I was gone because I was having an abortion? That I slept with Reed, Easton, *and* Gideon?

I'm no stranger to embarrassment—stripping at the age of fifteen taught me a huge lesson about humiliation—but knowing that everyone at school is saying all this horrible stuff about me has me blinking back tears.

I have Val, I remind myself, and she's the only person in Astor Park whose opinion matters. And Easton, I guess. He's barely left my side since I got back to Bayview, so I think I have no choice but to consider him a friend. Even if I do despise his brother.

After class, I head back to my locker to exchange textbooks because they don't all fit in my bag. Easton disappears down the hall, but not before squeezing my arm when we encounter yet another flurry of nasty whispers.

"So today's Easton's day?"

I tense up at the sound of Jordan Carrington's voice. I was wondering how long it would take for that bitch to roll out the unwelcome mat.

Rather than answer, I grab my World History text off the top shelf and replace it with my bio book.

"That's the arrangement, right? You alternate between Reed and Easton? Monday, Wednesday, and Friday, you do Reed.

Tuesday, Thursday, and Saturday, you do East." Jordan cocks her head. "What about Sundays? Are those reserved for one or both of the twins?"

I slam the locker door and turn to smile at her. "Nah, on Sundays I bone your boyfriend. Except for the times he's busy—then I do your dad."

Her eyes flash with anger. "Watch your mouth, bitch."

Keeping my smile in place becomes a strain. "Watch yours, Jordan. Unless you want me to smack you again?" I prompt, reminding her of the beatdown I gave her in the gym last month.

She releases a throaty laugh. "Go ahead and try. Let's see how far you get when you don't have Reed to protect you."

I take a step closer, but she doesn't even flinch. "I don't need Reed's protection. I never did."

"Oh, really?"

"Yeah, really." I jam one finger in the center of her chest, right between her perky boobs. "I'm capable of taking you down all by myself, Jordan."

"It's a whole new era here at Astor Park, *Ella*. The Royals don't call the shots anymore. *I* do. One word from me, and every single student at this school will be happy to make your life miserable."

"Gee, I'm terrified."

Her lips curve. "You should be."

"Whatever." I'm sick to death of this chick's power trips. "Get the hell out of my way."

She tosses her shiny brown hair over one shoulder. "What if I don't feel like it?"

"Everything okay here?" a male voice asks.

We both turn to see Sawyer standing there. His redheaded

girlfriend, Lauren, is with him. She glances uneasily at Jordan, then me.

"This doesn't concern you, little Royal." Jordan doesn't even look at him, but she does take the time to sneer at Lauren. "Doesn't concern you, either, Donovan, so why don't you and Sawyer get out of my face? Or is it Sebastian? I can never tell those two apart." An evil gleam lights her face. "What about you, sweetie? Can *you* tell them apart? Or do you keep your eyes closed when they're doing you?"

I'd wondered if Lauren knew about the twin switches Sawyer and Sebastian were pulling on her, and the expression on her face right now answers that question. Instead of shocked, she looks embarrassed and indignant.

But the girl has bigger balls than I thought, because she faces Jordan's mocking gaze and says, "Fuck off, Jordan." Then she clasps Sawyer's hand and drags him away from us.

Jordan laughs again. "That whole family is twisted, huh? But I bet you get off on that, just like that slut Lauren. Right, Ella? A dirty stripper like you probably enjoys getting tag-teamed by two Royals."

"Are we done here?" I ask tightly.

She winks at me. "Oh, sweetie, no. We're never going to be done. In fact, we're just getting started." She flutters her fingers in a dainty wave, then strolls down the hall without a backward look.

I watch her go, wondering what the hell kind of chaos I've come back to.

◆ ◆ ◆

AT LUNCH, VALERIE and I sit at a table in the corner of the room, where I try to pretend that we're the only two people who exist. It's hard, though, because I can feel everyone's eyes on me and it's making me nervous.

Val takes a bite of her tuna melt. "Reed's staring at you."

Of course he is. I shift around and spot him at a table jam-packed with football players. Easton's there, too, but he's all the way on the other side of the table instead of in his usual spot next to Reed.

I spare a glance at Reed, who's watching me with piercing blue eyes. The same eyes that grew heavy-lidded every time we kissed, that blazed hotly every time we were in the same room.

"Are you ever going to tell me what went down between you two?"

I tear my gaze away and force some pasta into my mouth. "Nope," I say lightly.

"Aw, come on, you know you can tell me anything," Val urges. "I'm a vault."

My hesitation doesn't stem from a lack of trust. Sharing just isn't natural for me. I'm more comfortable swallowing my emotions. But Val's expression is so earnest that I feel obligated to offer a few details. "We were together. He screwed up. We're not together anymore."

Her lips twitch. "Wow. Anyone ever tell you you're a terrible storyteller?"

I grimace. "It's all I've got right now."

"Fine, I won't bug you about it anymore. Just know that I'm here to listen whenever you're ready to talk." She uncaps her water bottle. "So what are we doing tonight?"

"Aren't you sick of me already?" I tease. After the disappointing meeting with Lucy, I went back to Val's and we pigged out on cake and binged all the *Step Up* movies. Easton wandered off in the middle of the second one and didn't come back.

"Hey, I'm in mourning." She glumly sticks out her lower lip. "I need you to distract me so I don't think about Tam. Halloween was our favorite holiday. We used to do couples costumes."

"Aw. Did he text you again?" He messaged her three times last night, but Valerie had ignored them.

"Constantly. Now he's talking about driving down so we can talk in person." She looks stricken. "Broken hearts suck."

Don't I know it.

As if on cue, my phone sounds the text message alert. I wince when I see Reed's name on the screen.

Don't read it, I order myself.

Like an idiot, I read it.

> Stop acting like u don't give a damn about me. We both know u do

I clench my teeth. Ugh. Arrogant ass.

Another message pops up: U missed me when u were gone. Same way I missed u. We'll get thru this

No, we won't. I want to shout at him to stop texting me, but the one thing I know about Reed Royal—he's a selfish jerk. He does what he wants, when he wants it.

And his next message is just a reminder of that.

> Brooke was a mistake. Happened before we met. Will never happen again

Just the sight of Brooke's name has me curling my fist around my phone. Before I can stop myself, I type back a blunt message.

I'll never forgive u for sleeping with her.

Leave me alone

"You know I'm still here, right?"

Val's dry remark brings on a guilty flush. I quickly shove my phone in my bag and pick up my fork again. "Sorry. I was just telling Reed to screw off."

She throws her head back and laughs. "God. I missed you, you know that?"

I laugh, too, and for the first time all day, it's actually genuine. "I missed you, too," I tell her, and I mean it.

✦ ✦ ✦

WHEN THE FINAL bell chimes, I'm more than ready to get the hell out of here. My first day back was about as fun as being waterboarded. The mean laughter, the whispers, the sneers and nasty looks. I'm going to lock myself in my bedroom, blast some music, and pretend that today never happened.

I don't even bother going to my locker. I shoulder my bag, text Val that she should let me know if she's coming over later, and hurry out to the parking lot.

Then I stop in my tracks, because Reed is leaning against the driver's side of my car.

"What do you want now?" I snap.

I'm sick and tired of him getting in my face all the time. And I hate how good he looks right now. The weather is growing cooler, so his dark hair is windblown and his sharp cheekbones are flushed from the cold.

He pushes his big, muscular body off the car and marches toward me. "Sawyer said Jordan was harassing you earlier."

"The only person who's harassing me is you." I give him an icy look. "Stop texting me. Stop talking to me. It's over."

He just shrugs. "If I really believed that, I'd back off. But I don't."

"I'll block your number," I warn.

"I'll get a new phone."

"I'll change my number."

He snorts. "You really think I won't be able to get it?"

I hug my bag against my chest like a shield. "It's over," I repeat. A ball of pain lodges in my throat. "You cheated on me."

"I never cheated on you," he says hoarsely. "I haven't touched Brooke in over six months."

He sounds so sincere. What if he's telling the truth? What if—

Don't be an idiot! an internal voice shouts. Ugh. Of course he's not being sincere, and I should know better than to get sucked in by his earnest face and the tiny wobble in his voice. Growing up, I watched my mom fall for the wrong guys over and over again. They lied to her. Used her. And as much as I loved her, I hated how stupid she could be when it came to men. It would take her months, almost a year sometimes, to figure out that the lying jerk in her bed wasn't worth her time, while I stood there on the sidelines and waited for her to come to her senses.

I refuse to be played like that.

"Go to hell, Reed," I mutter. "I'm done with you."

He moves even closer. "Yeah? So you're telling me you don't want me anymore?"

"That's exactly what I'm telling you." I sidestep his approach and practically fling myself at the car. But my escape attempt backfires, because he swiftly turns around and backs me up against the door.

The heat of his body sears right through my clothes. My pulse speeds up as he plants both palms against the car, trapping me between his arms.

"You're saying I don't turn you on anymore?" He dips his head and his warm breath fans over my neck. When I give an involuntary shiver, he laughs softly. "Admit it, you miss me."

I clamp my lips together.

Reed's cheek brushes mine as he keeps whispering in my ear. "You miss the way I kiss you. You miss me sliding in bed with you at night. You miss the way it feels when I put my mouth right *here*—" He presses his lips against my neck, and I shiver again. That gets me another husky chuckle. "Yeah, I'm sure I don't do anything for you at all, right, baby?"

"*Don't* call me that." I shove him angrily, ignoring the loud pounding of my heart. I hate the effect he has on me. "And leave me alone."

A low voice sounds from behind us. "You heard her. Leave her alone."

Easton stalks up to us and latches a steely hand on Reed's shoulder. Despite being a year younger, Easton is as tall and ripped as his brother. It takes zero effort for him to yank Reed away from me.

"This is a private conversation," Reed says, unfazed at being manhandled.

"Yeah?" Easton glances at me. "You in the mood to talk to our big bro, little sis?"

"Nope," I answer with forced cheerfulness.

Easton grins. "There you go, Reed. Conversation's over." The mocking glint in his eyes dissolves, replaced by irritation. "Besides, Dad just texted. He wants all of us to come home ASAP. He and Brooke have some announcement to make."

My gaze flies to Easton's. "Brooke?"

With a harsh laugh, he turns to Reed. "What, you didn't tell her?"

"Tell me what?" I demand. Why the hell is Brooke at the house?

Reed shoots his brother a stony look.

"Gee, I wonder why you didn't mention it." Easton shrugs at me. "Dad and Brooke got back together."

My whole body runs cold. What? Why would Callum ever get back together with that witch?

And how can I possibly face her again after what I witnessed in Reed's bedroom that night?

My legs feel wobbly and my hands begin to shake. I hope the boys don't notice how hard I'm trembling, that they don't see how shaken up I am by this news.

Going home is suddenly the last thing I want to do.

Thirteen

ONE BY ONE, our cars pull into the grand, circular driveway of the Royal estate. My convertible. Easton's pickup. Reed's Range Rover, and the Rover the twins share. I remain in the car as I watch the Royal brothers slam doors and disappear through the side door of the mansion.

I can't believe Brooke is in there. I can't believe Reed "forgot" to mention it. In all the times he's gotten in my face and mocked me about how he's going to win me back and how I still want him, he couldn't tell me that Brooke was back?

But of course he didn't say anything. He thinks if he pretends he never touched Brooke, if he pretends she doesn't exist, that maybe I'll forget about her.

I won't, though. Ella Harper doesn't forget. Ever.

I take a deep breath and order myself to get out of the car. The internal command fails, because I stay put. It's not until the side door swings open that I scramble out of the driver's seat.

"Ella," Brooke calls out, smiling from ear to ear.

I grab my backpack and round the car, trying to bulldoze past her, but she steps into my path. I've never wanted to punch anyone more than I want to punch this woman. She's as blond and fake as I remember, decked out in an expensive minidress, sky-high stilettos, and enough diamonds to fill a Tiffany shop.

"I have nothing to say to you," I announce.

She laughs. "Oh, darling, you don't mean that."

"Yes, I do. Now get out of my way."

"Not until we have a little girl chat," she chirps. "I can't have you going in there until we set a few things straight."

Disbelief makes my eyebrows soar. "There's nothing to set straight." For some reason, I find myself lowering my voice, even though she and Reed deserve that I scream it from the rooftops. "You slept with Callum's *son*."

"Did I?" She titters again. "Because it seems that if I did, and that if someone in this house knew about it"—she gives me a pointed look—"then Callum would have learned about it by now."

She's got me there. And now I'm pissed at myself for keeping my mouth shut. One word to Callum, and Brooke would be history. He'd throw her out on her ass faster than you can say *cheating shrew.*

But . . . he'd throw Reed out, too. He might even disown him.

God, I'm sick. I'm screwed in the head. Why else would I care what happens to Reed Royal?

Brooke smiles knowingly. "Oh, you poor pathetic girl. You're in love with him."

I clench my teeth. She's wrong. I don't love him anymore. I don't.

"I tried to warn you. I told you that the Royals would ruin you, but you didn't listen."

"And because of that, you punished me?" I say sarcastically.

"Punished you?" She blinks in what looks like genuine confusion. "What exactly do you think I did, sweetie?"

I gape at her. "You slept with Reed. I walked in on you two! Or have you conveniently forgotten that?"

Brooke waves a hand. "Oh, you mean the night you ran off? Sorry to disappoint you, but there was no . . . excitement . . . to be had that night."

"Y-you were naked," I stutter.

"I was proving a point." She rolls her eyes at my bewildered expression. "Reed needed to learn a lesson."

"That you're a cheating liar?"

"No, that this is my house." She gestures to the mansion behind us. "He doesn't call the shots anymore. I do." Brooke fingers a strand of her shiny golden hair before tucking it behind her ear. "I wanted to show him what happens when he gets out of line. I wanted him to recognize that I can destroy him without any effort. And see how easy it was? I take off my dress and poof! His relationship with you disappears. That, my darling, is called 'power.'"

I bite the inside of my cheek. I don't know what to believe anymore. Did Reed bargain for this with her? She'd lie and pretend she didn't sleep with him in exchange for . . . what? Does it matter? They slept together at some point. And if he's capable of betraying his own father like that, think of how easy it will be for him to betray *me*.

I can't take that chance. I know what I saw in his bedroom. Brooke was naked. And he just sat there and said nothing. If I let Reed and Brooke plant these seeds of doubt, it's only a matter of time before I do something stupid . . . like forgive him. And then he'll hurt me again and I'll have nobody to blame for it but myself.

"You slept with Callum's son," I repeat, letting my disgust for her show on my face. "Doesn't matter if you didn't hook up that night—you still cheated on him with his own son."

She just smiles.

Nausea shoots up my throat. "You're . . ." I trail off. Ugh. No insult in the world can do this woman justice.

"I'm what?" she mocks. "A tramp? A gold digger? Any more slut shaming you want to do? I don't understand why we girls can't stick together, but honestly, honey, your opinion of me doesn't matter. This will be my home soon and I'll be the one calling the shots. You should try to get on my good side." She arches one brow.

I remind myself that I've run into Brooke's kind a hundred times before. She's a backroom bully. Sweet to all the people with money, snotty to the girls who can't help her up the ladder, and downright evil to anyone who threatens her.

So I take courage in the fact that she finds me threatening, and direct an arched eyebrow right back. "Callum will never let you kick me out. And even if he did, I wouldn't care. I already tried to run away from here, remember?"

"But you came back, didn't you, darling?"

"Because he forced me to," I mumble.

"No, because you wanted to. You can claim to hate the Royals all you want, sweetie, but the truth is, you *want* to be part of this family. Any family, really. Poor orphan Ella needs someone to love her."

She's wrong. I don't need that. I was on my own for two years after Mom died. I can do it again. I'm fine being alone.

Right?

"A few gentle nudges and I guarantee Callum will come around to my way of thinking," Brooke says. "It's up to you which direction I nudge him in. Do you want to continue living the Royal lifestyle, or do you want to be shaking your ass for dollar bills again? You're in charge of your own destiny." She points a lacquered nail to an empty space next to her. "There's still room for you over here."

We both spin around at the sound of a car engine. Gideon's SUV comes to an abrupt stop behind Easton's truck. The eldest Royal brother hops out of the driver's seat, takes one look at us, and asks, "What's going on here?"

"Just welcoming Ella back into the fold," Brooke answers, winking at me. "Come here and give me a kiss, darling."

Gideon looks like he'd rather kiss a cactus, but he still trudges over and plants a cool peck on Brooke's cheek. "What's this all about?" he mutters. "I skipped my afternoon classes and drove three hours to get here, so it better be important."

"Oh, it's important." Brooke gives us a cryptic smile. "Let's go inside and your father and I will tell you all about it."

◆ ◆ ◆

FIVE MINUTES LATER, a grim-faced Callum ushers us into a room at the front of the house. His hand hovers protectively at the small of Brooke's back. And Brooke? She looks smugger than a cat at a fish market.

The room is impeccably decorated in what I've termed as *Southern Plantation chic*. The walls are covered in heavy cream wallpaper. There are several inches of molding that adorn the ceiling. The room is big enough that there are two seating areas, one near the floor-to-ceiling windows that are draped in peach silk fabric, and one closer to the doors. Brooke takes a seat in one of the light green-and-peach chairs by the fireplace.

Above the mantel is a gorgeous painting of Maria Royal.

There's something horribly wrong about Brooke sitting in this room, in front of that painting. Something sacrilegious.

After pouring a glass of whisky, Callum positions himself behind Brooke, one hand on the top of her chair and one hand clutched around a tumbler nearly overflowing with liquor.

Gideon wanders to stand near the windows, hands in his pockets as he stares out at the front lawn. Easton and I start walking toward him, but Callum's voice stops us.

"Sit down. You, too, Gideon."

Gideon doesn't move. He doesn't even acknowledge that Callum has spoken. Reed takes one look at his dad and one look at Gideon and makes up his mind in an instant. He walks over to his brother and stands beside him.

The lines are clearly drawn.

I watch as Callum's fingers curl into the back of the chair. His body sways toward his eldest sons, but he stays rooted in place at Brooke's side. What hold does she have on him?

She can't be *that* good in bed.

"Brooke—I mean, we—have an announcement."

Easton and I exchange a wary look. The twins are on my other side, wearing identical frowns of suspicion.

"Brooke is having a baby."

A collective whoosh greets that statement as we all inhale in shock.

When the last word leaves his mouth, Callum lifts the glass of liquor and drinks. And drinks. And drinks until the entire glass is empty.

Brooke looks happy, and her pleasure is awful.

Is it wrong to hit a pregnant woman? I fist my hands at my side in case someone, anyone, gives me the green light to vault over two sofas and a side table and whale on her until she cries for mercy. She's killing this family, and I hate her for that as much as anything.

"What's that got to do with us?" Easton finally asks. His voice is dripping with insolence.

"It's a Royal baby, which means it will have the Royal last name. We're getting married." Callum is implacable. I guess this is what he sounds like in the boardroom, but this isn't a business deal. It's his family.

Brooke raises her left hand and spreads her fingers.

By the window, Reed's entire body grows rigid. Beside me, Easton growls.

"That's Mom's ring!" Sebastian spits out.

"You can't give her Mom's ring." Sawyer picks up a vase from the side table and throws it across the room. It doesn't come anywhere near Brooke, but the crash makes us all flinch. "That's fucking bullshit."

"It's not her ring." Callum threads a shaky hand through his hair. "It might look like it, but your mother's ring is upstairs. I promise you that."

I gawk at him. What kind of man gives his new wife a ring that looks like his dead wife's ring? And what kind of woman wants that? This game that Brooke is playing is too twisted for me. It's like she's getting off on hurting everyone.

"Your promises aren't worth the dust under that chair," Gideon says to his father. He's cold and unyielding, a sharp contrast from his usual mild-mannered demeanor. Of all the Royal boys, Gid has always been the calmest. But he's not at all calm right now. "You can make all the babies you want with her, but they're not part of our family and never will be."

He pushes forward, striding all the way over to Brooke and Callum. I hold my breath as he looms in front of them.

"You will never belong here," he tells her, so matter-of-factly that it brings a frown to her lips. "No matter who you spread your legs for, you'll never be more than a whore from Salem Street."

Brooke smiles. "And you'll never be more than a rich man's forgotten son whose mother killed herself."

Gideon flinches. Then he spins on his heel and marches out of the room. The twins follow suit. Then Easton. Only Reed and I remain, and I can't help but glance in his direction. His expression is full of disgust. Anger. Disappointment.

But the one thing it's missing is . . . surprise.

Callum's announcement about a new Royal baby had shocked the hell out of everyone except Reed.

Our gazes lock, and in that moment, I see the truth in his blue eyes.

He'd already known.

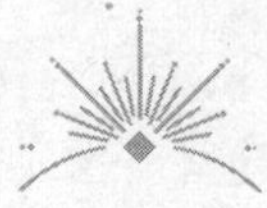

Fourteen

REED

THE MINUTE ELLA'S eyes swing toward me, I know she's jumped to the wrong conclusion.

I grab her wrist and drag her out of the parlor and into the room across the hall, which just so happens to be my mom's private suite—and the place Gid and I found her after . . . after she died. Perfect. This is exactly where my relationship with Ella will be saved. *Not.*

"Look—" I start, but she's off and running before I can get another syllable out.

"That's your baby, isn't it?" she hisses.

"No. I swear it. It's not mine."

"I don't believe you." Her hands are tiny fists at her side.

I want to reach for her, but I don't think that'll go over well. "I haven't touched her since you came here," I repeat for what feels like the thousandth time. "I was done with her even before that."

She slaps the nearest surface and dust fills the air. This room has been closed up for a long time. "How do you know it's not yours?"

I shift uncomfortably, because answering requires me to

dredge up a bad memory, but I don't have much choice. "When I saw her, she just had a small bump."

Ella pales, and I know she's remembering that night when she discovered Brooke naked in my room. "You don't know. You can't know. Not until you get a test done. I'm sick." She presses a hand to her stomach. "I feel actually, honest to God, sick to my stomach."

"It's not mine. It must be my dad's. Or, hell, it could be anyone's. She's willing to cheat on my dad," I say with desperation.

"So are you."

I suck in a breath. That's a direct hit and she knows it. But I'm not giving up. This is a fight I'm going to win even if I have to play dirty.

"I'm not going to deny that I was a dick. Maybe I still am, but I'm not the father of Brooke's baby. I didn't cheat on you. I kept a secret about my past from you, and it was a crappy thing to do. I know that. It was wrong. I'm sorry. Just . . . please, please forgive me," I plead. "Put both of us out of our misery."

"It doesn't matter anymore." There's a dullness in her face that scares me. She shakes her head. "Before I met you, my life was full of shitty things. But I dealt because what else could I do? It didn't matter that my dad was never around, because I had my mom. I told myself that I should be grateful when she died because she was in so much pain. Then I came here and I looked at you and thought, *I see myself beneath that hard, rough exterior*. This boy lost his mother. He's angry and hurt and I see him. Maybe he sees me, too."

She folds her arms around her middle—trying to hold something in, keep me out. I don't know anything other than she's hurting. I reach for her, but she flinches as if even the thought of my touch is too painful.

Fuck, she's hurting so bad and I did that to her.

"I did . . . *do* . . . see you," I whisper.

She's not listening. "And I thought, I'll just keep after him. Eventually I'll wear him down, convince him that we're a beautiful fairy tale. But we're not. We're nothing. We're *smoke*—insubstantial and meaningless." She flicks her fingers against each other in a soundless snap. "We aren't even a tragedy. We're less than nothing."

Her words make my heart ache. She's right. I should walk away, but I can't. And the fact that she's in so much pain tells me that she needs me. Only a coward would stop fighting now. I caused all this pain, but I know that I can take it away if she'd give me the chance.

I take a deep breath. "I can play this two ways. I can walk away. Or I can fight for you. Guess which one I'm doing?"

Ella glares at me in stony silence, so I keep talking. "I messed up. I should've been honest with you from the start. Brooke told me she was pregnant that night. I panicked. My whole brain shut down. I scrambled for a way out that didn't include me telling you that I ever touched her. I was ashamed. Okay? Ashamed. Is that what you wanted to hear?"

Her lips curl. "Yeah, well, you know what I am? I'm the stupid girl in the horror movie. You *made* me into that stupid girl." She points an accusing finger at me. "I'm the one running back into the house where the guy with the knife is. You warned me. Over and over again, you told me to stay away. But I couldn't listen. I thought I knew better."

"I was wrong. We shouldn't stay away from each other. We can't stay away from each other. You and I both know that."

I walk toward her and stop when my toes nearly touch hers. Then, in one swift movement, I haul her against me. Oh fuck.

She feels so good pressed up against me. I want to shove a hand in her soft hair and kiss the shit out of her, but she's gazing up at me with livid, burning eyes.

"Stop *touching* me," she snaps. "I'd rather die—"

I cover her mouth with my palm. "Don't say things you'll regret. Don't say things we can't come back from," I warn.

Her hand flies up and crashes against the side of my face. My chin jerks to the right on impact, but I don't let go. Her eyes are bright and her shoulders are shaking. I bet I look just as stupid and crazy and out of control at this moment as she does.

"What do you want from me? Tell me and I'll do it. Do you want me on my knees? Me kissing your feet?"

"No, keep your pride," she says snidely. "You'll need something to keep you warm at night. Oh wait, that's what you have Brooke for." She gives my chest a hard shove and scrambles away, and she's wresting the door open before I can reach her.

In the hall, Dad and Brooke grind to a halt. Dad looks at Ella's fleeing figure and then back at me with narrowed eyes. Brooke's all smiles.

Angrily, I stomp past them to find Gid. Maybe he has answers for me. At this point, he's the only brother left who'll talk to me.

I find him standing outside on the rocky ridge that separates the lawn from the sliver of sand we call a beach. The Atlantic is cold and dark, lit up only by a partially covered moon rising into the early evening sky.

He doesn't turn to look at me when he asks, "Is the baby yours?"

"Why does everyone think that?"

"Gee, bro, I can't imagine why anyone who knew you slept with Brooke might think that her baby is yours."

"It's not." I run a hand through my hair. "I haven't touched her in over six months. Not since St. Patrick's Day. We got lit, remember? I passed out upstairs. She climbed on top of me. I don't remember much about it except waking up naked with her next to me. Dad was outside, calling us in to dinner. I was gonna tell him then. That night. But I chickened out."

Gideon doesn't answer. He simply keeps staring at the water.

"I used to think that Dinah and Brooke were trying to destroy this family, but now I think it's us. We're the ones killing the family. I don't know how to make it better, Gid. Tell me." *Help me.* He doesn't speak, so I try again, desperate to make a connection. "Remember when Mom read us *The Swiss Family Robinson* and we walked up and down the coast trying to find a perfect cave to live in? It was all five of us. We were going to kill the whale, eat berries, make our own clothes out of Spanish moss and seaweed."

"We're not kids anymore and that book is racist as fuck."

"Okay, bad example. But we're still family. We used to fight together, conquer things together."

"You wanted to leave," he reminds me. "That's all you fucking talked about. Getting away from here. Now because Ella's around you think it's worth staying? What kind of loyalty do you have to your family?"

He jumps onto the sand and lets the falling night swallow him up, leaving me alone with my miserable thoughts.

Nobody forced me to sleep with Brooke. I made that decision all by myself. I took perverse satisfaction in figuratively sticking it to my dad by literally sticking it to his girlfriend.

I wanted him to suffer. He deserved to after everything he'd done to our family. He drove Mom to the brink with his cheating and lies. I feel like the lies were the worst. If he hadn't repeatedly promised that he wasn't involved in all those things Steve was doing, in all those whorehouses around the world with all those high-class escorts, models, and actresses that a billionaire's money can buy, maybe Mom would've left him.

And if she'd left, she'd probably still be alive today. But she's not. She's dead, and Dad's neglect and cheating killed her as solidly as the pills she took that night.

I press my lips together. Of course, my revenge is meaningless since I haven't had the balls to tell him about me and Brooke. And every time I think about him finding out I feel like puking.

I've spent the last couple of years trying to destroy everything around me. Who knew success would taste so bitter?

Fifteen

ELLA

"WHAT'S GOING ON?" Val demands at lunch on Friday. "And don't say 'nothing' because you all look like a royally depressed mess. Even Easton looks like someone kicked his puppy."

"Is that a euphemism?" I try joking.

Valerie glares at me. "No. Not really."

I pick at my meal. I haven't been able to eat much this week and I think it shows. Every time I try to eat, the vision of Brooke telling us all about her pregnancy pops up, except it isn't Callum at her side. It's Reed. And then my terrible mind runs with it, showing me images of Reed holding the baby, pushing a stroller in the park with Brooke looking like a fitness model beside him, the two of them cooing over their stupid baby's first steps.

No wonder I can't eat.

This morning when I pulled my jeans on, they felt loose. The clothes are wearing me instead of the other way around.

I'm not ready to tell Val about how the entire Royal household is rotting from the inside out, but if I don't give her something she might stab me with her fork. "I thought being an only child sucked, but family drama is a hundred times worse."

"Reed?" she asks.

"Not just him. It's everyone." I hate the tension in the house. The way the brothers don't look at each other over breakfast. And I can't even escape because I've lost my job. I guess I should start looking for a new one. This time it's not because I need the money, but because every time I walk into the house, I feel like a hundred-pound weight descends on my shoulders. And it's going to be even worse once the baby arrives. I don't know how I'm going to deal with that.

"Life sucks, but if it makes you feel any better, I blocked Tam's phone number."

"You did?" *It's about time*. Tam's stupid suggestion of having an open relationship was basically his way of keeping Val locked down while he spread his skanky ass all over his college campus, and she doesn't deserve that. "Because that does make me feel better."

"Yup, and it felt good. I was tormenting myself reading all his texts and I could feel myself weakening."

"You know you can do better."

"I know." She takes a sip of her Diet Coke. "So last night I blocked him and I slept well for the first time in a long time. I woke up this morning and, yeah, it still hurt, but the pain wasn't as bad."

"It's going to get better." The words come out limply. That used to be my personal mantra.

I don't know if I believe it anymore.

She fiddles with the can. "I hope so. Is there a real-life block button? Because it could come in real handy right about now."

"Sunglasses. Really big sunglasses," I advise. "Or, wait, even better—a shield." I could use one at home against Reed.

A reluctant smile spreads across her face as she considers my silly suggestion. "Wouldn't it be awkward trying to maneuver that thing?"

"Nah, it's brilliant. Let's patent the sucker and make millions."

"Done." She holds out her hand and I slap my palm against hers.

"God, Val. I think you're the best thing that happened to me since I moved here."

"I know." She gets a speculative look in her eyes, slides a glance toward the football table, and then returns to me. "Let's go to the game tonight."

"Um, no thanks. I take back every good thing I've said about you."

"Why not?"

"First, I don't like football. Second, I don't want to cheer for people I don't like. Third, other than you, all the rest of Astor Park can die in a fiery blaze."

"You can pick me up at six thirty."

"No. I don't want to go to the game."

"Aw, come on. Both of us need a distraction. You need one from Reed and I need one from Tam. Everyone goes to the Riders games. We can inspect the man stock that's available and pick one to ease our broken hearts with."

"Can't we just eat a barrel of ice cream?"

"We'll do both. We're going to eat our ice cream and get eaten."

She waggles her eyebrows at me, and I laugh reluctantly, but inwardly my heart's protesting. The only touch I want is Reed's. The cheating bastard. Dammit. Maybe I do need a distraction.

"Okay, let's go."

✦ ✦ ✦

"GET OUT OF the car," Val orders when she climbs into the passenger seat later that night. "I need to get a better look at this outfit."

"You'll see it when we get to the game."

"Are you doing this to make Reed come in his football pants or to make the girls at Astor Park freak out?"

I ignore the reference to Reed. I definitely wasn't thinking of how I wanted to make him burn with jealousy. Nuh-uh. Not at all.

"You told me I'm supposed to pick out a new man tonight. This is my man-hunting outfit." I wave a hand toward my clothes.

I paired striped knee socks over black leggings topped with an old jersey I found at the secondhand store I hit after school. I couldn't tuck the material into the top of the leggings without it looking like I had a bunch of socks stuffed down my pants, so I bought a big black belt and bunched the jersey around my hips.

Two loose braids and smeared eye black—which in my case was a load of black eyeliner over a heavy priming base so it wouldn't budge—under my eyes complete my pinup football look.

"I suggested one man, not a whole herd," Val says wryly. "But maybe this works for my benefit. You pick the one you want and you can leave the rest for me."

"Very funny."

"Seriously. I'm thinking we need to get the twins to escort us inside. I'm afraid of what the girls are gonna do when they get a load of you."

Val's prediction isn't that far off the mark. The football girlfriends scowl at me when we walk past the area where the girlfriends and parents wait for the players to run from the locker room onto the field.

A few insults—"slut," "trailer trash," and "what do you expect?"—trickle down the crowd from the other girls.

"These chicks are so jealous they won't even have to shove their fingers down their throats tonight," Val snarks. "Their jealousy will eat away at all their extra calories."

I shrug. "I've heard worse and I don't really care."

"You shouldn't. Next week we'll be surrounded by a whole team of slutty football players."

"I'll have to up my game, then." I don't mind a challenge.

When we arrive at the student section, Jordan turns us away.

"You can't sit with us," she announces.

I roll my eyes. "Why, because I'm too trashy for your precious bleachers?"

"That, too." She smirks. "But also because you're wearing the wrong colors."

I look up at the mass of students and realize she's right. They're all situated so that the color of their T-shirts spells out an *A* in gold against a black background. I'm wearing a white jersey and Val's wearing a cropped gray knit sweater. Jordan's in a black catsuit, and the only thing missing from her latex dominatrix gear is a whip and a chair.

"I guess we missed the memo." Because there had to be one, seeing as how everyone else fits perfectly into Jordan's scheme. I'm reluctantly impressed. It can't be easy to wrangle a couple hundred students into wearing color-coordinated shirts depending on where they're sitting on the stands.

"Maybe you should check the Astor stories once in a while." She turns with a swish of her glossy hair.

I didn't even know there was an Astor social media account.

"Come on," Val says, tugging my arm. "We'll sit with the parents."

We find a place at the top where we can eat popcorn and pretend to cheer for the Riders. "What on earth is Jordan wearing?" I giggle. "Is she a part-time S&M mistress?"

"Nah." Val throws a few kernels of popcorn into her mouth. "The dance team performs at halftime before the band so I'm guessing that's their costume."

She's right. When halftime comes around, Jordan and her squad put on a routine with so much boob and ass shaking that I feel like I should slip some of Daddy G's business cards in their gym bags in case their trust funds ever dry up.

"They'd get at least the five-dollar tips," I whisper to Val behind my hand.

"Only five dollars? I'd want at least twenty per dude before I'd strip."

"What are you talking about? You'd strip for free," I tease. Val has told me before that she has exhibitionist tendencies. When we go to the Moonglow club's eighteen-and-over night, Val makes me dance in the cages suspended from the ceiling.

"True. But I wouldn't mind getting paid." She gives me a thoughtful look. "How much did you say you earned while you were working at these clubs?"

"I didn't. And stripping is a lot different from cage dancing in front of a bunch of hot high school and college guys," I caution. Most strip clubs reek of desperation and regret and I'm not just referring to the strippers' dressing room. The guys on the floor waving their singles around over their eight-dollar steak lunches are as needy as the girls on the stage.

Val wrinkles her nose. "I don't know. It'd be nice to have the extra cash, and you must've been making serious bank to be able to support yourself and your mom on it."

"The money is the only good thing about it. Besides, you wouldn't want to strip around here. Think if someone saw you and then you had to have classes with him or something. That'd be a hundred different kinds of awkward."

She sighs. "It was just an idea."

I feel a stab of sympathy. I know that Val's status as the poor relation really bugs her. I wish I could give her part of my stash—it's not like I need it—but she's not the kind of person who'd accept a handout. She'd see it as charity, which she already has to accept from her aunt and uncle.

"How about I hire you to be my bodyguard? Because everyone's looking at me right now like they want to murder me. Especially that one over there." I jerk my head toward the second row of the student section, where a familiar golden-haired girl keeps swiveling around to frown at me.

"Ha. Abby wouldn't hurt a flea. She's too passive. Do you think she wears that Eeyore expression when she comes?"

I slap a hand over my mouth to muffle my shout of laughter.

But it's true. Reed's ex is pale, quiet, and mild-mannered, as opposite from me as you can get. Someone said that Abby reminds them of Reed's mom. At one time that made me nervous as hell, because Reed adored his mom. These days, I don't give a crap about trying to impress Reed Royal.

Abby obviously still does, though. And she obviously views me as competition, because she won't stop staring at me. If she'd asked, I could've given her a pretty good tip about how to win Reed over. First and foremost, don't sleep with his brother.

"Did she really hook up with Easton when I was gone?" I ask Val.

"Yup. What an idiot, right? I mean, that's a surefire way to send Reed running in the opposite direction." Val purses her lips. "Or, wait, maybe not. You made out with Easton and that didn't scare Reed off." Then she changes her tune again. "But you're special. Abby isn't. No way is Reed getting back together with her now."

"Even Abby is too good for him," I grumble. "He deserves to be alone for all of eternity."

Val snickers.

"Actually, I was really hoping someone would break his legs in the game, but unfortunately it looks like he's still up and walking around."

"We could break them."

"Take a baseball bat to him in the middle of the night?" I say wistfully.

"Sounds like you've already got this all planned out."

"I might've fantasized about it a few times," I admit.

"After we're done with Reed, can we drive up to State?"

"Obvs. Then we'll put an ad online offering our services to other women. We'll name our bat 'Vengeance.'"

"Your bloodthirstiness is turning me on so much right now."

"Save it for one of the herd," I tell her. "You have your eye on any of them?"

"No. I'm still considering my options." Meaning the only thing she can see right now is Tam. I have the same problem, except my vision is blocked by Reed.

We slump in the bleacher seats and turn our attention back to the game.

The Riders win, as expected, and talk after the game immediately turns toward Winter Formal, which Astor Park puts on after Thanksgiving and before Christmas. The dance talk is like foreplay for Jordan. She's glowing when Val and I descend the stadium steps. Our progress is slowed by all the parents stopping to tell Jordan how much they liked her routine and how talented she is.

Jordan thrusts out her boobs a little more with each compliment. The dads stare at her with lusty hunger and she looks like she's getting off on it.

"Nice show," I tell Jordan as we draw even with her. She looks pretty fantastic in her formfitting costume, and there's a dewy glow on her cheeks left over from the exertion on the field.

Her eyes flick over me with disdain and then dismissal. She turns to her cousin. "You're too good for this piece of trash, Val. Why don't you come to Shea's party with me?"

"Pass. I wouldn't climb into your car if we were on Fury Road and the War Boys were after me."

A few kids snort with laughter behind us. That only makes Jordan angrier.

"I can't believe we're related."

"I know. I wonder about it, too, sometimes. How someone so nice, like me, could end up with a bitch like you for a cousin."

Jordan lunges at Val, and I stupidly step between them. Jordan's fist hits the back of my head at the same time that Val charges forward. I bounce off them and land against the railing.

"Holy shit," some random guy yells. "Girl fight!"

The stands empty and suddenly it's pure chaos. Popcorn is flying everywhere. There are arms and hands and nails in my face. A strong arm lifts me down over the fence, where someone else catches me and swings me out of the way. I look up to see Reed.

Easton comes up on my other side and slings his arm around my shoulder, separating me from Reed. They proceed to trade scowls.

"So are we going to the Montgomerys' party?" Easton asks me.

"I told you, I don't like dressing up."

He snickers and points to my getup. "Looks like you're already in costume, little sis."

Oh man. He totally has a point.

"Come on," he coaxes. "It'll be fun."

I cave. "Fine. Whatever. Where's Val?" I turn back to the stands to see that the administrators have broken up the fight.

An arm jerks me around. Reed again. "What the hell are you wearing? Whose jersey is that?" he demands.

"It's just a secondhand—"

"Take it off."

"What? No way."

I look to Easton for help, but he's frowning. "Now that I think about it, you can't wear another school's jersey to our games. That's bad voodoo."

"You won," I remind him.

"Take it off right now," Reed orders. His voice is muffled because he's trying to tug his own jersey up over his head.

"Forget it. I'm not putting your jersey on."

"Oh yes, you are." His shoulder pads are up around his ears. "Dammit, East, help me out."

Easton ignores him. "You need a ride, sis?"

"She'll ride with me," Reed says firmly. He shoves his jersey back down and his expression dares me to challenge him.

So I challenge him. "Sorry, pal, but that's not happening."

"Don't call me 'pal.'"

"Don't give me orders."

He gives me another order. "Val can drive your car to the party. You're coming with me."

"Oh my God!" I burst out. "What's it going to take for you to get the message, Reed? We're *over.*" My frustration and annoyance are reaching all-time highs. "I already have my eye on someone else."

His nostrils flare. "Like hell you do."

I look at the line of players standing along the track watching us, and an evil thought pops into my mind. My eyes narrow in on Wade, the quarterback. Wade's a whore. Straight up, he had to use Reed's Range Rover for sex one night outside the club because, according to Reed, Wade couldn't wait to get home before banging some girl.

Smirking at Reed, I move away from the Royals, waltz right up to Wade, and launch myself at him.

His muscular arms close reflexively around me. And when I bend down to kiss him, his lips part automatically. He tastes like sweat, smells like grass, and is a pretty fantastic kisser. His tongue stays firmly in his mouth, but he can use his lips like a master.

No wonder girls leave perfectly nice clubs to have sex with him in a stranger's car. I grip his hair and tighten my legs around his waist. He groans in response and his fingers bite into my ass.

Cheering breaks out, only to be cut off abruptly. The next thing I know, Reed is ripping me out of Wade's arms.

"What the hell, Carlisle?" he growls.

Wade shrugs ruefully. "She jumped me. I couldn't let her fall."

"You don't touch her. No one touches her." Reed throws his helmet at some poor player's stomach and advances on Wade, his hands fisted.

The big blond quarterback laughs and puts up his hands. "I didn't encourage her, man."

Reed glares and then points a finger at the rest of the team. "Ella is a Royal. She belongs to me. If any of you assholes want her, you have to go through me."

My jaw drops. "Screw you, Reed. I don't belong to anyone, least of all you." I kick him in the back of the knee, then turn to look at the line of football players. "I'm available. Who wants a go with the trashy stripper? I know tricks that even porn stars don't."

Eyes light up but then immediately transfer to Reed. Whatever his expression is, it causes every gaze to drop to the ground. Not a single guy steps out of line.

"Cowards," I mutter.

Then I whirl away and stomp toward Val, who's grinning at me from the sidelines. Screw these Astor Park kids. Screw them all to hell.

Sixteen

SAVANNAH AND SHEA Montgomery live in an inland mansion on the grounds of the country club. At the main gate, Val reaches across me to hand the guard a white envelope. He shines some special light on it and apparently the secret message he reads with his special country club decoder ring lets us through.

"Seriously, Val? What the hell is that?"

She flicks the invitation in my lap. The heavy cream paper is completely blank. "UV ink. So it can't be copied."

"Really?" I run my fingers over the stock and feel nothing but the paper itself. "What's so special about a high school party that there need to be guards and gates and top-secret invitations?"

I toss the invite onto the dash and pull through the now-open gate.

"They like to limit the crowd," she replies.

"Wish they'd use their powers to keep assholes out," I mutter. I haven't seen Daniel Delacorte yet, but I know he's still at school, walking the halls of Astor as if nothing happened between us.

"If the asshole has money, he's getting in."

She's right, but it doesn't make me happier. The pounding bass pouring out of the Montgomery house greets us even before we turn onto their cul-de-sac. We have to park at the end of a long line of cars leading up a hill.

Val guides me through the main room and onto the porch. The Montgomery house is ultra-modern, all weird angles and planes and windows and steel. The backyard pool is lit up from underneath and there are spouts of water springing out of the concrete to arc into the water, but no one is swimming because it's too cold.

"I'm getting something to drink. What do you want?" Val asks, pointing to a cooler.

"Beer is fine."

I spot Reed in the far corner of the porch. A fairy with big-ass wings and a floral crown is talking to him. Ugh. It's Abby. Their heads are bent close enough that his dark brown hair is brushing the edges of her petals. That sounds vaguely pornographic. The scene is sickeningly similar to one of the first memories I have of Reed.

Abby was his last girlfriend. Maybe she was his only girlfriend. Reed, unlike Easton, is picky. He slept with Abby, and then Brooke.

I don't know the rest of his sexual history. Maybe that was it. Maybe he lost his virginity to Abby. Maybe there's a bond that will always draw them back together.

Daniel, the rapist, once said those two belong together.

Is that true?

Do I care?

Of course I do. And I hate myself for it.

I turn away before I do something outrageous, like march

over to them and tear Abby's hair out and order Reed to stop talking to her because he's mine.

I'm not sure that was ever true, even during those private times when his fingers were in my hair and his tongue was in my mouth and his hand was between my legs.

Inside, the house is filled with tight corsets, fake-blood-spattered clothes, and probably even some socks padding out jockstraps. Almost everyone has a costume on, except for a few. The nonconformists include the Royals. Those boys wear T-shirts and shredded jeans. When I first saw them, I labeled them thugs. They don't look like prep-school kids. They look like dockworkers with their heavy muscles, broad shoulders, and messy hair.

People turn as we walk in, and I instantly regret my outfit. I'm the only slutty football player here, so once again I've made a spectacle of myself. It's strange because in the past I've been so good at blending in, but ever since I came here I've been doing things that unwittingly put me in the spotlight.

Fighting with Jordan.

Making out with Easton.

Hooking up with Reed.

Running away.

Wearing this ridiculous outfit.

I grab Val. "I need to change. Or at least wash my face." The heavy black stripes under my eyes look dumb compared to the perfectly made-up faces of all these princesses and ballerinas. It's like Disney threw up in here—the adult, after-hours Disney.

"You look gorgeous," Val protests.

"No. If I'm going to make it through these next two years, I need to tone it down."

Val shakes her head in disagreement but points a hand down the hall. "I'll wait here for you."

It's easy to find the bathroom because there's already a line. I slump against the wall. Why am I trying to make everyone notice me? Is it because I want Reed to pay attention?

The line shortens and finally the two girls in front of me push inside. I hear a snippet of conversation as the door opens.

"Abby with Easton? I don't believe you. Abby would never ruin her chances of getting back with Reed by sleeping with his brother."

"Why? It worked for that Ella girl. She made out with East at Moonglow and then, bam, she was with Reed."

"So, what, like, Easton preps the girls for his brother?"

"Who knows. Maybe they're like the twins, which is gross." There's a long pause. "Oh my God, Cynthie! You think that's hot?"

"I don't know. Like, come on, you wouldn't want to be the meat in that sandwich? If it's wrong, maybe I don't want to be right."

There's complete silence and then a huge fit of laughter followed by one of the girls saying, "Fuck, marry, kill the Royals."

The door swings shut, but I can still hear them. I make a mental note to turn on the faucet when I pee since the walls here are tissue thin.

"There are five of them, Anna," Cynthie complains.

"So pick three."

"Fine. Fuck Reed, kill Gideon, and marry Easton."

Something seizes up inside me at the thought of another girl with Reed. Hard enough to see him with Abby. I don't need to envision him with a whole line of girls waiting to screw him.

"Easton's a dog," Anna protests.

"He's a doll," Cynthie says. "And reformed bad boys make the best husbands according to my maw-maw. Now you."

Okay, maybe Cynthie isn't all that bad. Easton really is the sweetest guy under all that bravado.

"Marry Gideon, because he's the oldest and will end up running the Royal business. Screw Easton, because he has to have learned something for all the time he's spent up girls' skirts. Kill the twins."

"Both of them?"

"Pretty much."

I wince. Harsh. Anna is harsh.

"Abby and Reed looked cozy outside, didn't they?" a honeyed voice whispers in my ear, interrupting my eavesdropping.

Ugh. Jordan Carrington. She's not in costume, which is a shame. She would've made a fantastic witch.

"Don't you have a boiling pot to stir?" I ask sweetly.

"Don't you have a Royal to screw?"

"Maybe one or two," I say in a breezy voice. "I bet that drives you crazy, doesn't it, Jordan? That the Royals will screw everyone but you?"

Her face flushes for a second, but she recovers quickly. "Are you seriously bragging about your sluttiness?" She rolls her eyes. "You should write a book about all your experience. It'll be a real feminist empowerment story. *Fifty Shades of Banging: The High School Years.*"

"Only fifty? That seems like a low number for a slut like me."

Jordan flicks a curtain of dark hair over her shoulder. "I was giving you the benefit of the doubt. Figured that even you couldn't be so insecure that you needed three hundred guys to prove your worth."

I wonder if she'd believe me if I told her I'm still a virgin. Probably not.

But it's true. Before Reed, I hadn't even given so much as a blowjob.

We did a lot together, but not the final deed. I told him I was ready, but he wanted to wait. At the time, I thought it was because he was thoughtful. Now . . . well, I don't have the first clue why he didn't want my virginity.

Maybe the girls in the bathroom are right. Maybe Reed likes Easton to break them in for him. That thought churns painfully in my stomach.

"Your snarky little insults don't work on me, Jordan." I straighten from the wall. I'm taller than her, and I use it to my advantage. "I fight back, remember? And I fight dirty. So go ahead, come at me. Let's see what happens."

"I'm shaking in my boots," she parries, but there's a note of concern. We both hear it.

I allow a vicious smile to spread. "You should be."

The door to the bathroom opens, and I brush by the two gossipers into the powder room. My hands are shaking and sweaty. I wipe them against my shirt and then stare at my reflection in the mirror.

Astor Park is not my crowd. It will never be my crowd. So why am I trying to change myself to fit in? Even if I dressed exactly like Jordan and wore soft makeup and pretty clothes, I still wouldn't get the kids here to accept me.

I'm always going to be the trashy interloper.

I use the toilet, wash my hands, and then leave—without changing one thing.

Back in the main room, I survey the crowd. Tonight the football players are the gods. I don't know if that's true in other months, if in December, after football is over, the school revolves around the basketball team or the lacrosse team or whatever other sport. But tonight, the rulers are the broad-shouldered football guys. My gaze takes in several. Their eyes meet mine and skip away.

When I look behind me, I'm not surprised to see Reed. He's leaning against a wall and glaring at every male in the room.

I march over to him. "You said you'd do anything for me."

"I would," he says gruffly.

"Yeah? Then prove it."

"Leave you alone?" he guesses, a resigned look in his eyes.

"Yep. Don't talk to me. Don't touch me. Don't even look at me, or I swear to God I'll find the first guy I can and screw him right in front of you."

Something in my face or my voice must convey my seriousness because Reed gives me an abrupt nod. "For tonight, then."

"Whatever," I mutter, and then I stalk away.

Seventeen

"WHAT'S GOOD?" VAL asks when I step onto the porch. She presents me with a bottle of cold beer.

"I can't find one guy who'll look me in the eye." I scan the crowd and spot Easton on the other side of the porch. His hand is on Shea Montgomery's hip and they're looking intently at each other. "I guess Reed really did lay down the law."

"We should go over to Harrisville," Val suggests.

"What's that?"

"Local college about thirty minutes away. No one there gives a rat's ass about the Astor Park social hierarchy." She pauses. "But I am kinda surprised that anyone is listening to Reed. Word was that the Royals were on their way out."

I take a sip of my beer before answering. "You realize how ridiculous that sounds, right?"

"It's not, though. This pecking order is set at birth. Even before. The governor of our state went to Astor. The judges he appoints are guys or girls he went to school with. What prep school you went to matters at the bigger, better colleges. What jobs you get depends on the clubs you belonged to. The more secret and exclusive, the better. That's why I live with the

Carringtons for nine months out of the year. So I can give my kids the privileged start in life that my parents didn't have."

"I guess. But you can still be happy without all this." I wave the bottle toward the party. "I was happy before I came here."

"Mmmm." Val makes a disbelieving noise. At my frown, she says, "Were you really happy by yourself? With your sick mom to take care of? Maybe you were coping, but you can't tell me you were truly, blissfully happy."

"Maybe I wasn't blissfully happy, but I was definitely happier than I am now."

She gives a tiny shrug. "Okay, but the point is still the same. Astor is a smaller version of what we're all going to face when we're adults. These jerks are going to run our world unless we do something about it."

I exhale an irritated sigh, mostly because she's right. So how am I going to survive? I can't run away, so I guess that means I have to face these people and deal with them. "If the Royals are on their way out, who's on the rise?"

"Jordan, of course. She's dating Scott Gastonburg." Val gestures to a tall boy leaning against a fireplace mantel.

I narrow my eyes at him. He looks really familiar in his cowboy getup, except the last time I saw him, he didn't have his jaw wired shut. The last time I saw him was at the club and he was on the floor getting his face bashed in by Reed.

"I can see why they're a couple," I say cattily. "She does all the talking and he can only smile and nod. The perfect boyfriend." I don't feel guilty at all that Reed broke this guy's face. Scott said horrible things about me. Not as horrible as Jordan did, but still bad.

Val smirks and drinks her wine cooler in silent agreement.

Then she tips her chin toward another guy sitting on the arm of a sofa. "What do you think of him?"

"I have no idea who he is. Nice cheekbones, though." The boy Val's referring to has ink-black hair and is wearing a pirate's costume complete with a dangerous-looking sword strapped to his waist. The gleam off the metal hilt seems too real for a costume piece.

"Right? That's Hiro Kamenashi. His family's part of the conglomerate of Ikoto Autos. They opened a manufacturing plant two years ago and apparently have more money than some small countries."

"Is he nice?"

She shrugs. "Don't know. Heard he has a decent dick, though. Hold my drink. I'm going in."

I grab her wine cooler before it drops to the floor and watch as Val slides through the crowd and taps Hiro on the shoulder. A few seconds later, she's leading him into the next room, where couples are grinding against each other.

I feel a pull in my belly. If Reed and I were together, we'd be in there. Our bodies would be glued together. I'd feel his excitement press against me. He'd hear my desire in the shortness of my breaths and my soft, irrepressible moans.

We'd go outside and find a dark corner, where his fingers would slip beneath my shirt and my hands would map out the hard planes of his muscles. And in the dark, away from the crowd, his mouth would seal itself against mine and we would dance away all my feelings of loss and loneliness.

I lied to Valerie. I *have* experienced moments of blissful happiness. The problem is that the fall off the cliff of joy hurts like a bitch.

I shake myself to get rid of dangerous thoughts about Reed and look around the room again for my Hiro. This time when I spot Easton, he's leaning against a pillar on the porch and it's not Shea between his legs. It's Savannah, Gideon's ex, dressed in an ethereal white gown. She looks gorgeous but sad, like the abandoned princess she is.

Easton, you dumb shit.

But I'm as dumb as he is, looking for some guy to put my arms around to make me feel better. Well, I already have someone who cares about me and I care about him, too. And I'm not going to let him make another mistake tonight.

"Hey, Easton," I say as I approach.

He rolls his head lazily toward me. His eyes are completely unfocused. Shit. I have no clue what he's on, and the boy is nearly a foot taller than me and a hundred pounds heavier. I can't just drag him off.

So I improvise. "Val found a hottie and I need a dance partner."

"Not interested." His hand slides up Savannah's side until his thumb rests under her boob.

Her mouth is set in a mulish line, daring me to call her out on this.

And I do, because both of them will regret this tomorrow. "Come on," I urge Easton. "I'm hungry. Let's go find something to eat."

He leans forward and kisses Savannah's shoulder. He's done listening to me, if he ever started.

I try Savannah instead. "This isn't going to make you feel better. They may have the same last name, but they aren't the same person."

Her defiant expression wavers for a moment, until Easton

drawls in a voice loud enough to carry, "What, you're the only girl we can pass around?"

A few giggles and a gasp put a smile on his mouth. He's hit his mark, just as he intended. Maybe he's not so high, after all. He knows exactly what he's doing and apparently Savannah does, too.

"Fine, screw up your lives. Both of you."

My hurt expression must penetrate whatever drug-fog he's in, because his face pales with regret. "Ella—"

I push past a couple of gawking students and run smack into Jordan, who's drinking a vodka mixer and smirking at me.

"Jealous that your Royals are moving on? Everyone knows you were always just temporary." With the glass still between her fingers, she flicks some nonexistent speck on my shoulder. The icy liquid sloshes over the brim to trickle underneath the neckline of my jersey and between my breasts. "Slumming it is fun for a night or two, but after a while the stench just gets too strong to handle."

"You would know, wouldn't you?" I say tersely, backing away.

"Actually, I'm just hypothesizing, because getting dirty isn't my thing. Neither is getting wet."

Jordan smiles as she empties her drink down the front of my jersey.

As outrage jolts through me, my hand shoots out and fists her silk blouse. I drag her to me and rub my wet chest all over her. "Guess we're both wet now," I chirp.

"This is a thousand-dollar Balmain!" she screeches as she shoves me away. "You're such a bitch."

I give her a mean smile. "You say that like it's a bad thing."

Then I stalk off in search of Val before Jordan can come up with another insult. I find my friend in the middle of the dance floor with Hiro's hands all over her butt.

It takes several hard taps to get Val's attention.

"What's wrong?" she asks.

"I want to leave. I can't stay here another minute."

Val looks reluctantly at Hiro and then back to me. "Okay. Let me run to the bathroom and I'll be ready."

Hiro steps forward. "Why don't I drive you home? I've got Tina and her boyfriend, Cooper, with me."

Val gives me a pleading glance. "Is that okay?"

"Of course," I say, but I don't mean it. I need a friend to lean on. I want someone to hold my hand, brush the hair out of my face, find me a towel. I want to commiserate with someone about what a bitch Jordan is, and for someone to tell me that it's okay that I don't like her.

But Val's my friend and she needs something tonight, too, something that I can't give her. So I offer a reassuring smile and then walk away with the vodka mixer trickling between my boobs.

The crowd doesn't part for me like a scene in the movie. I have to push and shove past cops, robbers, superheroes, and werewolves. More than a little beer is spilled on or near me, and by the time I reach the front door, I smell like I've been dunked in a vat of yeast.

I stomp down the asphalt toward my car. My heel gets caught in a crack and my ankle decides to give way.

Cursing under my breath, I rip off my shoes and finish the rest of the walk barefoot, not even caring that the tiny pebbles stick to the bottoms of my feet like little pointed leeches. When I get to the convertible, I toss the shoes in the backseat and grab the door handle.

Ew!

What is that? My hand comes away sticky. I fumble with my

phone in my left hand and shine the screen against my right. There's something gooey and yellowish spread all over my fingers and—are those ants?

Gross!

I yelp and swipe my hand against my jersey, only now my palm is sticky and covered in fabric fibers. Grimly, I shine my phone on the car door. Honey is running down the side of it, and a line of ants swarm around the handle and into the crevice of the door.

With a sense of foreboding, I lean over the top of the open convertible. The phone doesn't illuminate much, but I see more ants and shiny speckles of what looks like glitter on top of a pool of honey on the expensive leather. The back of the driver's seat is coated with the same shit.

It's too much. All of it. This town. These fucking kids. This whole ridiculous life that's supposed to be so much better than the one I had before because I've got a fat wallet. I tip my head back and release the scream of frustration that's been building since I rode that stupid bus back into Bayside.

"Ella!" Running footsteps pound on the pavement. "What's wrong? Who hurt you? Where is he? I'll kill him—" Reed stumbles to a halt when he realizes I'm alone.

"Why are you following me?" I demand. He's the last person I want to see right now with ants crawling all around my feet, spilled beer drying on my skin, and my hand feeling gross and sticky.

"I've been yelling your name for the last five minutes, but you were so lost in your head that you didn't hear me." He grabs my shoulders. "Are you hurt?"

His hands run down my arms and then onto my hips. He turns me and I let him because I'm so hungry for someone to care about me that even this feels lovely. And I hate myself for it.

I jerk away and stumble against the car door. "Don't touch me. I'm fine. I screamed because of this." I flip an angry hand toward the car.

He peers into the convertible, shining his own phone on the mess. "Who did this?" he growls.

"Maybe you did," I mutter, even as my brain tells me how silly the accusation is. Reed has no reason to destroy my car.

"My dad gave you that car," he says with an irritated sigh, confirming my thoughts. "Why would I ruin your wheels?"

"Who knows why you do anything?" I answer snidely. "I can't even begin to guess what goes on in your sick mind."

He looks like he's struggling to keep his cool. Why he has any struggle, I have no clue. I'm the one dealing with an ant-infested car while he was cozying up to his ex-girlfriend.

"You sleep with Abby while I was gone?" The question slips out before I can stop it.

I regret it a hundred times more when a ghost of a smile flits across his face. "No."

Then what were you two whispering about back there? I scream silently. I force myself to turn away and focus on fixing the problem. I don't need Reed, or anyone else for that matter. I've been taking care of myself for years.

I wipe my hand again and then thumb my way to the search engine on my phone. Awkwardly, I type in the word *taxi*.

"Not going to ask me what we were talking about?"

Nope. I've learned my lesson. I select the top service and call.

"Yellow Cab, can I help you?"

"I'm at—" I cover the mouthpiece. "What's the name of this place?"

"Ma'am? I'll need an address," the dispatcher says impatiently.

"Just a minute," I mutter into the mouthpiece.

Reed shakes his head and pulls the phone out of my hand. "Sorry. Wrong number." He hangs up and sticks the phone in the pocket of his jeans. "Abby was apologizing for hooking up with East. I told her not to worry about it."

"You should worry about it. Give me my phone back."

He ignores my request. "I've got other things on my mind. Like wondering why my girl is kissing my quarterback."

"Because he's hot." I stare at Reed's pocket, wondering how I'm getting my phone out of there. My gaze drifts to the left, where there's another noticeable bulge. One that seems to grow as I stare at it. One that I remember pressed against me, hard and hot . . .

Parts of my body start to tighten and tingle. I clench my thighs together.

"You don't like him," Reed says hoarsely.

"You don't know what I like."

"Oh, yeah, I do." Snake-quick, he wraps an arm around my waist.

His mouth slams against mine.

I grip his head to push him away, but instead I hold him there. We don't kiss so much as try to kill each other with our lips and tongues and teeth. His hands dig into my arms. My fingers gouge his scalp. That steel in his jeans is no longer a memory but a reality, and my whole body rejoices. Oh my God, I've missed this. His lips on mine. His warm body pressed up against me. I missed it and I hate myself for it.

I wrench my mouth away from him. "Stop kissing me," I order.

His lips curve upward. "Let go of me, then."

And when I don't do it immediately, he kisses me again and his tongue slides through my parted lips. This time his hand is at the waistband of my leggings, yanking them down. I fumble for the bottom of his shirt, seeking his bare skin. Groaning, he hoists me up and my legs somehow close around his waist.

I feel the cool metal of the car hood under my bared butt. Reed's fingers are squeezing my thighs and the tightness I felt before starts to ache. I thrash under his rough embrace, wanting something, searching for something, reaching for it. But it's elusive.

His mouth leaves mine to find my neck and then my shoulder. "That's right, baby. You're mine," he growls against my skin.

Yes, I'm his. His . . . *baby*?

"No. No, I'm not." I wiggle out from underneath his body, breathless and ashamed as I frantically tug my leggings up. "You have a baby and it's not me."

He stands up slowly, not bothering to pull down his shirt or button the jeans that I've apparently undone. "For the last fucking time, Ella—I didn't get that woman pregnant. Why won't you believe me?"

His voice rings with so much sincerity that I almost believe him. *Almost* being the key word. My mind suddenly snaps back to all those times Mom begged me to give her latest cheating boyfriend a second chance. *He's changed, sweetie. He's different. It was a misunderstanding. The woman was actually his sister.*

I never understood why she couldn't see through the lies, but now I wonder if maybe she wanted to believe in love so badly that she convinced herself that her slimy boyfriend was telling the truth just so she could have someone around.

"Of course you're going to deny it. What else are you going

to say?" I let out a shaky breath. "Let's just forget this ever happened."

"You really think I could forget this?" His voice is low, edgy. "You kissed me back. You still want me."

"Don't flatter yourself. I would've kissed anyone just now. Did kiss anyone. Remember? If it was Wade here and not you, I'd be kissing him instead."

Reed frowns. "Wade's a good guy. Don't break his heart to get back at me. That's not who you are."

"You don't know who I am."

"Yeah, I do. You said it yourself—I see you. I see your hurt and your loneliness. I see your pride, and the way it stops you from leaning on anyone. I see your big heart, and how you want to save the world, including an ass like me." His voice catches. "I'm done playing games, Ella. No other girls exist in this world for me. If you see me talking to one, know that I'm talking about you. If you see me walking next to someone, I'm wishing it was you." He steps toward me. "You're the only one for me."

"I don't believe you."

"How can I change your mind?"

I push at him. He's standing way too close to me, and I need distance.

"Do you want me to beg? Because I'll do that." He starts to lower himself to the ground.

"Dude! Royal's *whipped*," a loud voice crows. The comment is followed by a whip sound and lots of drunken laughter. A group of guys stumble past us on their way to the side of the mansion.

I grab Reed before he can hit his knees. As much as I hate him, I hate the Astor kids more. But Reed doesn't seem bothered at all that these jerks overheard him. He just smirks and flips up his middle finger.

Tears prick my eyes, and I avert my face so he can't see them. "I hate this place," I whisper. "Astor is officially the stupidest school in the entire world."

Silence weighs heavy between us until he sighs deeply. "Come on. I'll take you home."

Since my car is disgustingly out of commission, I slump in defeat and climb into his SUV, but I make sure to sit as far away from him as possible.

"What happened to your jersey?" he asks gruffly. "It's soaking wet."

"Jordan happened."

His hands tighten around the wheel. "I'll deal with her."

"How?"

"You let me worry about that."

I stare out the window and shut down the flutters of hope that are trying to rise in my heart. This is Reed Royal. He's a guy who screwed his dad's girlfriend. He has no morals or principles. All he cares about is what he can get for himself.

So no, I won't allow myself to hope. My heart can't take it. Not again.

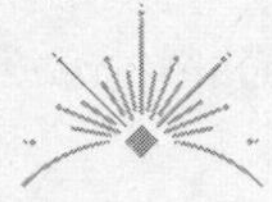

Eighteen

REED

WINNING MY GIRL back is taking longer than I thought it would. And it's harder, too. I thought that the kiss at Shea's party signaled a change of heart. If anything, it ended up having the opposite effect. Ella still doesn't believe me, and short of a DNA test, I don't know how I'm going to convince her.

Dad hasn't mentioned a paternity test, but he's got to be getting one, right? He can't tie himself to that snake without some kind of proof.

I spent the entire miserable weekend getting ignored by everyone in the family except my dad and Brooke. Ella, Easton, the twins, Gid. They're all pissed at me.

Don't get me wrong, I deserve it. One hundred percent. Sleeping with Brooke was the stupidest decision I ever made. The fact that I've always been choosy as hell when it comes to chicks makes it even worse, because someone like Brooke shouldn't have made the short list. I should've resisted her. I should've resisted the urge to punish my dad. I know from experience that every boneheaded thing I do only ends with me punishing myself.

But I did it and I can't change that. I can hate myself for it,

I can feel like shit every time I remember it, but I can't rewrite the past.

And Ella can't hold it against me forever, right?

"You're staring."

I turn to find Wade rolling his eyes at me. Yeah. Busted. I was totally staring at Ella's table. She's sitting with Val on the opposite side of the dining hall, and I know she chose that spot on purpose. She's putting as much distance between us as humanly possible.

And she positioned her chair so that her back is to the room. To me. She wants me to know it's over, but we both know it's not. She hated me before and still fell for me. Nothing's really changed between us. We're still sparring, still circling each other like well-matched opponents, but we're there, in the ring, together. And that's all that matters.

"I'm allowed to stare." I scowl at him. "You, on the other hand, are not. So keep your eyes off my girl. Your lips, too."

He just grins. "Hey, it's not my fault she shoved her tongue in my mouth."

I growl. "Bring it up again and I'll lay you out."

"You'd never hurt your quarterback," Wade taunts, laughing as he rises from his chair. "I'll catch you bros later. Got someone waiting for me in the bathroom."

All the guys roll their eyes. Wade is notorious for his bathroom hookups.

"Hey, East," someone else says from the other end of the table. "Heard you hooked up with Savannah Montgomery."

I jolt upright. Seriously? First Abby, and now Sav?

When Abby pulled me aside at the party, it was to apologize for hooking up with East. She claimed she was mad at me and that it was her way of lashing out. It was hard to stop myself from saying, *I don't give a damn who you screw.* But it's true, I don't. I was over Abby even before Ella entered the picture, and I honestly don't care who she sleeps with.

What I do care about is East. My brother's out of control and there's nothing I can do to stop it. That's what keeps me up at night. Well, that, and Ella.

Speaking of Ella, one of my teammates suddenly mentions her name. I drop any pretense that I'm not interested and turn to face the two football players who are gossiping like they're at a Junior League luncheon.

"What about Ella?" I demand.

Neiman Halloway, a sophomore O-lineman, grimaces. "Just heard she had a bad time of it in Speech today."

"What happened?" I fold my arms across my chest and glare at the two players. If they don't start talking, they're going to wear imprints of their lunch trays on their faces.

Neiman clears his throat. "I wasn't there, but my sister's in her class. Said that Ella had to give a speech today about the people she looked up to or some shit. She wrote it about her mom, and, ah . . ." He shifts uncomfortably.

"Spit it out. I'm not gonna punch you for repeating what went on in class, but I might beat the crap out of you if you don't stop wasting my time."

From the other side of the table, East is also listening intently, but he doesn't meet my eyes when I try to catch his gaze.

"Right. Okay. So I guess some kids were busting her ass, you know? Saying shit like, 'I look up to strippers, too. Usually when they're grinding on my face.' And my sister says one of the Pastels asked if Ella had any home videos of her mom teaching her how to blow clients."

I can feel my face grow darker and angrier at every word he

says. I remind myself that he's just the messenger and I can't kill the messenger.

Neiman's paler than a ghost by now. "And then some girl told her that her mom died of shame because Ella's such a slut."

I catch a flash of movement from the corner of my eye and turn to see Ella and Val making their way across the gleaming hardwood floor, empty trays in hand.

I'm tempted to chase after her, but as much as I want to comfort her, I know she's not interested in hearing from me. Besides, comfort can only do so much.

Wade was right—something's got to change here at school. Before she left, no one but maybe Jordan would've dared to talk to Ella like that.

I turn back to the guys. "That it?" I ask between gritted teeth.

Neiman and his friend exchange a worried glance.

No, that wasn't it, I guess. I brace myself for the rest.

His friend picks up the story. "When we were walking out, someone asked Daniel Delacorte if dollar bills fell out when Ella spread her legs for him. He said, no, she's too cheap. Only quarters."

I stick my fists on my knees because I'm afraid if I lose control, I'm going to destroy this whole fucking school. "Text your sister," I bark at Neiman. "I want some names."

Neiman has his phone out faster than when he lunges at an opposing defense that's after his quarterback. He taps out a quick message, and we sit there for nearly a minute waiting for a response. By the time his phone beeps, I'm ready to murder someone.

"Skip Henley is the one who said the dollar-bill thing—"

Neiman doesn't even finish the sentence before I'm on my

feet. My peripheral vision shows East standing up, too, but I hold up a hand to stop him.

"I've got this," I growl.

Something—grudging respect?—flickers through his eyes. Huh. Maybe my relationship with my brother isn't completely unsalvageable.

I scan the dining hall until I find my target. Skip Henley. Kid's been on my radar for a while now. He's got a big mouth and likes to brag about the chicks he's hooked up with—in degrading detail.

I stalk across the room toward Henley's table, which falls silent at my approach.

"Henley," I say coolly.

Skip warily twists around. He looks preppy as hell with his perfectly gelled hair and clean-shaven pretty-boy face. "Yeah?"

"You have Speech before lunch?"

He nods. "Yeah. So what?"

"So here's the deal." I pat my chest. "I'm gonna give you one shot. One free shot. Anywhere you like. And then I'm gonna beat you so bad, your own mother won't be able to recognize you."

He looks around, frantic for an escape. But he's not getting past me, and whatever friends he once had pretend they don't know him. Everyone at the table averts their gazes, fiddles with their phones, picks at their food. Skip's on his own, and he knows it.

"I don't know what you think I did," he starts, "but—"

"Oh, you need a reminder? Sure. Let me help you out, bro—you talked trash about Ella Harper."

Panic flares briefly in his eyes, but then it hardens into indignation. He realizes he doesn't have many options, so he decides to double down on his stupidity. "So what?" he says again. "I was just speaking the truth. We all know that your girl has spent so much time on her back she's got the word 'Sealy' imprinted on her skin—"

I'm hauling him out of his chair before he can finish. My fingers bunch up the collar of his shirt, fisting the material as I bring his face close to mine. "You've either got balls of steel or a death wish. My vote's on the second one."

"Fuck you," Henley shouts, his spittle flying toward my face. "You think you run this school, Royal? You think you can bring some whore to our place and shove her down our throats? My great-granddaddy knew General Lee! I'm not going to associate with trash like her."

Then he launches himself at me with a roar, and I let him take his shot. It's weak, like he is. Like all bullies really are. That's why they're bullies. Because they're insecure idiots who try to make themselves feel better.

His fist glances off my jaw because he doesn't know how to throw a punch. Laughing, I grab the dickhead by the throat and drag him against me.

"Does your daddy not love you enough to teach you how to fight, Skippy? Watch. This is a jab." I punch his face twice in succession. "See how that works?"

I hear a loud snicker behind us and recognize it as Easton's. My brother is enjoying the show.

Henley whimpers in pain and backs away from me. The smell of urine fills the air.

"Jesus Christ, he just pissed himself!" someone yells.

Disgusted, I grab Skip by the nape of his neck, kick his legs out from under him and slam him face-first on the ground. My knee digs into his spine as I bend my head toward him. "You say one word to Ella or any of her friends, and I'll do a lot worse to you than a couple jabs to the face, you got me?"

He nods, weeping pitifully.

"Good." I shove him as I get to my feet. "That goes for the rest of you," I announce to the crowd. "You're all gonna clean up your acts starting today, or what happened to this jackass will look like a fucking tea party."

The entire dining hall is dead silent, and the nervous, fearful eyes I see all around me bring a wave of satisfaction. Wade was right about another thing—these kids need a leader, someone to stop them from devouring each other.

I might not have applied for the job, but it's mine, whether I like it or not.

✦ ✦ ✦

INSTEAD OF GOING to class, I head for the men's room on the first floor near the gym. There's no stated rule that this bathroom is solely for the football team, but it's worked out that way.

And Wade makes good use of it. He has Government this period, and since his mom started sleeping with the teacher, he hasn't stepped one foot into the classroom. He says after all the carbs at lunch, it's either sleep or screw and the latter's more fun.

I make a production as I enter to alert the occupants that they're not alone, but it doesn't affect Wade at all. I hear breathy moans, interspersed with "yes, Wade, please, Wade" chanted out in a familiar rhythm.

Bored, I lean against the sinks and watch the closed door to one of the stalls rattle noisily as Wade starts giving it to her hard. From the sound of the voice, I'm guessing his post-lunch hookup is with Rachel Cohen.

Wade has the attention span of a peanut, but when he's with a girl, he gives it his all. You can't ask for more than that. I check my watch. I don't want to miss next period.

I pound on the door. "Almost done, kids?"

The noise pauses and I hear a muffled cry of surprise along with a hushed reassurance. "I got you, babe . . ." A rustling and then, ". . . there you go. Feels good, don't it. Don't worry about ol' Reed out there . . . Ahh, you like that. You want me to open the door . . . No? Okay, but he's out there. He can hear you. Damn, you like that a lot. Yeah, babe, let go."

A soft moan escapes and there's more shuffling followed by a long, low groan. The finale is signaled by the sound of a toilet flushing.

The door opens and I catch Wade's eyes and tap on my watch. He gives me a nod and finishes zipping his pants, then pulls Rachel in his arms and gives her a wet, noisy kiss. "Damn, babe, that was spectacular."

She sighs against him. I recognize that sound. Heard a similar one from Ella when we fooled around. I'm dying to hear it again, and it pisses me off a little that she's not letting me in.

I clear my throat loudly.

Wade half walks, half carries Rachel over to the door.

"I'll see you after class?" she asks with hope in her eyes.

"You bet, babe." He pauses and then looks over his shoulder at me.

I shake my head no.

He shrugs as if to say, *Doesn't hurt to ask*. "I'll be over after dinner. Keep this hot for me, okay?" He pats the front of her shortened uniform skirt. "I'll be thinking of you all afternoon. It's gonna be a rough time."

Even after all these years with Wade, I can't tell if he's sincere or just that smooth.

"You mean a hard time," she coos.

Okay, that's enough.

"Wade," I say impatiently.

"I'll see you, Rach. I've got to confab with Reed here or I promise we'd be going another round."

She hesitates and Wade has to physically push her out the door. After it shuts, he shoves the waste can in front of it and saunters over. I turn the faucets on to prevent little ears from listening in.

I get straight to the point. "Ella's car was honey-bombed on Friday night at the Montgomerys' party, and I just threw down with some asshole who crucified her during Speech. What the hell is going on?"

"Seriously? Did you not hear a word I said to you the last time we talked about this? Actually, you did—and you said you didn't care," he says pointedly.

"Well, now I care. I want to know why Ella is a target again. Everyone knows I'm willing to give a beating to anyone who looks sideways at her, so I don't understand why she's being jacked around."

Wade sticks his hands under the faucet and washes them, taking his own sweet time before answering.

"Wade," I warn.

"Okay, don't hit me." He holds up his hands. "Look at this pretty face." He pats his chin. "There'll be no more Rachels in the bathroom if this kisser gets ruined."

I stare down at Wade, who's two inches shorter than me. "Why are people messing with Ella?" I press.

He shrugs. "People used to be terrified of you. Now? Not so much."

"What's that supposed to mean?"

"It means Delacorte still has all his teeth and he tried to rape your girl. Jordan says what she wants and there's no repercussions. Everyone thinks you're done with Ella, and since you stopped standing up for people, they aren't gonna return the favor. Ella's fair game."

"Anything else?"

Wade shrugs ruefully. "Isn't that enough?"

I nod in frustration. "Yeah, it's plenty."

"You gonna do anything about it?"

"What do you think?" I nudge the wastebasket away from the door.

"I think if you Royals stood as a united front, then everyone would just chill. No one really likes what's happening here, but everyone's scared or lazy. And frankly, buddy, you fall into the latter category."

I clench my teeth tight, but he's not wrong. Gideon was a way more active enforcer at school than I am. He paid attention. He figured out who was behind shit and made sure they fell in line. Usually I was the one delivering the messages.

After he left, everyone assumed I was in charge and I didn't do much to prove if they were right or wrong. Until now.

I twist to face him. "You're right. I've been a lazy asshole."

Wade grins. "I'm always right. So what're you gonna do about it?"

"Not sure yet. But don't worry, shit's gonna change." I give him a deadly look. "I'm on it."

Nineteen

ELLA

I GET HOME from school and make a beeline for my room, where I throw myself on the bed and curl up on my side. I just want to pretend that this entire day from hell never happened. Every time I think I can't feel any more humiliated, the jerks at Astor Park Prep prove me wrong.

I won't cry, though. Nope. Not shedding a single tear. I'm not giving them that kind of power over me.

Still, Speech class sucked on a whole new level. The slurs against my mom were almost too much for me to handle. I can't believe the teacher stood there like a dummy for five minutes before shutting the class down.

Maybe I should've gone over to Val's like she'd wanted me to. We could've sat on her bed eating ice cream and gossiping about her new crush, which suddenly sounds a lot better than sulking in my room all night.

Plus, I wouldn't be tensing up every time I hear footsteps in the hall. I can't believe I kissed Reed the other night. No, I more than kissed him. He had my pants down and his hands on my butt. Who knows how much further I would have let him go if the whole *baby* thing hadn't popped up between us?

What if he's actually the father of Brooke's baby? How can I ever live in the same house as Reed and Brooke and their secret baby that poor Callum will be unknowingly raising as his own?

God. When did my life become such a soap opera?

I squeeze my face tightly between both my palms until I can feel my teeth press against my cheek. That pain doesn't make the one in my heart go away. I . . . miss Reed. I'm angry at myself for it, but I can't stop it, either. All that stuff I told him about how I thought he *saw* me . . . I still feel that way. Reed fixes those intense blue eyes on me, and it's like he can see into my soul. He sees past the tough front I hide behind. He sees my fears and my vulnerability and he doesn't judge me for it.

And I honestly believed I could see him, too. Was I imagining it? Those moments of laughter where we both let our guards down, that raw look in his eyes when he told me he wished he could be worthy, the peaceful sensation that washed over me when we fell asleep together . . .

Was it all in my imagination?

I grab my math book out of my backpack and force myself to concentrate. Afterward, I treat myself by watching two mindless episodes of *The Bachelor*, but it's no fun when Val isn't sitting beside me making wisecracks about the contestants.

"Ella." Callum's voice sounds from the hall, followed by a sharp knock on my door. "Dinner's ready. You need to come down."

"I'm not hungry," I call back.

"Come down," he repeats. "We have guests."

I frown at the door. Callum's not usually super parental with me, but right now, his tone is stern and fatherly.

"We're eating on the patio," he adds, and then I hear him

knocking on other doors and gathering the troops. He's personally collecting each one of us, and he sounds a bit . . . worried.

I sit up warily, wondering who our "guests" are. Brooke, obviously, because that witch has been over almost every night since she and Callum dropped their baby bomb.

But who else? As far as I know, Callum's only friend was Steve, and he's dead.

Sighing, I heave myself off the mattress and quickly change out of my school uniform into something more dinner appropriate. Unfortunately, I keep forgetting to go shopping, so I'm stuck wearing one of the dresses from my shopping spree with Brooke.

I walk into the hall at the same time Reed and Easton are leaving their rooms. I ignore them both and they ignore each other and it's a silent, stony trudge down the stairs.

When we step onto the patio, I immediately understand why Callum was worried. We have two dinner guests: Brooke . . . and Dinah O'Halloran. Oh hell no. Steve's widow hates me.

Beside me, Reed's entire body stiffens. His blue eyes shift from one blond bitch to the other.

"What's the occasion?" he asks coolly.

Brooke offers us a broad smile. "Celebrating the engagement, silly!" She flips her hair over her shoulder. "Unofficially, of course, because there'll be a proper engagement party once we get the details squared away. Somewhere decadent, like the Palace or maybe the King Edward? What do you think, Dinah? Do we want a modern venue, or someplace more distinguished?"

Dinah lifts her nose in distaste. "The King Edward Hotel has lost its appeal, Brookie. It used to be far more exclusive, but now that they've reduced their rates, the clientele is downmarket."

My jaw falls open. Is that how they categorize people? Like goods in a shopping mall?

Callum glances at me and the boys. "Sit," he commands. "You're being rude."

I snap my mouth shut and scan the available seats. Brooke and Dinah are on either side of Callum, while Sawyer and Sebastian—both wearing sullen expressions—lucked out with seats on the opposite end of the table.

Reed and Easton bypass the empty chairs near the women and flop down beside the twins. This leaves me with two not-so-appealing options, but I decide Dinah is the lesser of two bitches and reluctantly take the seat next to hers.

I get situated just as Gideon stalks through the French doors. "Evening," he mutters.

Callum nods in approval. "I'm glad you were able to make it, Gid." There's an edge in his voice.

Gideon's tone is even sharper. "Because you really left me much of a choice, right, Dad?" His jaw ticks when he realizes the only available seat is next to Brooke. His future stepmother.

She pats the chair. "Come sit, darling. Let me pour you a glass of wine."

"I'll have water," he says tightly.

An awkward silence falls over the table once we're all settled. Every single Royal boy is sporting a deep scowl. Callum watches them, looking disappointed.

What did he expect, though? His sons have barely spoken to him since the baby announcement. I've seen the twins cringe every time Brooke flashes her shiny diamond around. Easton's drunk more often than he's sober. Gideon apparently needs to be bullied into coming home. And Reed slept with Callum's girlfriend two or three or a hundred times.

So yeah. Callum's out of his mind if he thinks this big, happy family dinner will be anything other than a total disaster.

"Thank you so much for inviting me tonight," Dinah chirps to Callum. "It's been ages since I visited the Royal palace."

The bite to her words reveals exactly how she feels about the lack of invitations rolling her way. She looks beautiful tonight, despite the venom in her green eyes. Her golden hair is swept up, and two diamond earrings dangle from her earlobes. She's wearing a white dress with a deep-cut V that shows off both her tan and her cleavage.

I can see why my father was drawn to her. Dinah looks like a sexy angel. I wonder how long it took him to realize she was actually the devil.

Callum must have hired caterers for this dinner, because three uniformed women I don't recognize sashay onto the patio and begin serving us. It makes me feel awkward, and I have to pin myself to the chair so I don't jump up and help them.

Then the nine of us settle in to eat. Is the food delicious? I have no idea. I don't pay attention to what I'm shoving into my mouth. If anything, I'm trying not to throw up. Brooke is gabbing away about the new Royal baby and it's making me sick.

"If it's a boy, I'd like his middle name to be Emerson, after Callum's father, God rest his soul," Brooke is telling Dinah. "Don't you think that has a nice ring to it? Callum Emerson Royal the Second."

She's planning on naming the baby Callum? *Why not Reed?* I want to crack. Then I clench my fingers around my water glass, because the thought of Reed actually being this kid's biological dad is rage-inducing. And nauseating. And just plain awful.

Reed claims that the last time he was with Brooke was more

than six months ago, and she's definitely not that far along. So maybe they *didn't* have sex the night I walked in on them. He says they didn't. Brooke says they didn't.

Maybe they're telling the truth?

Yes, Ella, and Mom's last boyfriend was totally *holding hands with his* sister *and not cheating on Mom. Idiot.*

"Ella?"

I lift my head and find Callum eyeing me. "Sorry, what?"

"Brooke asked you a question," he prompts.

I reluctantly glance at Brooke, who winks at me. "I asked if you had any suggestions for girls' names."

"No," I mutter. "Sorry. I'm bad with names."

"Boys?" she asks the Royals. "Any ideas?"

Not a single one of them answers. The twins pretend they're too focused on stuffing their faces, but Reed, Gideon, and Easton flat-out ignore her.

Since I'm the only one who contributed to the conversation—if you can call six measly words a contribution—I quickly become the focus of the adults.

"I'm disappointed that you don't visit the penthouse more often," Dinah tells me. "I'd really like to get to know my husband's daughter."

She says *daughter* as if it's a dirty word. Callum's features tighten, but his mouth remains firmly shut.

"I haven't been invited." I strive for an equally cool tone.

Dinah's gaze darkens. "You don't need an invitation," she answers sweetly. "The penthouse is half yours, remember?"

"I guess."

At my cloudy expression, she shrugs and turns to Gideon. "How's college, darling? It's been ages since I've seen you. Tell me everything you've been up to."

"College is fine," he says curtly.

"You have a swim meet coming up, no?" Dinah runs her fingers over the stem of her glass. "I think Brooke might have mentioned it?"

A muscle in his jaw flexes before he answers. "Yes, that's right."

Brooke speaks up, her eyes twinkling. "Maybe we should all drive up to cheer him on. What do you think, Callum?"

"Ah . . . yes. That sounds . . . great."

Reed snorts quietly.

Callum throws a warning glance in his direction.

I pretty much hate everyone at the table right now.

The tension thickens and thickens, until I feel like the walls are closing in on me and I'm suffocating from the inside out. And we're outdoors, dammit.

"I wish you'd gotten to know your father," Dinah says. "Steve was such a . . . formidable man. And loyal. So very loyal. Right, Callum?"

Callum nods and pours himself another glass of wine. I'm pretty sure he's on his second bottle. Brooke, meanwhile, is drinking sparkling water because of the pregnancy.

"Best man I ever knew," Callum says hoarsely.

"Not very good at managing his money, though," Dinah remarks. Her green eyes narrow at me for a moment. "Do you take after your mother or father, Ella?"

"My mother," I answer tersely, but how the hell would I know?

"Of course you have to say that," she muses. "After all, Steve didn't know about you. You literally did not exist for him for most of your life."

Nice, subtle jab there, Dinah. But you know what? I grew up around catty women who were constantly afraid that their one asset—their looks—was quickly fading. I can take whatever she dishes out.

I smile. "He came around. I mean, he did leave me everything he could."

And he would have left me more if you didn't have a boatload of lawyers making sure every loose penny fell into your purse.

Her answering smile is full of teeth. "I was thinking about you the other day." *Please, don't.* "And how much alike we are. My mother wasn't well when I was young, and we moved around as much as you did. She made poor life decisions. There were often . . ." She pauses and takes a sip of her drink.

Against all of our wills, we're listening to her every word, and she clearly revels in the attention.

"Often people that drifted in and out of my life that weren't always the best sort of influence. Sometimes these men wanted things from me that a child should never be asked to give."

Dinah looks at me expectantly. I guess she's like one of those old-timey Southern preachers who need affirmation to make sure their message is getting through.

"That's too bad," I mutter.

She's right, though. Her story is similar to my own past. But I refuse to feel sorry for her. Her life is a far cry from that now.

"It is, isn't it?" She dabs the side of her mouth with a napkin. "I'd love to give you some advice, from one lost girl to another. You don't need to wait for what you want in life, because if you do, you'll end up like our mothers—used and, ultimately, dead. And I'm sure you don't want that, do you, Ella?"

Callum sets his fork against the table with more force than necessary. "I don't think this is appropriate dinner conversation."

Dinah waves a dismissive hand. "It's girl talk, Callum. I'm giving Ella some of my hard-won wisdom."

And warning me that she's going to try to take everything Steve left me.

"Is this the plot of some Lifetime movie?" Easton interjects before I can respond. "Because I blocked that channel on my TV."

"Samesy," Sawyer says. "Where's the dessert?"

"Well, if we're bored of my life story and Ella's, how about we talk about you boys? I know Easton and the twins like to play the field. What about you two? Reed? Gideon? Are you boys seeing anyone special or breaking hearts like your little brothers?" She gives a teasing laugh. Nobody else joins in.

"We're both single," Gideon grinds out.

That gets Brooke's attention. She twirls a strand of hair around her finger, shooting me an impish look as the waitstaff carts out our desserts. "And you, Ella? Found that special someone yet?"

Callum is eyeing me, too, now. It figures this would be the moment he decides to take his drunken face out of his wine bottle.

I lower my head to my dessert as if the tiramisu on my plate is the most interesting thing I've ever seen. "No, I'm not seeing anyone."

There's another lull in the conversation. I scarf down my cake as quickly as I can, and I notice from the corner of my eye that all the Royal boys are doing the same.

Gideon beats us all, dropping his fork on his empty plate and scraping his chair back. "I need to make a phone call."

His father frowns. "We're about to serve coffee."

"Don't want any," Gid mumbles. He hightails it off the patio as if he can't get away fast enough.

Reed opens his mouth to speak but Callum silences him with a look. *You're not going anywhere*, it says. And Reed angrily slumps back in his seat.

The catering staff comes out with trays of fancy-pants lattes featuring actual designs created out of the foam. Mine's a leaf. Brooke's is a tree but should've been a pitchfork.

"Excuse me," Dinah says as the coffee is served. "I need to use the little girls' room."

Reed catches my gaze and we both roll our eyes, and I instantly regret the moment of camaraderie because it brings a pleased half smile to his lips.

This time, it's Easton and I who beat out the brothers, slurping our lattes back in record time. We slam our cups down and speak at the same time.

"I'll help the caterers with these dishes—"

"I'll take in this tray—"

We glare at each other for a moment, but our mutual need to flee inspires another bonding moment.

"Ella and I will take care of this," Easton finishes, and I nod in gratitude.

Callum is quick to protest. "The waitstaff is perfectly capable of—"

But Easton and I are already gathering up random plates and cups.

As we hurry toward the French doors, I hear Reed's grumble of annoyance tickling my back.

"Great minds think alike," Easton murmurs.

I flash him a quick scowl. "Oh, so now we're friends again?"

His expression flickers with guilt. When we reach the kitchen, he sets the plates in the sink, glances discreetly at the catering staff, and lowers his voice. "I'm sorry about what I said at Shea's party. I was . . . wasted."

"You're not allowed to use that as an excuse," I retort. "You're *always* wasted and you've never said anything like that to me before."

His cheeks redden. "I'm sorry. I'm an asshole."

"Yup."

"Forgive me?"

He dons his trademark little-boy look that usually makes people melt, but I'm not letting him off the hook that easily. The comment he'd made the other night was mean. And hurtful. So I shake my head at him and walk out of the kitchen.

"Ella. Come on. Wait." He catches up to me in the hall and takes hold of my arm. "You know I say stupid shit without thinking."

My face heats up. "You pretty much told everyone at that party that I'm a slut, Easton."

He moans. "I know. I messed up, okay? You know I don't think that about you. I . . ." His features crease. "I like you. You're my baby sis. Please don't be mad at me."

Before I can respond, a soft noise snags my attention. It sounded like a groan. Or maybe a sigh?

I glance toward the end of the hall. There are only three rooms in this section of the house: a small powder room, the walk-in pantry, and a closet.

"Did you hear that?" I ask Easton.

He nods grimly.

Something compels me to creep farther down the corridor. I pause in front of the pantry, but I don't hear anything behind the door. Same with the closet. The bathroom, though . . .

Easton and I both freeze when we hear the moan. It's a woman, from the sound of it. My blood runs cold, because there are six females in the Royal mansion right now and five of them are accounted for. Brooke's on the patio. The waitresses are in the kitchen. And I'm right here.

Which means . . .

I turn to Easton with wide eyes, suddenly feeling sick to my stomach.

He must have put two and two together, because his mouth falls open slightly.

"Easton," I hiss when he reaches for the doorknob.

He holds the index finger of his free hand to his mouth. Then, to my horror, he turns the knob and eases the door open about an inch.

An inch is all we need. An inch is plenty for us to catch a glimpse of the couple inside the bathroom. Dinah's blond head. Gid's dark one. His hands digging into her hips. Her body arching toward him.

With disgust in his eyes, Easton soundlessly closes the bathroom door and stumbles backward as if he was just slapped in the face.

In unspoken agreement, we don't say a word until we're a safe distance away.

"Oh my God," I whisper in horror. "What the *hell* is Gideon—"

Easton clamps a hand over my mouth. "Shut up," he says in a low voice. "We didn't see anything, you got it?"

His hand is trembling as it drops away. He gives me one last punishing look, then spins on his heel and disappears into the foyer. A few seconds later, the front door slams.

Twenty

THE PHONE RINGS at midnight. I'm not asleep. When I close my eyes, all I can see is Gideon's and Dinah's heads and his hands on her ass. It's too close to how I picture Brooke and Reed, and I wonder if that's where Reed got his stupid idea in the first place.

I stretch my arm out and grab the phone off the nightstand. The display shows Val's pursed lips blowing me a kiss.

"Hey, girl, what's up?" I whisper into the phone.

Silence greets me.

I sit up. "Val?"

After a shuddering breath and a half sob, I hear, "Ella, it's me. Val."

"I know. I saw your name on my phone. What's wrong? Where are you?" I'm out of bed and pulling on my leggings as I wait for her response.

"South Industrial Boulevard outside some warehouse. There's a rave."

"What happened? Do you need a ride?"

"Yeah. I'm sorry to call you." She sounds miserable. "I caught a ride out here because I heard Tam was in town, but I couldn't find him, my ride took off, and it's a bad scene."

I sigh but offer no judgment. After all, wasn't I kissing Reed just a few nights ago? I'm so ashamed of it that I haven't even been able to confess this to my best friend.

"I'll be there as soon as I can," I promise.

She starts to say something and then stops.

"What?" I ask, grabbing my keys off the dresser.

"It's just . . . this is a rough place. You might want to bring someone with you."

Does she mean Reed? Yeah right. I'd cut off my leg before asking him for help. "I'll check if Easton is home."

"Good. I'll wait for you here."

I find my shoes, throw open my door, and grind to a halt when I see Reed slumped against the wall. The door strikes the wall before I can catch it and the sharp sound jerks him out of sleep.

Hooded eyes take in my clothes, bag, and keys. "Where're we going?" he drawls, instantly alert.

"I'm going to get something to eat." As lies go, that one sucks, but I'm sticking with it. "Easton around?" I ask casually. "Maybe he's hungry."

Reed pushes to his feet. "He might be. You'll have to call him, though, because last I heard he was going out for drinks with Wade and the guys."

Damn. "Why aren't you there? And why are you lurking outside my room like a creeper?"

He shoots me a look of disbelief. "Isn't it obvious?"

I shut my mouth, because it *is* obvious but, more important, I'm afraid if I open my mouth again, a whole slew of questions will fall out. Like how long has he been doing this, and is it because he's afraid I'm going to run away or because he just wants to be as close as possible to me? I'm even more afraid of the answers.

And I have Val to pick up, so I turn and head downstairs. Wordlessly, Reed follows me.

He's my silent shadow across the grand foyer and its giant chandelier, past the dining room that's never used, and into the kitchen where I once sat on Reed's lap wishing I was having him for breakfast instead of whatever dish Sandra had created.

"Go upstairs, Reed. I don't need you."

"Whose wheels are you taking?"

I stop short and he nearly steps on the back of my feet. "Oh."

My honey, glitter, and ant–infested car is undrivable, I realize. I'd parked it in the garage that I've never seen Callum use because I needed time to find a place that could clean it and I had no idea how to explain the mess to Callum in the meantime.

He reaches over and plucks my now-useless car keys out of my hand and pockets them. "Come on. I've got you."

Val's warning that I should bring someone tickles my conscience, but I don't want to ask Reed for anything. "Can't I just borrow your car?"

"First, it's not a car—it's an SUV. Second, no."

I don't have time to argue. Val needs me. And apparently, I need Reed. But I don't have to be gracious about it, so I huff an angry sigh and stomp into the mudroom, grabbing the first jacket I can find. The minute I zip it up, I realize it's Reed's. Great. Now my nose is filled with his scent.

"Fine, but when we get there, you have to stay in the car."

He grunts his response, which could either be agreement or *I'm not going to argue with you until I have you in the car.*

"So where are we going?" he asks as I buckle in. I give him the address, and he slides me a wry look in return. "I didn't realize the wharf was the only place to get fast food at midnight."

"Heard it was the best in town," I answer airily.

"You and I both know that you aren't going out to pick up food. Want to tell me what's going on?"

"Not particularly, no."

I expect him to shoot back some retort like *My car, my rules*, but instead he remains silent. His fingers flex around the steering wheel, squeezing the leather-wrapped circle. He's probably imagining it's my neck and that if he squeezes tight enough, I'll eventually spill my guts and say, *Oh, gosh, Reed, I don't care that you screwed your daddy's girlfriend and maybe got her pregnant. Come inside my bedroom and take my virginity.*

Well, if he even still wants my V-card. I mean, yeah, he *says* he wants me, but what does that mean? Is it just a matter of pride for him? A girl who turns him down is a prick to his ego so he pursues her to build his image back up?

It's not like I can rely on my instincts anymore. After all, I let Reed in even when he was being an asshole to me. I definitely can't trust him now that he's being nice.

I should've listened to him when he told me to stay away, but I was lonely and stupid and there was something in him that called to me. I thought . . . I don't know what I thought. Maybe my estrogen levels were super high and I got caught up in some kind of hormonal episode. Or maybe it's just how I'm wired. I spent my whole life watching my mom make one bad decision after the other when it came to men. Is it really a surprise that I'm doing the same thing?

Reed reaches across the console to squeeze my knee. "You're gonna hurt your brain, thinking that hard."

His touch makes my pulse speed up, so I move my knee

away to dislodge his hand. He gets the message and returns his grip to the steering wheel while I stare at the dashboard, trying to squash the regret that fills me.

"My problem isn't that I'm thinking too hard—it's that I'm not thinking enough," I mumble.

"You don't have problems, Ella. Not the way you think you do. You're fine the way you are."

The compliment sends a warm rush to my belly. Sweet, nice Reed is more potent and dangerous than asshole Reed. I can't deal with this right now. I'm tired and my defenses are low.

"Don't be nice to me. That's not who you are."

To my surprise, Reed laughs. It's not a hearty one and it's tinged with a shade of bitterness, but it's still a laugh. "I don't know who I am anymore. I think I'm lost. I think my brothers are lost, too."

My heart flips. Oh no. Vulnerable Reed is even more dangerous. I scramble for a subject change. "Is that what's wrong with Easton?"

"If I knew what's up with East, I wouldn't be going with you in the middle of the night to haul him out of whatever trouble he's in. So if you have some ideas on how to fix him, please, I'm all ears."

"We're not rescuing Easton right now," I admit. "And if you want ideas about how to help him, ask someone else. I don't have the first clue what's going on with him." All I know is that Easton told me once he has addiction issues. He misses his mother desperately, loves his brothers, and is sickened by what he saw in the bathroom tonight.

It's on the tip of my tongue to ask Reed about it. If he knows. But as with so many other things that go on in that household, I feel the less I know, the better.

"I don't think he likes to be left out," I offer reluctantly. "There's the twins and there's you and Gideon. Maybe he feels like he doesn't belong."

I know that feeling, and it might explain why Easton was so upset at seeing Gideon and Dinah together. Why he's hooking up with Abby and Savannah. Why he's drinking and smoking himself senseless. Maybe he's trying to get a closer sense of his brothers and doing it in his own special messed-up Easton way.

Reed grunts. "I guess I've never thought of it that way."

He taps his fingers on the steering wheel and then abruptly changes the subject. "You haven't told my dad about your car yet."

"How do you know I haven't?"

"Because he'd be stomping around the house and making a thousand phone calls. And your ant-infested car wouldn't be stashed in the garage where Dad can't see it."

"I've been calling around to find a place that will clean it up."

"I'll take care of it."

Any response I might have is cut short by the scene we pull up to. Cars are peeling out of a parking lot, and we hear the faint wail of sirens in the distance. When Reed slows down, I jerk open the door and hop out. Hitting the ground running, I yell, "Val! Val! Where are you?"

A slender figure separates itself from a straggly bush lining the sidewalk and throws itself at me.

"Oh my God, I thought you'd never get here!" Val sobs in my ear.

I pull back to see a bruise forming beside her left eye and a red mark on her forehead. "What happened?" I exclaim.

"I'll tell you in the car. Please let's go."

"Of course." I wrap my arm around her, but when we start for the car, Val stumbles, nearly taking me with her.

Reed appears at my side and lifts Val into his arms. He nods toward the car. "Let's go."

This time I don't hesitate to listen to him. The sirens are getting closer and there are people jostling us, running around, racing away.

Reed hurries to his Rover. While I hold open the car door, he slides Val into the backseat. I climb in after her as Reed jumps into the driver's seat.

"Don't take me home. Please, I can't deal with Jordan tonight," Val whimpers.

"Of course not. You can stay with me."

Reed gives me a nod that he's heard me, and he takes off, heading north toward home.

"Who did this to you, Val?" he demands. "I'm gonna kick his ass."

Val leans her head back against the seat. She's exhausted, emotionally and physically.

"You don't have to talk about it." I rub my hand down her bare arm. Her cute outfit—a crop top and embroidered shorts—looks intact. I don't see any signs of injury other than the ones on her face.

"It's fine." She gives me a sad smile. "I ran into an ex of Tam's. We got into a ridiculous fight, so if you're going to kick anyone's ass, it'll be mine."

She closes her eyes and silent tears rain down her face. I slide over and wrap one arm around her, holding her close for the rest of the drive.

When we get home, I help her up to the bedroom, and she

collapses on my bed. I pull her shoes off, strip off her shorts and top, and grab a bottle of water from my fridge. She takes it with a grateful smile.

"Do you want Astor football or this old Iron Man T-shirt?"

She looks pointedly at the football T-shirt but gestures to the other one. "Iron Man, please."

I toss her Iron Man, glad she doesn't ask why I still have one of Reed's old workout shirts. My answer would be that it's comfortable. I mean, it really is comfortable, but anyone with half a brain would guess I've kept it for other reasons.

Val slips under the covers just as Reed appears with a pill bottle. "Valium," he says, walking through the door I'd left open.

I don't ask why he has a prescription for it. I just shake out one pill and give it to Val.

"You two need anything else?"

"No thanks," I answer.

He shifts from one foot to the other and then reluctantly leaves.

Val falls asleep almost immediately, but I'm too wired to crash. I curl up next to her and just lie there for a while, until a noise in the hall captures my attention. Careful not to wake my friend, I creep across the room and crack the door open.

Sure enough, Reed is settling down outside my door.

"Go to bed," I hiss.

He opens one eye. "I am in bed."

"There's no bed in the hall."

"Don't need one."

"Fine." I start to slam the door but remember Val at the last second. The door closes with a soft snick and I lean against it, forcing myself to remember how I don't love him. How he was cruel to me. How I spent my weeks away tormented with visions of him and Brooke together and wanting to just curl up and die but instead getting up every morning to hustle and find work.

And now he's sitting outside my door, trying to make me believe he's changed.

I wrench open the door again and stomp out. "Why are you here?" The words come out like a plea rather than an accusation.

Reed stands up. He's wearing a black tank and track pants that ride low on his hips, and his biceps flex when he reaches for me. "You know why."

The fire in his eyes simultaneously turns me on and fuels my anger. "Don't touch me."

He lets his arm drop, and I hate the disappointment that I feel. *Get it together, Ella!*

"Fine," he rasps. "You do the touching."

My eyes widen as he starts tearing off his clothes right there in the hall.

Naked Reed with his rippling chest and his rock-hard thighs and that thin line of hair that arrows down to his waistband? No. No. *No!*

"Put this back on," I order, throwing his shirt back in his face.

"No." He snatches it out of the air and tosses it aside.

And then he pulls me against him.

Every inch of him is hard. Every inch.

I expect another hot, frantic make-out, like the one in Savannah's driveway, but Reed surprises me. His touch is gentle as he skims his fingers over my cheek. His breathing thins, and then those fingers tenderly slide through my hair, angling my head perfectly for his kiss.

It's the sweetest kiss we've ever shared. Slow. Soft. The

featherlight brush of his lips, the tentative swirl of his tongue. I can feel him shaking, but I don't know if it's because he's nervous or excited or both.

I scream at myself to move, to push him away. If I call for help, maybe he'll stop kissing me like I'm the single-most important person in his world.

But I don't do any of that. My stupid body melts against his. My stupid lips part for him.

Take what he can give you and then send him on his way, a little voice whispers. *Use him.*

Isn't that a convenient excuse?

But in the haze of my growing need, I give in a tiny inch and Reed takes full advantage, hoisting me up and carrying me to his bedroom. He kicks his door shut behind him and lowers me onto his mattress.

"I missed you," he whispers, and I open my eyes to find that his are shining with emotion. "Tell me you missed me, too."

I swallow the words before they can leave my mouth.

The disappointment on his face fades quickly. "It's okay, you don't have to tell me. You can show me."

His hand leaves my hair and moves between my legs, and when his fingers curl up, I can't stop from rocking my hips. He grunts in pleasure against my mouth and rubs that aching spot, making me whimper.

I hate that he still has power over me. I hate that I no longer feel in control over anything. I hate that I'm here. That my mom is gone. That I fell for Reed in the first place.

Tears start trickling out, sliding down to where our mouths meet.

"Are you crying?" Reed abruptly breaks away from me.

I can't stop myself from gripping him tighter. It's like some part of me is saying that I've had too much loss in my life so I might as well hang on to the scraps Reed Royal is willing to give me.

But I can't stop crying, either. The tears fall, fast and furious. Reed swipes them away, but they keep coming.

"Please stop crying, baby. Please," he begs.

I try. I hold my breath, but the unshed tears rack my body with a wave of shudders.

"I'm done. I won't touch you again. Promise. Ella, you're killing me."

He pushes my head against his chest and strokes my hair. It takes more time than I'd like to admit to get myself under control, and all the while Reed is apologizing and repeating his promise to keep away.

This is what I want, I tell myself, but his vow to not touch me again only makes me cry harder.

I finally gather enough composure to push him away. "I'm sorry," I whisper.

He gazes back with sad eyes.

I heave myself off the mattress and back away from the bed, gaining some much-needed distance. My head grows clearer the farther away from Reed that I get. "We need to leave each other alone. We're not good for each other."

"What does that mean?"

"You know what it means."

He stands and puts his hands on his hips. I avert my eyes from his naked body and perfect face. If he could turn ugly overnight, that would be so helpful.

"So you're gonna be okay with me hooking up with someone else? Putting my mouth on some other girl. Having her hands all over me."

I almost barf on the cream carpet. I force myself to breathe through my nose. And lie. "Yes."

I feel the weight of his stare for what seems like forever. I want to leap after him and beg him to stay, but for my own self-preservation, I keep my head down and my feet firmly rooted.

"No, you won't," Reed says quietly. "You're hurting and pushing me away, but I'm not giving up."

He walks over to me, and I brace myself. But he only kisses me on the forehead and then leaves me alone in his room.

His last words hang in the air. I slump to the floor and draw my knees tight to my chest. I'm upset he didn't try to press me. I know I would've given in. I'm upset that he's still swearing to pursue me.

No, that's not right. I'm upset at myself for feeling the warm glow over his declaration that no matter what I throw at him, he's going to win me back.

Twenty-One

I HAUL MYSELF to my room and manage to fall asleep two hours before the alarm rings for us to get up and go to school. I stick a hand out from the covers and fumble for my phone. Hitting snooze, I peer over to the other side. Val's half off the bed, one leg stuck out from under the comforter and one arm hanging over the edge of the mattress.

I shake her shoulder. "Time to get up, Sleeping Beauty."

"No. Don't wanna," she mumbles.

"School starts in . . ." It takes my slow mind a minute to make the calculation. ". . . an hour ten."

"Wake me up in twenty, then."

I force myself out of bed, grab a bottle of water from my mini fridge, and duck into the bathroom. I blink a few times until the mirror version of me comes into focus.

There's no evidence on my skin of Reed's touch. There's no mark on my neck where his mouth sucked. There's no outward evidence of my weakness. I press a finger against my lower lip and pretend it's Reed's.

Val appears behind me, saving me from my own idiotic imagination. The bruise over her eye is ugly.

"I know you told Reed last night that you got into a fight, but if someone hurt you, I'm going to kill them." I'm not even joking.

"Then you'll need to start with me, because this"—she points to her forehead—"is the result of me headbashing Tam's ex."

I wince. "Maybe use a beer bottle next time? Or better yet, take me with you." I meet her eyes in the mirror. "You never mentioned a rave at school. Why didn't you ask me to go? I would've backed you up."

"I didn't know about the party until late last night. I got a text from a girl who goes to Jefferson—that's where Tam went to school—and she said she swore she saw him. I didn't even stop to think about what I was doing. I got dressed, caught a ride with Jordan, who was on her way to Gastonburg's house, and the next thing I know I'm in some stupid catfight with a stranger over Tam."

"I thought you said it was an ex, not a stranger. Was she from his college?"

Val looks like she was punched in the gut. "No. I think he's been cheating on me this whole time. That's why I called her his ex."

"Oh no." I place my arm around her, and she curls into my chest.

"I'm so stupid."

You're not the only one.

I clear my throat. "I kissed Reed last night."

"Really?" Her voice is almost hopeful.

"Yeah. He's been sleeping outside my room. That's creepy, right?"

Val pulls back so I can see her wide eyes. "Super creepy," she agrees, but she doesn't sound convincing.

I sag against the counter. "No, I don't think it's creepy,

either. I should, but instead I think it's weirdly . . . sweet that he's so intent on making sure I don't run off again that he's literally sleeping on the floor outside my door." I rub my forehead, embarrassed by my own weakness.

"He beat up Skip Henley for you yesterday."

I blink in surprise. "What?"

Val shifts, looking embarrassed. "I didn't say anything because I know you don't like talking about Reed, but . . . yeah. He punched Skippy in the middle of the dining room for harassing you in Speech class."

A flurry of emotions flies through me. Joy. Satisfaction, because those nasty comments in Speech yesterday were so brutal. And then there's guilt, because . . . dammit, because I've been pushing Reed away since I got back and meanwhile he's sleeping protectively outside my door and fighting other boys in my honor.

Maybe I . . . God, does he deserve another chance?

"Just figured you might feel better knowing he did that," Val says with a shrug. "And hey, at least Reed didn't cheat on you and he's not trying to avoid all contact with you. He's not a liar like Tam." Val squeezes my arm. "Do you have a toothbrush I can borrow? It feels like an animal died in my mouth."

I lean down to rummage under the sink, where I find a basket of pretty wrapped soaps and a stack of new toothbrushes. I hand her one and then apply toothpaste to my own electric brush. While Val brushes her teeth and washes her face, I go back to the bedroom and stare at my closet full of Brooke-picked clothes. I don't see anything, though. All I can think about is the phrase: *Reed didn't cheat on you.*

When Val said it, my first instinct wasn't to deny it.

Because it's true.

I don't believe anymore that he cheated on me. I don't know if the baby is his. But . . . if I believe that he didn't cheat on me then I should believe him when he says he's not the baby daddy.

And Val is right about another thing—Reed's not a liar. The one thing that he hasn't done in our time together is lie to me. He's been so blunt in telling me that he plans to leave town after graduation, that he's not good with relationships, that he destroys the people around him.

And he's not talking about girls or any kind of juvenile bullshit. In a burst of insight, I realize he's talking about his parents. He loved them desperately, and they both failed him.

His mother killed herself, leaving five sons to cope with the loss. His father drowns himself in liquor and horrible women. Is it any wonder that Reed told me that sex was just sex? That he tried to use it as a weapon? He uses it to punish himself and others. He's living up to the legacy left to him by his weak parents, but there's a struggle inside of him—and it's that struggle that spoke to me.

"You're about to drool on yourself," Val remarks as she exits the bathroom.

I swipe a guilty hand across my face and run to the sink to spit and swish out my mouth. Admitting to Val that I still have feelings for Reed is one thing, admitting to her that I'm thinking about forgiving him is an entirely different story. One that I don't know the ending to.

"What do you think is going to be in my locker today?" I ask as I join her in front of my closet. "Garbage? Day-old food? Used tampons?"

Val points to her bruise. "What about this? I look like I'm a poster child for abused girlfriends."

"I can cover that. I've done it before." At her outraged

expression, I hurry to explain. "Not to my mom or myself, but girls she worked with."

"Ugh."

"I know."

I turn away from the closet. "You know what? I'm thinking I want to skip again and hit the mall today. What do you think?"

Her mouth slowly spreads into a smile. "I'm thinking I want to eat a big yeasty pretzel and have Froyo for lunch."

We knock fists together. "Do we fake being sick?"

"Nah. We're just skipping. We're going to the mall, eating terrible things, maxing out our guardians' credit cards. Then we're going to get makeovers at Sephora. Afterward, we're going over to the pier and stuffing our faces full of shellfish until we're only attractive to marine life."

I give her a big grin. "I'm *so* on board with this."

✦ ✦ ✦

"HOW WAS YOUR shopping trip?"

I spin around at the sound of Brooke's voice. I was in the process of making myself a snack, but as usual, her presence kills my appetite. I shove my bowl of corn chips aside and move away from the counter.

Brooke waltzes toward me in her four-inch heels. I wonder if she'll still wear stilettos when she's eight months pregnant, waddling around on heels with her huge belly. Probably. She's vain enough that she'd probably take the risk of tripping and falling, even while knocked up.

Ugh. Why am I even thinking about Brooke's pregnancy? It's only making me queasier.

"The silent treatment? Really?" Brooke laughs on her way to the refrigerator. "I expected better from you, Ella."

I roll my eyes at her back. "Like you really care how my day was. I'm just saving us the trouble of making small talk neither of us cares about."

Brooke grabs a pitcher of filtered water and goes to pour herself a tall glass. "Actually, I've been anxiously waiting for a chance to talk to you."

Uh-huh. I'm sure.

"Callum and I were talking the other night, and we thought it would be a good idea if you and Dinah planned my baby shower."

My spine goes rigid. Is she kidding me?

"It'd be a nice bonding opportunity for the two of you," Brooke goes on. "Callum agrees."

Yeah right. There's no way this was Callum's idea. The day he took me to meet Steve's widow, he drank himself into a coma in the car and begged me not to listen to a word Dinah O'Halloran said.

Brooke eyes me expectantly. "What do you think, sweetie?"

"What do I think?" I echo in a syrupy tone. "I think I'd like to see some paternity test results before I waste my time on a baby shower."

Her delicate jaw tightens. "That was uncalled-for."

"Nah, I don't think it was." I prop a hip against the counter, then shrug. "You might have fooled Callum into believing this is a Royal baby, but I've got my doubts, *sweetie*."

"Oh, it's a Royal baby, all right. But are you *sure* you want to know which Royal's DNA made up half this bundle of love?" She pats her tiny baby bump and smiles at me.

My hands clench into fists. She's struck a nerve, and she knows it.

You can't hit a pregnant woman, says the firm voice in my head.

I swallow my rising anger and force my fingers to relax.

Brooke nods in approval, as if she voodoo'd her way into my head and knows how badly I want to smack her. "So, back to this baby shower," she says, as if that bit of ugliness didn't just happen. "You should really consider helping Dinah plan it. She wasn't happy with the way you treated her at dinner."

"I barely said a word to her."

"Exactly." Brooke frowns at me. "Dinah isn't someone you want as an enemy, Ella."

I frown right back. "What does that mean?"

"It means she doesn't take kindly to rudeness, and your behavior—you and the boys—seriously pissed her off."

She didn't look pissed when she was having sex with Callum's son in the hall bathroom, I almost spit out.

"When I spoke her to the next morning, she even brought up the C-word," Brooke says in a singsong voice.

My jaw drops. Wow. Dinah called me a—

"Contest," Brooke supplies, chuckling at my horrified expression.

I stare blankly at her.

"Dinah threatened to contest Steven's will," she clarifies. "And if she goes through with it, I guarantee you that she'll tie it up in court for years. By the time she's done, there'll be no money left for either one of you—the lawyers will get it all. I've already advised her against it, but Dinah's always been stubborn, and she was incredibly offended by the way you treated her."

"What does she care?" I shake my head in annoyance. "I don't know her and I didn't know Steve."

Brooke sips her water. "Feel lucky about that second one. Not knowing Steve."

My brow furrows. As much as I hate getting drawn into a conversation with the she-devil, I can't deny that my curiosity is piqued every time someone mentions my biological father. "Why?"

"Because despite what Callum Royal thinks, Steve was a terrible friend."

Given that her source is probably Dinah, who I think is one step up from Brooke in the demon stakes, I don't trust a word of this, but I smile prettily and nod because that's the easiest way out of this discussion.

"If you say so."

"It's the truth. You're lucky he's dead. I'd hate to see what he would do to an innocent, young girl like you." The bluntly stated words, so different from her usual saccharine delivery, raise the hairs on the back of my neck.

"I know Dinah is mad about the will, but I had nothing to do with that."

Brooke's mouth twists into an ugly line. "Steve would've left it to a turtle if it meant keeping it away from Dinah. Him leaving it to you was the shock. Even Callum thought the money would go to his sons."

That stops me short. Is that why Gideon doesn't like me? Because he thinks I stole his inheritance?

"The boys already have a ton from Callum," I point out.

Brooke shakes her head in mock dismay. "You can never have enough in this world. Haven't you learned that yet?" She sets her mug on the counter between us. "It's not too late, Ella. Dinah and I can be your family. You don't need to stay here with these men. They're poisonous. They'll use you up and hurt you."

I stare back at her in disbelief. "No one has hurt me more than you have. You're trying to tear this family apart and I don't understand why. What's your end game here? What do you have against them?"

She sighs, like I'm a dumb child. "My end game is survival, and Lord, I've tried to teach that to you, too. I tried and tried to tell you to get away. Everything I did when you were around was to help you." Her tone changes. It's no longer sweet, but hard and biting. "But I see you're like all the others. So blinded by those dazzling Royal smiles that you can't see your own salvation. My mama told me you can't cast your pearls before the swine."

"And I'm swine because I think the Royals aren't going to be the end of me?"

"You're ignorant and lost in your own teen lust, which is sad, but"—she gives a delicate shrug—"I can't make you wise. You'll have to learn those hard lessons on your own."

"You're not really cut out to be a teacher. And you should probably concentrate on looking after yourself, because once the paternity test comes back, I can't see Callum's wallet staying open for you." I grab my bowl of corn chips and start for the door.

"And you look out for yourself," she calls after me, "because I'm not going to give you a shoulder to cry on when Reed breaks your heart. Or maybe you should give Gideon a try. I have it on good authority he's an animal in the sack."

I can't keep the shock off my face.

Brooke roars with laughter. "You're such a child. The horror on your face is adorable. Here's one last piece of advice—ignore the Royal boys. They're bad for you. Let Dinah and me help you with your money, and we'll all live happily ever after."

"I'd trust Reed before I'd ever trust you."

She's unfazed by my biting retort. Instead, she beams and continues as if I didn't speak at all. "Play your cards right, and you can be a bridesmaid at my wedding. Won't that be fun?"

Ha. I'd rather walk barefoot on a ten-mile road made of lava than be her bridesmaid.

"No thanks."

Her eyes burn a hole into my back as I walk out of the kitchen and straight into Reed's smiling face.

"Knew you still had feelings for me," he murmurs.

I want to deny it, to tell him he's delusional, but the words die in my throat. I can't tell him what he wants to hear. I'm too . . . raw from all the things swirling around in my head. I'm not ready to have this conversation with him.

"You stood up for me just now," he presses when I don't respond.

I shake my head. "I didn't stand up for you. I stood up for myself."

Twenty-Two

REED

I STOOD UP for myself.

Two days after Ella said those words to me, I still can't stop thinking about them. And I can't stop thinking about that night in my bedroom, either. Her tears. How she insisted we weren't good for each other.

She's right. Well, half right. She's definitely good for me, but what good am I for her? I was an ass to her when she first showed up. I lashed out and treated her like crap because I hated that my father brought Steve's bastard into our house when he couldn't be bothered to pay attention to his existing children. Dad clearly cared about her, so my brothers and I did the opposite—we shunned her.

And yeah, I changed my tune. I gave in to the attraction. My guard dropped lower and lower until I was completely under her spell. But even after I fell for her, I still kept secrets. I still pushed her away more than once. I still let her run off instead of immediately explaining about Brooke.

I told Ella I was going to win her back, but what the hell am I really doing to make it happen? I put my fist in Henley's jaw on her behalf, but what do I really have to offer someone like her? She's perfectly fine taking care of herself.

But the thing is, the reason she's always fighting her own battles and standing up for herself is because . . . nobody has ever done it for her.

Today, that's about to change.

"You're really not gonna drop me at home first?" Wade grumbles from the passenger side of my Range Rover. He's glaring at every car in the parking lot as I pull up in front of the French Twist.

"Why the hell would I?" The bakery is literally five minutes from school, while Wade's mansion is twenty minutes in the other direction. "I'll be five minutes."

"I've got someone waiting for me back at my place."

"Who?" I challenge.

"Rachel." He grins sheepishly. "And her friend Dana."

I snicker. "Guess you shouldn't have smashed up your Porsche last night, then. But you did, and now you're stuck being my bitch boy until you have wheels again."

He gives me the finger. "I'm late for a threesome because of you, Royal. I'll never forgive you."

"I'm crying a river." I leave the keys in the engine and open the door. "Wait here. I won't be long."

"You better not be."

The bakery is surprisingly deserted when I stride inside. Usually it's packed around this time, but I spot only a couple of Astor Park kids, plus a trio of old ladies at a table in the corner.

Ella's former boss frowns as I approach the counter. "Mr. Royal," she says politely. "How can I help you?"

I take an awkward breath. "I'm here to apologize."

Her eyebrows rise. "I see. I'll be honest—you don't strike me as the type of boy who knows the meaning of that word."

"Trust me, I know how to say I'm sorry." I offer a rueful smile. "I'm pretty sure those are the only two words I've been saying lately."

That gets me a reluctant smile in return.

"Look, it's my fault Ella ran off," I explain in a rush. "I don't know if she told you, but she and I were sort of going out."

Lucy nods. "She didn't tell me, but I knew she was seeing someone. That last week before she left, I'd never seen her look happier."

Guilt arrows through me. Yeah, Ella had been happy. Until I took that happiness and turned it into something ugly. Like I always do.

"I messed up." I force myself to man up and look Lucy in the eye. "Ella wasn't sick. She ran away because I didn't leave her any other choice. But I'm telling you right now—she feels terrible about letting you down."

"Did she send you here to tell me that?" Lucy asks, frowning again.

I choke out a laugh. "Are you kidding me? She'd kill me if she knew I was here. Have you ever met anyone with more pride than Ella Harper?"

Lucy presses her lips together as if fighting back a laugh.

"She loved this job," I say earnestly. "Everyone in my family, myself included, didn't want her to work. It's, uh, a status thing." I'm a prick. We rich people are the worst, I realize. "But she took the job anyway, because that's the kind of person Ella is. She doesn't like accepting handouts or sitting on her ass all day like everyone else at Astor Park. And she really liked having you as her boss."

"I enjoyed having her here," Lucy says grudgingly. "*But*. That doesn't change the fact that she left me short-handed for more than two weeks."

"My fault," I repeat. "Seriously, I take all the blame for this. And I feel sick about it, too. I hate that I cost her a job she really cared about. So I'm asking you to reconsider firing her. Please."

"I've already hired a replacement, Reed. I can't afford to take on two employees."

Disappointment fills my gut. "Oh. I understand."

"But . . ."

Just like that, I feel a burst of hope. "But what?"

"Kenneth is only able to work afternoons," Lucy says, and it's obvious she's not thrilled with that. "I haven't been able to find anyone who can fill the five thirty a.m. shifts that Ella used to do." She smiles. "Not many teenagers want to wake up at the crack of dawn."

"Ella does," I say instantly. "Her work ethic is intense. You know that."

Lucy looks thoughtful. "Yes, I guess I do know that."

I rest both hands against the counter and eye her hopefully. "So you'll give her another shot?"

She doesn't answer right away. Then she says, "I'll think about it."

Since that's all I can ask for, I shake her hand, thank her for her time, and leave the bakery with a smile on my face.

✦ ✦ ✦

FOR THE FIRST time since the engagement and pregnancy news, our house is Brooke-free. Brooke and her evil hench-woman, Dinah, are going to Paris for two weeks to look for a wedding dress. When Dad tells us the news, the twins release a happy whoop. Our father glares at them, then announces that we're all having dinner together on the patio. I shrug and head outside, because as long as Brooke and Dinah aren't eating with us, I've got no issues with dinner.

Our housekeeper, Sandra, places two huge casserole dishes on the patio table, which is already set for seven. "I'm heading out now," she tells Callum. "But I left enough food in the freezer to last you boys until the end of the weekend."

"Aw, Sandy, no. You're going on vacation again?" Sawyer asks in dismay.

"I wouldn't exactly call it a vacation." She sighs. "My sister just had a baby and I'm going to San Francisco to help her out for a week. I foresee many sleepless nights in my future."

"Take as much time as you need," Dad says with a warm smile. "An extra week, if you need it."

Sandra snorts. "Uh-huh, and then I'll come back and find out that these two"—she gestures at the twins—"tried to burn down my kitchen again." Her tone firms. "I'll see you all next week, Royals."

Dad chuckles as the plump, dark-haired woman marches to the back door. Voices waft out of the kitchen, and then Ella hurries out the French doors.

"Sorry I'm late," she says breathlessly. "I was on the phone." She slides into the seat next to Callum's. "You won't believe who called me!"

Dad gives her an indulgent smile. I, on the other hand, am hiding my grin, because I don't want to give anything away. But I'm pretty sure I know who called.

"Lucy!" Her blue eyes dance with excitement. "She's willing to give me a second chance at the bakery. Can you believe that?"

"Really?" I say blandly. "That's great news."

From the corner of my eye, I notice East shooting me a strange look, but he doesn't say anything.

"It's news, all right," Dad says in an unhappy voice.

Ella frowns at him. "You're not happy that I got my job back?"

"I never wanted you to have a job in the first place," he grumbles. "I'd like it if you focused all your time on your studies."

"Are we back to this again?" She sighs loudly and reaches for the serving spoon. "I'm perfectly capable of holding a job and going to school at the same time. Now who wants lasagna?"

"Me," the twins say in unison.

As Ella serves up food for everyone, I notice that my father and brothers are watching her every move. The twins are smiling. Dad looks pleased. East seems upset, though. Is he not glad that Ella's back? He lost his freaking mind after she ran, so shouldn't her presence make him happy?

"Why so quiet, East?" Dad prompts once we all start eating.

My brother shrugs. "Got nothing to say."

The twins snicker. "Since when?" Seb cracks.

Another shrug.

"Is everything okay with you?" Dad pushes.

"Uh-huh. Everything's A-okay in Easton Land."

His cheerful tone worries me. I know my brother. I know he's hurting right now, and when he's hurting, he gets out of control. After Mom died, he hit the bottle hard. Then he started with the oxy. The gambling. The brawls. The never-ending stream of hookups.

Gideon and I managed to rein him in. We flushed the pills down the toilet. I started fighting more so I could keep an eye on him when he was down at the docks. I thought we'd gotten him under control, but now he's spiraling again, and it kills me to see it.

Dad gives up on East and turns to Sawyer. "I haven't seen Lauren around lately. Did you two break up?"

"Nah, we're still together."

That's all Sawyer is willing to share on that subject, and Dad once again hits a wall. "Reed? Easton?" he prompts. "How's the season going? I'm hoping to catch the game this Friday. I've already asked Dottie to clear my schedule."

I can't hide my surprise. Dad used to come to all our games when Mom was alive—they'd sit behind the home bench together and cheer like maniacs—but ever since she died, he hasn't stepped foot in the stadium. It's like he just stopped caring. Or maybe he never cared to begin with, and Mom was the one who dragged him to the games.

Beside me, East is equally skeptical. "What's your angle?"

Dad's expression collapses. I think he might be genuinely hurt. "No angle," he says tightly. "It's just been a while since I've seen my boys play."

East snorts.

An uncomfortable silence falls over the table, until Ella finally breaks it in a tentative voice. "Callum," she starts. "Can we talk after dinner?"

"Of course. What about?"

She stares down at her plate. "Um. About my . . . inheritance. I had some questions for you about it."

"Of course," he says again, but this time his expression is brighter.

The rest of dinner passes quickly. Afterward, the twins disappear into the game room while Ella and my dad duck into his study. That leaves me and East to clean up. Normally, we'd be trying to make the task less boring by cracking jokes and talking about bullshit, but East doesn't say a word as we load the dishwasher and shove the leftovers in the fridge.

Fuck. I miss my brother. We've hardly spoken since Ella came back. Hell, we were barely speaking before that. I hate it. My life feels unbalanced when East and I are on the outs.

He closes the fridge and stalks toward the doorway, but I stop him before he can leave the kitchen. "East," I say roughly.

He slowly turns around. "What?"

"We ever gonna be cool again?"

Either I imagine it, or I glimpse a flicker of remorse in his eyes. But it's gone before I can be sure. "I need a smoke," he mutters.

My chest sags in defeat as he turns away again. But he doesn't walk out. He speaks without looking at me. "You coming?"

I hurry after him, hoping my eagerness doesn't show. But, hell, this is the first time he's wanted to be around me in ages.

We leave the house through the side door and walk out to the carport. "Where we going?" I ask.

"Nowhere." East flicks the back latch of his pickup, then hops up to sit on the truck bed. He fishes a small tin out of his pocket, flips it open, and pulls out a neatly rolled joint and a lighter.

After a beat, I hop up beside him.

He lights up and takes a long hit, then speaks through the curls of smoke that seep from his lips. "You got Ella her job back."

"Who told you that?"

"Wade." He passes me the joint. "I went over to his place after school."

"Thought he had a threesome lined up."

"Turned into a foursome."

I exhale a cloud of smoke. "Yeah? I thought you were only interested in tapping Royal exes these days."

He simply shrugs. "Nobody ever said I was smart."

"Nobody ever said you were vindictive, either," I point out quietly. "I get it. You're pissed at me, and that's why you made a move on Abby. But Savannah? You know Gid's not over her."

East has the decency to look guilty. "Wasn't thinking of Gid when I hit on Sav," he admits. "Wasn't thinking at all, actually."

I hand the joint back. "You gonna be honest and tell Gid about it?"

My brother offers a harsh smile. "I'll be honest with Gid when he decides to be honest with me."

What the hell does that mean? I don't touch the comment, though, because I didn't come out here to fix East's relationship with Gideon. I came out here to save *my* relationship with East.

"I was wrong," I tell him.

He wrinkles his forehead. "Wrong about what?"

"Everything." I grab the joint and take a deep pull that leaves me light-headed. On the exhalation, I blurt out every bone-headed move I've made this year. "I shouldn't have hooked up with Brooke. Shouldn't have hid it from you. Shouldn't have hid it from Ella." The weed loosens not just the cobwebs in my head, but my tongue. "It's my fault she ran off. I drove her away."

"Yeah. You did."

"I'm sorry."

He doesn't answer.

"I know it scared you when she left. It hurt you." I turn to study his tense profile, and I tense up, too, as something occurs to me. "Do you love her?" I ask hoarsely.

His head whirls toward me. "No."

"You sure about that?"

"I don't. Not the way you do."

I relax, just slightly. "Still. You care about her."

Of course he does. We all do, because that girl flew into our house like a whirlwind and made everything come alive again. She brought steel and fire. She made us laugh again. She gave us a purpose—at first, it was us uniting against her. Then it turned into us standing beside her. Protecting her. Loving her.

"She made me happy."

Helplessly, I nod. "I know."

"And then she left. She left us and she didn't look back. Like . . ."

Like Mom, I finish for him, and a jolt of agony arrows through my chest.

"Whatever," East mumbles. "It's no biggie, okay? She's back now, so it's all good."

He's lying. I can tell he's still terrified that Ella might pack up and leave again.

It terrifies me, too. Ella's barely spoken to me since the night we kissed. The night she cried. Cried so hard that it broke my fucking heart. I don't know how to make it better with her. I don't know how to make it better for East. Or for Gideon.

But what I do know is that this isn't just about Ella. Easton's abandonment issues run deeper than that.

"Mom's not coming back," I force myself to say.

"No shit, Reed. She's goddamn dead." Easton starts to laugh, but it's a hard, humorless sound. "I killed her."

Jesus. "How many joints did you smoke today, little brother? 'Cause you're talking crazy right now."

His eyes are grim. "Nah, I've never been saner." Another laugh pops out, but we both know he's not getting amusement out of any of this. "Mom would still be here if it weren't for me."

"That's not true, East."

"Yeah, it is." He takes a quick drag. Blows out another gray cloud. "It was my oxy, man. She took it and OD'd."

I look over sharply. "What the fuck are you talking about?"

"She found my stash. A few days before she died. She was in my room putting away some laundry, and the shit was in my sock drawer and she found it. Confronted me, confiscated it, and threatened to send me to rehab if she ever caught me with 'scrips again. I figured she flushed the pills, but . . ." He shrugs.

"East . . ." I trail off. Does he really believe this? Has he believed it for two whole years? I draw a slow breath. "Mom didn't OD on oxy."

He narrows his eyes. "Dad said she did."

"That was just one of the things she was on. I saw the tox report. She died of a whole combination of shit. And even if it was just oxy, you know she could've easily gotten her own prescription." I snatch the joint from his lax hand and suck deeply on it. "Besides, we both know it was my fault. You said it yourself—I'm the one who killed her."

"I said that to hurt you."

"Worked."

Easton studies my profile. "Why'd you think it was you?"

Shame crawls up my spine. "Just felt like I wasn't enough," I admit. "I knew you were hooked on pills. I knew something was wrong with Gid. Night before she died, she and Dad argued over a fight I got in. My fighting bugged her. I liked it too much.

She knew that and she hated it. I . . . I was just added stress for her."

"You're not the reason she died. She was messed up way before that."

"Yeah? Well, you're not the reason, either."

We go quiet for several moments. It's awkward now, and my skin is starting to itch. Royals don't sit around talking about their feelings. We bury them. Pretend nothing touches us.

East taps out the joint and tucks the roach into his little tin. "I'm going inside," he mumbles. "Turning in early."

It's barely eight o'clock, but I don't question him. "Night," I say.

He pauses near the side door. "You wanna ride to practice tomorrow?"

I almost choke on a sudden rush of happiness. Fuck, I'm a sappy loser, but . . . we haven't ridden together in weeks. "Sure. See you in the morning."

He disappears into the house. I stay seated on his truck, but my joy and relief are short-lived. I always knew I'd fix stuff with East. I expect to fix things with Ella, too. And the twins. Gid. My brothers never stay pissed at me for long, no matter how royally I screw up.

But sitting here trading confessions with East reminds me that I'm still keeping a secret from my dad. Worse, I was so desperate to make sure that secret stayed hidden that I actually encouraged him to bring Brooke back into our lives.

I suddenly feel like hurling, and it has nothing to do with emotions or all the weed I smoked. Brooke's back because I was too chickenshit to own up to my mistakes. Why didn't I just tell her to screw off? So what if she tells the world that I'm the father of her kid? One DNA test and her story would go up in flames.

Instead, I made a deal with her. I urged my father to take her back just so he wouldn't find out what I did. So Ella wouldn't find out. But Ella knows the truth now. And . . . I take a breath . . . maybe it's time Dad knew the truth, too.

Twenty-Three

ELLA

AFTER A POINTLESS and frustrating conversation with Callum, I stomp upstairs and throw myself on the bed. Callum is ticked off that I got a job and that I want to give my inheritance back. He lectured me for twenty minutes about it before I interrupted by asking him if he's trying to control me because he can't control his sons. That went over really well.

I don't get what the big deal is. It's my inheritance, isn't it? And I don't want it. As long as I have Steve's money, people like Dinah and Brooke will always be trying to take it from me. So let them. What do I care?

I give myself an hour-long pity party before finally sitting up to text Val.

What're u up to

BBQ with the fam. It's terrible

Jordan tormenting u

No, she's upstairs packing. She's visiting her grandmother—dad's side. They send her off there periodically bc the old bat is rich rich rich. From the way they talk about her I think she's a bag of skin stuffed with rolled up hundies

I laugh.

Sounds like she'll live forever.

Possibly. I think she's 80 now.

All this $$$ makes me anxious. I feel like if the Royals didn't have any they'd all be happier.

Babe no one's happy if they're poor.

I ponder that thought. When Mom was alive, I was happy. Yeah, we had problems, and at times they seemed insurmountable, but we had a lot of laughter in our lives. There was never any doubt in my mind that she loved me with everything in her. It's that unadulterated love that I miss. The pure, sweet, unshakable love that she had for me kept me warm at night and filled my empty stomach during the day.

There's no guarantee of happiness just bc you're rich either

Actual studies show u can buy happiness

Okay! I give. Let's buy some happiness with my $$

We were happy shopping the other day. I'm game for the mall if u are. But not tonight. Tonight I have to suffer. Auntie is glaring at me right now. Gotta go

I drop the phone on my bed and stare at the ceiling. I guess money can make things better to a certain extent. Maybe I'm approaching this the wrong way. Maybe I can buy the Royals happiness by buying Brooke off. She wants security in the form of the Royal bank account, right? What if I could get her to leave by offering her my inheritance? Callum doesn't want it. I could live without it. I think . . . hmm, I think this might be a quality idea. I just wish I had someone to run it past.

I drum my fingers against the coverlet. There *is* someone who knows Brooke better than I do, and he happens to live in this house.

Argh. Is this an excuse to talk to Reed? Maybe. I push the thought aside and get up to find him.

It's not easy. The Royals have scattered. Seb and Sawyer are probably at Lauren's house. Easton's door is locked and the music in his room is so loud he doesn't hear my knock. Or maybe he does and is ignoring me. Down the hall, I peek into Reed's room. His door is open, but he's not around.

I wander around the big house until I finally hear some noise. It's coming from the exercise room. A rhythmic thudding leads me down the stairs into the basement. The door is propped open, and I spot Reed pummeling his fists against a large bag. Sweat drips down his face and his upper body glistens.

Ugh, he's so hot.

I tell my hormones to settle down and push the door open. His head swings toward me immediately.

"Hey," I say quietly.

He catches the bag and steps back, wiping a wrapped hand across his face. His eyes are red and I wonder if some of the moisture on his face might be from something other than sweat.

"What's up?" he asks, and his voice cracks. Using the pretense of needing a drink, he ducks his head and grabs a water bottle.

"The twins are gone. And Easton's door is locked."

He nods. "The twins went to see Lauren. Easton is . . ." He pauses, searching for the right words. "Easton is—" He stops again and shakes his head.

"What's wrong?" I demand. "Is he okay?"

"More okay than he was a couple hours ago."

"Are . . . *you* okay?"

There's a beat. Then he slowly shakes his head again.

Despite the warning bells in my head, I take a step closer to him. This is bad. My defenses have crumbled. I can feel myself surrendering to him. He keeps drawing me in with his addictive kisses and his strength and the vulnerability he's stopped trying to hide from me.

"What happened?" I ask.

I see him swallow. "I . . ." He clears his throat. "I tried to tell him."

"Tell who what?"

"My dad. I walked right up to his study, all ready to tell him what I did."

"What you did?" I echo stupidly.

"Brooke," he spits out. "I was going to tell him about Brooke. But I chickened out. I stood there at his door and couldn't bring myself to knock. I kept picturing his disgust and his disappointment and . . . so I bailed. I turned around and came down here and now I'm pounding this bag and pretending I'm not a coward and a selfish asshole."

A sigh lodges in my throat. "Reed."

"What?" he mutters. "You know it's true. Isn't that why you hate me? 'Cause I'm a selfish ass?"

"I . . . don't hate you," I whisper.

Something flares in his eyes. Surprise? Hope, maybe? Then it fades, replaced with a cloud of sorrow. "You said you'd never forgive me," he reminds me.

"For what?" My lips twist into a bitter smile. "For having sex with someone before me? For trying to warn me away?"

He rubs his lips together uncertainly. "For everything. For not telling you about Brooke. For not being there for you when you needed me. For taking advantage of you the night Daniel drugged—"

"I knew what I was doing that night," I interrupt. "If I said no at any time, you wouldn't have touched me. I wanted it to happen, so please don't make me feel bad by turning it into something it's not."

He tosses the bottle to the side and closes the distance between us. "Fine. I'm not sorry about that night anyway. I have a lot to apologize for, but I won't lie to you. That was one of the most incredible nights of my life." He raises a hand toward my cheek. "And every day that I woke up after that was better because I could look forward to holding you that night."

I know what he means. After we both dropped our guards, things were so . . . perfect. I'd never had a real boyfriend before, and every second I spent with Reed, kissing, talking, falling asleep together, was new and wonderful and I loved it.

"I miss my mom," he says in a choked voice. "I didn't realize how much until you came along. I think you were my mirror. I looked at you and how strong you were and I realized I didn't have an ounce of your steel in me."

"That's not true. You don't give yourself enough credit."

"Maybe you give me too much?"

I can't help but laugh. "I don't think that's been the case for a while."

He grins back ruefully. "Yeah, you got me there." Then his face sobers up. "I want to tell you about my mom. You up for that?"

I nod slowly. I'm not sure what's happening between us right now, but whatever it is, it feels . . . right. Something about this guy has always felt right, even when it was wrong, even when I swore I'd never fall for him again.

"Let me shower." He releases me. "Don't go anywhere," he murmurs as he backs away. "Promise?"

"I promise."

He escapes into the attached bathroom. If it was me or Val, the shower would've taken at least twenty minutes, but Reed is done in literally two minutes. He's still wet when he comes striding out with one towel wrapped around his waist and another in his hand that he uses to rub against his short hair.

The water runs in an interesting path down his chest, over his ridged abs and then stopping at the terry cloth at his waist.

The towel looks securely fastened, but I'm pretty sure that with one tug, the thing would give way.

"Your room or mine?"

I jerk my head up. He grins at me, but doesn't say a word. Smart boy.

"Mine," I answer.

He holds out his hand. "Lead the way."

Twenty-Four

UPSTAIRS, REED DUCKS into his room to get changed while I grab a couple of sodas from my mini fridge and wait for him. When he returns, I hand him a Diet Coke and he settles on the bed beside me, angling his broad body so we're facing each other.

"You know my dad cheated on my mom, right?"

I hesitate. According to Callum, he never touched another woman when he was married to Maria, but for some reason, his sons refuse to believe him.

Reed sees the doubt on my face. "It's true. He screwed around on her while he jetted all over the world with Uncle Steve, who, by the way, was cheating on Dinah from day one."

I swallow a lump of unhappiness. I hate hearing stuff like that about my father, which is weird because I didn't even know the guy.

"Dinah didn't care, though. She married Uncle Steve for his money, everyone knew it. And she had her own pieces of ass on the side. But Mom was different. She *cared*."

"Did she have proof that Callum was cheating?" I ask tentatively.

"He was gone all the time, and he was always with Steve, a guy who couldn't keep his dick in his pants."

I wince. "That's not real proof, Reed. It's just suspicion. Why are you so sure he's guilty?"

"Because he is." Reed's adamant. I want to argue some more, but he doesn't give me the chance. "Mom was depressed, and she was taking a lot of pills."

"I heard there was a mix-up with her prescription? And her doctor went to jail or something?"

"There was no mix-up," he says bitterly. "She was on meds for depression and insomnia, but she started self-dosing, taking more than she was supposed to. And she was drinking a lot, too . . ." His voice shakes. "It got worse and worse, and Dad was never home, so it was up to us to take care of her."

"It's awful to be helpless," I murmur, thinking about how I had to take care of my mom when she was sick.

Realization flares in his eyes as he recognizes that I know exactly how he feels—watching someone you love be eaten by a disease that is out of control and knowing you can't do a damn thing about it.

"Yeah. Worst thing in the world."

"How do you know it wasn't an accident?" I ask.

He takes a deep, slow breath. "She told us—Gid and I—that she loved us but couldn't take it anymore. That she was so, so sorry." His mouth twists into an ugly shape. "Those words are meaningless, aren't they?" His eyes shut in self-disgust, like he's remembering how many times he's said those same words to me since I came back to Bayview.

Maria's goodbye probably did more harm than good. If she'd died without professing her love and regret, maybe Gideon and Reed would have been able to convince themselves that her death was an accident. Instead, they were burdened with guilt that somehow they weren't enough to keep her alive.

Maria was as bad as Callum, I realize. Just as selfish. Just as needy. Is it any surprise that her kids are flawed in the same way?

"I hated him for what he did to her. We all did. And then six months after she died, he started bringing Brooke around. I wanted to kill him for that. It was like he was spitting on Mom's grave."

I exhale shakily, wondering how Callum could be so stupid. Couldn't he have waited a bit longer before parading his new girlfriend in front of his sons?

"They were together for about a year when Brooke started hitting on me," Reed admits. "I was wrong. I know I was wrong. The really ironic part is that I was doing it to get back at my dad, but I could never bring myself to tell him."

"Why did you sit there and not say anything that night?" I burst out. "Why did you let me think the worst?"

He lifts his head to meet my eyes. "I was ashamed. I knew I had to tell you about Brooke, and I was scared you'd hate me for it. Then she told me about being pregnant. I knew it couldn't be mine, but I . . . froze. I couldn't move. Literally. I tried but couldn't. And then I got pissed, so pissed, at myself, at her, at *you*."

I tense up. "At me?"

"Yeah, for being everything I wish I could be." His voice thickens. "Look, Royals are known for their money, their looks, and that's about it. We cave at the first sign of pressure. Dad's business is about to go under, so he starts sleeping around. Mom starts over-medicating and then . . . dies. I—" He visibly swallows. "I was pissed at my dad, so I slept with his girlfriend."

I grit my teeth but don't say a word.

"I heard the door slam and it was like I was released from this prison. I went racing after you. I stayed up all night looking for you."

But I was already gone, sitting on a bus, determined to get as far away from Bayview as possible.

"I'm sorry." He takes my hand and laces his fingers through mine. "I'm sorry I hurt you. I'm sorry I didn't tell you the truth earlier."

I release a shaky breath. "Reed?"

"Yeah?"

"I forgive you."

His breath hitches. "You do?"

I nod.

Reed's hand trembles as it cups my chin. "Thank you."

His thumb rubs an arc across my cheekbone, swiping away a tear I hadn't realized slipped out.

The emotion lining my throat makes it hard to get my next words out. "I want to forget—"

He kisses me before I can finish the sentence. Warm lips crash onto mine, and I instinctively wrap my arms around his strong shoulders, pulling him closer.

His breath tickles my lips. "I missed this. I missed *you*."

Then he's kissing me again. Everywhere. His mouth grazes my cheeks and my throat and even my closed eyelids. It's a sweet, leisurely exploration, and I drink it up. One of his thighs slides between my legs to press against the unbearable ache.

"Reed," I whisper, but I don't know what I'm asking for.

He does. "Not tonight."

I squeeze my thighs together around his leg. His body vibrates against mine as he releases a groan. Then he moves over and lies beside me, pulling my head against his chest.

It feels good to be in his arms again. I've missed this, too. But I'm afraid this moment of happiness won't last, because there are still so many obstacles in our lives.

"Reed?"

"Mmmm?"

"What are we going to do about Brooke?"

"I don't know."

"What if I give her my inheritance?"

His breath hitches. "Dad would never let you do that."

"I know." My shoulders slump into the mattress. "I tried to give it to him. Brooke told me Callum expected Steve's share to go to the Royals."

Reed peers down at me. "Please tell me he said no."

"He said no."

"Good. We don't need that money. It's yours. We have plenty."

"Brooke says you can never have enough."

"Brooke's a money-sucking bitch."

Frustration bubbles up inside me. "Why did he take her back? Just because she's pregnant? It's not like we're living a hundred years ago. Even Callum knows he doesn't have to marry someone just because he knocked her up."

Reed tenses.

I instantly lift my head. "What did you do?" I demand.

"I made a deal with her," he admits. "She'd shut up about saying the baby was mine—which is a lie—and in exchange I'd put in a good word with my dad."

"Oh my God. That was a terrible idea."

"I know. I'm a dumbass, but I was desperate. I would've agreed to anything at that point."

"Obviously," I say darkly.

The two of us go quiet for a second.

"We need to find a way to get rid of her." His voice is low and ominous. "I can't have that woman living in my house. I don't want her anywhere near you."

I bite my lip, because I'm worried that if the truth gets out, things won't go well for Reed. Callum already thinks he's been too lenient with the boys, and if he finds out about Reed and Brooke, it'll be just another sign that he needs to pull the reins tighter. I don't know if I disagree with Callum's line of thinking. The Royal boys could handle a little discipline in their lives. The problem is, I don't know what path Callum would take. Military school?

I can't imagine living in this giant museum without the guys here. I guess I'm a little selfish, too.

"Don't do anything you'll regret later," I warn.

His arm tightens around me. "I'm not making promises I can't keep. You know I'd do anything for you. For us."

I wriggle closer to Reed. I just got him back, and I don't want to fight. Not tonight. I twine my fingers through his. "Are you sure everyone was okay with me getting Steve's half of the company?"

"Yeah, why?"

"Because Gideon doesn't like me."

"Actually, babe, you've got that all wrong. Gid doesn't think I'm good for you."

Is that Gideon's problem? He's never been mean to me, but he's definitely kept his distance.

"Why does he think that?" I ask uneasily.

"Gid's life isn't great right now. He's got . . . issues."

Issues? Like screwing my dad's widow? I wonder if Reed knows about that.

"What issues?"

"He's not in a good place."

Yeah, this isn't making me happy. I blow a lock of hair out of my face. "I think we need to be done with the secrets between us."

Reed raises his free hand. "I swear if I could tell you the details, I would. But they're Gideon's issues, not mine."

I sit up. "No more secrets," I repeat, firmer this time. "You want me to start? Fine, I'll start."

"Start with what—"

"Easton and I caught Gideon and Dinah having sex," I interrupt.

He sits up, too. "You serious? And you're just telling me this *now*?"

I study his face. "You don't look surprised." My tone sharpens. "Why aren't you surprised, Reed? Did you know?"

He hesitates.

"You knew," I accuse.

Reed shrugs.

I angrily shove my hair out of my eyes. "Why is he with Dinah?" I demand. "And why does he care if you and I are together? The night I caught you with Brooke, Gideon asked to meet me—did he tell you that? That's why I was coming to your room that night, to talk to you about it."

"No, he didn't tell me," Reed says with a frown. "What did he say to you?"

"He told me to stay away from you. He said you would hurt me, and that too many people have already gotten hurt. What did he mean by that?"

He shrugs again.

"Reed," I warn. "I swear, if you don't tell me what's going on, we are *not* getting back together. I can't handle any more lies. I mean it."

He lets out a breath. "Right after Mom died, Gideon and I snuck into a fundraiser my dad was supposed to attend but bailed on. He was too busy with Steve somewhere. We got wasted."

I grumble in annoyance. "What does that have to do with any of this?"

"You wanted to know what's going on with Gid. I'm telling you." Reed scowls at me. "Dinah was at that fundraiser."

"Oh." I bite my lip. Shoot, maybe I don't want to know the details after all.

"Yeah. She'd kinda been hitting on Gid for a while, and she caught him coming out of the bathroom and they . . . uh, made out for a bit."

"Reeeeeeed," I say with a bucketful of exasperation. "Is this where you got your *I'm going to screw my dad's girlfriend* idea?"

His guilty expression gives him away. "Maybe." He sighs. "Anyway, after that, she wouldn't leave Gid alone. She'd corner him constantly and make these sleazy comments about how she liked fresh, young, ripe things."

I can't keep a disgusted look off my face. "That's really gross."

"No shit. She wanted more. Like, she was—is—seriously obsessed with him. After that party, she was shameless about trying to seduce him. He told me so many sick stories about it, you don't even want to know. But he fell for Savannah and wanted nothing to do with Steve's gold digger. So then one night she asks Gid to come over, says she has something to show him. My dad and Steve were out of town, as usual. Gid went over to the penthouse." Reed pauses. "He came home that night and told me he slept with Dinah."

"Ew. *Why*?"

"Because she blackmailed him," Reed says flatly.

"Are you serious? With *what*?"

"Pictures. She got her hands on Gid's phone. I guess he left it in the kitchen or something when she was over one time. Dinah snooped around and found all these pictures that Sav and Gid were sending each other."

"Dirty pictures?"

"Yeah."

"So?" I'm still confused. "People text dirty pictures to each other all the time."

"But they're cracking down on it. These two kids down in Raleigh were charged with seven counts of child porn when the girl's parents found out they were sexting. The girl's full ride to UNC was yanked. If it was only Gid's neck on the line, he probably would've told Dinah to go to hell, but Dinah swore she'd drag Sav into it and even release the pics to the entire school."

I feel even sicker now. "So Dinah blackmailed him into bed with her?"

"Pretty much. It's been over a year now. He broke it off with Sav and she was devastated."

I think of Savannah, who's such a brittle, hard-edged girl. Her smiles are thin and her words are cutting. If she truly loved Gideon, then the pain she's going through must be horrible. "That's so awful."

Reed makes a face. "He's gonna kill me for telling you all this."

"I'm glad you did," I say sternly. "Because now we can come up with a plan."

"A plan for what?"

"To save Gideon from Dinah. We can't let her keep doing this to him. Otherwise he's going to lose his mind."

"Sometimes I feel like this is some part of a plan that Brooke and Dinah have. Like they divvied us up and decided they'd ruin the Royals, one at a time. Steve included." Reed shakes his head. "It sounds crazy when I say it out loud."

"You really think Brooke and Dinah planned this?"

"They're friends. I think Dad was screwing Brooke before Mom died, but I don't know anything about them. Steve showed up with Dinah one day and she had a ring on her finger. Marrying her didn't slow him down, though."

"What else do we know about Dinah? And where do you think she's keeping the evidence she has against Gid? Do you think she's shown it to anyone?"

"I doubt it, otherwise Gid would've been arrested ages ago."

"If we can get our hands on those pictures, Dinah has nothing. No leverage at all." I think it over. "How do we find them? Would she be dumb enough to keep them at the penthouse? Smart enough to make copies?"

"I don't know. But you might be right. If we can find all the stuff she has on him and get rid of it, we could put this thing behind us."

"But what about Brooke?"

"Brooke," he repeats with disgust. "We need a paternity test. I don't understand why Dad won't get one."

"I don't, either." I chew on the end of my thumb until Reed pulls it out of my mouth.

"You're going to gnaw your finger off if you think about it any more. Can we stop talking about Brooke and Dinah? At least for a bit."

"Why?"

His gaze heats up. "Because there're better ways to spend our time right now."

"Like what—"

Before I can finish, he rolls me over and presses his lips against my neck. "Like that," he whispers.

I gasp. "Oh . . . okay."

His clever fingers find a bare patch of skin above my waistband, and while a stronger girl might've been able to repress a shiver, I've never been able to resist Reed before. Seems pointless to try now. Especially when I enjoy his touch so much.

He burrows his nose against my neck and continues his slow sweep across my waist as if he's happy to do nothing more than this. And for a while that's all I need, too. I let the silence sink in around us and enjoy the simple touch. In the peace comes the realization this is the first time in forever that I've had a quiet moment with another person.

"Do you really forgive me?" he asks.

I stroke a hand over his glossy, dark hair. When I look at Reed and his muscular frame and his hard face, sometimes I forget that he's got a heart that's as fragile as mine. But guys aren't supposed to be emotional so they hide their feelings behind seriousness, crudeness, or dickish behavior. "I really forgive you."

"Even though I'm an asshole?"

"Are you done being an asshole to me?" I tug on his hair a little harder than necessary.

He dips his head as if to say, *I deserved that.* "I was done with that a long time ago. Right after our first kiss. I haven't even looked at a single other girl since I met you, Ella."

"Good. And if you treat me like the goddess I am and don't cheat on me, then yes, I'm cool with this."

"I can be a handful."

Meaning he loves too deeply and he's afraid I'm going to bug out on him again—like I did before, like his mom did permanently. "Yeah . . . but you're my handful," I whisper.

His laughter is muffled as his mouth moves along my collarbone, dotting my chest with soft kisses. The soft lace of my bra suddenly feels scratchy and rough. I shift restlessly. He moves lower, his chest pushing into the softness of my abdomen, resting against the ache between my legs.

My fingers clutch against his hair, not sure if I want to pull him up to my mouth or push him lower. But Reed has his own plans. He lifts the hem of my shirt, dragging the fabric up much too slowly. Impatient, I grab the bottom and whip it over my head.

He grins. "Have I mentioned how much I like your night gear?"

"It's comfortable," I say defensively.

"Mmmhmmm," he murmurs, but the smug smile stays on his face as he reaches behind his back and tugs his own shirt off.

I forget what smart-ass remark I was going to say and stroke a hand over his chest.

He closes his eyes and shudders. His hands hang at his sides, clenching and unclenching. Waiting for me? I like this—that he's on my leash until I tell him to go.

"Touch me," I murmur.

His eyes snap open and the heat in them makes me gasp. He pushes me backward and attacks my yoga pants as if they've personally offended him. I lift my hips and push the spandex down my legs because I don't want anything between us, either. I want all of him pressed against me.

His fingers reach behind and release the clasp of my bra.

Then his mouth covers me, and my whole body starts to tremble. When he kisses my nipple, I make a choked, desperate sound and dig my fingers into his shoulders.

I was wrong. His touch doesn't soothe. It makes me wilder, hotter, more out of control than I've ever been. And the lower he moves, the hotter I get.

"Reed," I moan, my head thrown back.

"Shhh," he says. "Let me."

Let him what? Move down until his shoulders are pushing me more open than I'd ever thought would be okay? Until his mouth is right *there* and his tongue is doing the most amazing things to that one throbbing spot? Let him touch me in ways I once thought would be awkward and uncomfortable?

He groans out his own delight as I let him work me into a mindless mess. My back arches and my toes curl and I grip the sheets as a rush of pure bliss runs through me.

Eventually he rises, leaving me shaking and gasping. He lies down on his side next to me, and I don't miss the tent situation in his boxers.

Reed grins when he catches me staring. "Just ignore it. It'll go away soon."

I slide closer. "Why would we want to ignore it?"

He tenses when I put my hand over him. "I wanted tonight to be about you," he protests, but his eyes are fiery as my fingers slide inside his boxers.

"Well, I want it to be about us," I whisper.

He feels so good in my hand, and I can tell by his heavy eyelids and ragged breathing that he's enjoying every second of this.

"Ella . . ." He pushes his hips forward. "Fuck. Faster."

Watching his face is the most thrilling thing ever. His

cheeks are flushed and his eyes are hazy, and when I kiss him, his tongue tangles with mine until we're both breathless.

The throbbing between my legs starts up again and Reed seems to sense it, because his fingers find me and then we're frantically trying to drive each other wild. And it works. I clutch him tighter, because if I'm going to lose it, I'm taking him with me. His mouth is on mine and we move in perfect sync until I'm lost, drowning in a state of blissful happiness.

Twenty-Five

"HAVE YOU SEEN Reed?" Callum asks someone in the hall.

The sound of his voice so close to my door jerks me upright. A heavy arm clotheslines me, sending me straight back to the mattress.

"Probably went to football practice," Easton replies.

"Huh, it's early. Shouldn't you be at practice, too?"

"Trying to, but someone's grilling me about my brother's whereabouts," is Easton's snarky response.

Callum grunts or laughs or huffs a breath. I can't really tell. I shake Reed's shoulder until his eyes snap open.

"It's your dad," I hiss.

He shuts his eyes in response and rubs his cheek against my hand.

Callum speaks up again. "I got a call from Franklin Auto Body saying Reed brought in a car, but I see his Rover out there. Ella's car is missing. She hasn't run off again, has she?" There's a strained note in his voice. I wonder if I upset him over the money talk. Or maybe he thinks he upset *me* and that's why he's worried I might've run.

"Nah, Ella's car had an unfortunate honey accident and she was too embarrassed to tell you. Reed took it in for her."

"Honey accident?"

"Yeah, don't worry about it, Dad," Easton says, and then their footsteps fade down the hall.

I glance at the clock, which tells me I need to get moving if I want to make it to the bakery on time. Lucy gave me a second chance, and there's no way I'm blowing it again. I crawl out from under Reed's possessive arm and realize I'm in my underwear.

Walking around barely dressed in front of Reed is somehow more awkward than taking my clothes off for a bunch of strangers. I find his discarded T-shirt still clinging to the edge of the bed and quickly slip it on.

Reed rolls onto his back and tucks his hands under his head. He watches with intent interest as I buzz around the room getting ready.

"You didn't need to cover up for me," he drawls.

"I didn't cover up for you. I covered up for me."

He laughs, a low, sexy, gravelly thing. "You still have your V-card, little Miss Innocent."

"I don't feel very innocent," I mutter.

"You don't look it, either."

I duck in front of the wide mirror that hangs over my desk. My hair is crazy wild. It looks like a family of forest animals took up residence in it. "Oh my God! Is this what sex hair really looks like?" Though is it still considered sex hair when you didn't have sex?

Behind me, Reed rises from the bed, looking way too good at this time of the morning. He brushes aside some of my sex hair and presses a hot kiss against my neck.

"You look gorgeous and hot and if I stay in here any longer, your virginity will be on the floor somewhere next to yesterday's panties."

Then he gives my butt a hard slap and saunters out of my room wearing only his boxers. Thankfully, he isn't greeted with any horrified exclamations from Callum.

With Reed gone, I dunk my hair under the sink, throw on a pair of jeans, sneakers, and a rather smutty black-lace top that I used to wear at a truck stop where I worked before Callum found me.

Reed walks by my room as I step out. He stops, runs his eyes over my body, and then holds up a finger. "Hold it right there."

I don't stay, because as I've told Reed a million times before, I'm not a dog.

I follow him to his room, where I find him rifling around in his closet. "What are you doing?"

"Looking for a uniform."

I roll my eyes. "There're no uniforms on Fridays."

Friday is the one day we're allowed to break out our non-school-issued wardrobes, though Headmaster Beringer seems to prefer everyone wearing something to support the football team on game day.

"Doesn't mean you should be wearing something that will cause a riot at school." Reed emerges with a button-down shirt in white with tiny blue checks. "Don't suppose you'd wear my jersey, would you?"

I make a face. I'm not ready to declare to the world that I'm back together with Reed Royal. I already have enough shit to deal with at school and I'm not sure how this is going to complicate things.

Reed sighs but doesn't argue.

I let him push my arms into the shirt and then flap the excess fabric in his face. "How am I supposed to wear this?"

He waves his index finger in a circle. "Do the thing with the sleeves. The roll-up thing. Aren't boyfriend clothes supposed to be in?"

His use of the word *boyfriend* has me feeling twenty degrees warmer, but I can't let Reed know how easily he affects me or he'll use it against me all the time. "It's boyfriend jeans, and fine, but just this once," I grumble, scrunching up the sleeves so I can actually use my hands at the bakery today without Reed's cuffs getting in all the flour.

We grab a couple snacks from the kitchen before heading out.

"So what do you want to do this weekend?" Reed asks once we get on the road to the bakery.

"I don't want to go to an Astor party." I wrinkle my nose. "And we should do something with Val because Tam's an asshole and I don't want her to be alone."

"There's a farm that has a big maze and a pumpkin toss we could go to."

"'We'? As in you and your brothers 'we'?" I ask hopefully.

"Yeah, all of us. We'll take our testosterone out on the fruit and then you and I can go make out in the maze."

"You sound very sure of yourself."

He smirks. "I have scratches on my back this morning."

"You do not!" I exclaim and then suck in breath. "Do you?" I ask quietly, looking at my nails.

Reed keeps smiling but wisely changes the subject. "How is Val anyway?"

I tuck my hands under my thighs. "Not good. She misses her ex." I wish she could see how much better off she is without that cheating Tam, but I don't hand out relationship advice. In the back rooms of strip clubs, more than one friendship is ruined when a woman tries to point out obvious flaws in her friend's man.

A sudden thought strikes me. Reed is a year older than I am. Next year I'll still be at Astor Park and he'll be gone. He once said he wanted to put an ocean between him and Bayview. I know why now, but the thought of him being so far away is gut-wrenching.

"Am I going to have to worry about you at college?" I ask nervously.

"No." He reaches over and places a hand on my knee to give me a reassuring squeeze. "Val's man wants to try a bunch of different stuff out, but I've already . . ." He pauses and searches for the right word. "I don't mean this to sound bad about your dad, but Steve had all the women he wanted in the world and none of that made him happy. I don't need to sleep around to know what I want."

His words, *gah*, his words are like sunshine baking sweetness into every pore of my body. Suddenly I pray that I didn't make a mistake agreeing to give him another chance. If he hurts me again, I don't think I'll survive it.

Reed pulls to a stop outside of the bakery and leans over to curl his hand around the back of my neck. Before I can protest, he plants a hard, possessive kiss against my lips.

"Meet you at the parking lot," he growls against my mouth.

He doesn't wait for an answer, but speeds off to practice. I give myself another mental head slap for enjoying his caveman behavior, but I can't keep the smile off my face as I enter the bakery.

✦ ✦ ✦

THE MORNING GOES by quickly. I thought it would drag while I moped and missed Reed's company, but instead I'm energized. Maybe that's what good almost-sex does for a person.

I wonder how I'll feel after the real thing. Like a superhero? Like I could leap tall buildings with one jump and single-handedly hold up falling airplanes in the sky?

The fact that I found a pair of used panties in my locker doesn't even bother me. I mean, I'm going to have to start wearing rubber gloves everywhere, but even my tormenters at Astor Park Prep can't get me down now.

"Did you get laid last night?" Val demands as we set down our lunch trays later.

Do I have a sign on my forehead? "Why? What do you see?"

"You have this sick, happy face that people who get it regularly and get it good wear." She slumps with disgust into her seat.

"I didn't get laid last night," I promise her.

"You did something." She inspects me carefully, as if there's some evidence of Reed's fingers on my face. "With him?" She tips her head in the direction of the cashier, where Reed is paying for his lunch. My face must have given it away, because she groans. "You did. You took him back. *Why?*"

My spine feels all prickly. Val isn't usually judgmental, but right now her disapproval is written all over her face. "What, are you going to unfriend me now?" I say sarcastically.

Her expression instantly softens. "No! Of course not. But I don't understand. You said you couldn't forgive him."

"I guess I was wrong." I sigh. "I love him, Val. Maybe it makes me the dumbest girl on the planet, but I really want to try to make things work with him. I . . . miss him."

She makes a frustrated noise. "I miss Tam, too. Look at the stupid shit I did the other night, and for what? We can't take these assholes back or we'll never be able to live with ourselves."

"I know, and trust me, if I was sitting in your seat, I'd be rolling my eyes, too." I nibble on the corner of my lip. I can't reveal exactly what Reed's issues are, because that's private, but I want Val to understand. The only reason she's pressing me is that she cares, which I really do appreciate.

"So what is it? Is he just really good at groveling?"

Why did I forgive Reed? It wasn't because he had a sad story and that he made me feel good, because those aren't reasons to be with anyone who treated a girl the way Reed treated me.

My connection to him is . . . complicated. Even I can't make sense of it half the time. I just know that I get him on a deeper level, that his loss speaks to mine. That his happiness stirs my own. That his struggle to find some sense in this crazy world is as familiar to me as my own skin.

Carefully, I try to explain this to Val. "I took him back because I don't know if there's anyone I understand better or who gets me in the same way. You don't know this, but a couple weeks after I got here, I had a meltdown all over Reed and started hitting him in the car."

Val's lips twitch. "Seriously?"

I'm glad to see her smiling. Val's friendship is as important as anything these days. "Seriously. He held me off with one hand while still driving us home. And even when he said he hated me, he still drove me to school every day. I don't know how to explain it, but I feel like we're the same. Some days I'm hormonal and weepy and some days he's an asshole, but we're made out of the same bits of flesh and bone and screwed-up emotions."

"Have you even tried another guy?"

"No. And even if I did, it wouldn't work. He wouldn't be . . . Reed."

She sighs, but it's a sound of acceptance. "I'm not going to pretend to understand, but I decided after the other night that I'm moving on."

"You might want to wait until your bruise fades. How'd you even explain that to your family?"

"I said I walked into a door. It's true enough, except the door was some girl's face."

"Are we going to the game tonight?"

She pokes at her quinoa veggie bowl. "I don't know. I think I'm done with Astor guys."

"How about the hottie sitting next to Easton?" I ask.

She peers past my shoulders. "Liam Hunter?"

"He looks . . . intense."

"He is intense. And probably at the top of my list of guys to avoid. He's like Tam. A poor boy with a big chip on his shoulder who wants to make it big. He'd use me up like Kleenex and then toss me away." She uncaps her water bottle. "What I need is a rich boy, because they don't attach to people, only things. If they don't attach to me, then I won't attach to them."

I start to tell her that isn't how it works, that you can fall in love with people who can't stand you. Look at me and Reed. I fell for him while he was pushing me away and treating me awfully. I kept loving him despite finding out some pretty horrible things. But Val isn't hearing me. She's still wrapped up in her hurt and that's the only voice in her head right now.

"You need a rich boy to use, I'm your man."

We both twist around to see Wade sidling up to our table.

Val gives him a cool appraisal. I can tell she likes what she sees, but that's not much of a surprise. Wade is hot. "If I used you, then you'd have to abstain from other girls."

"What do you mean?" he asks, looking genuinely confused. Fidelity is obviously a foreign concept to him.

"She means that while the two of you are using each other,

you don't go outside of that friends-with-benefits relationship," I explain.

He frowns. "But—"

Val cuts him off. "Forget it, Wade. I'd do things to you that would blow your mind, and then you'd never be able to enjoy yourself again because you'd keep comparing all your other girls to me and coming up short."

His mouth hangs open.

I grin, because this is the first time I've ever seen someone get the better of Wade. "She knows things," I confirm, even though I don't have a clue what I'm talking about.

"You know things," he croaks out.

Val nods. "I do."

Wade instantly falls on one knee. "Oh, dear maiden. Please allow me to insert my member into your cavern of pleasure and take you to heights only the immortals have known."

Val stands and picks up her tray. "If that's your idea of dirty talk, you've got a lot to learn. Come with me."

She walks off.

Wade turns to me and silently mouths, *Dirty talk*, with childish glee.

I shrug and raise my hands, and he runs after Val. Like literally sprints.

"Do I want to know what that was all about?" Reed asks, setting his tray down next to mine.

"I don't think so. Honestly, I'm not even sure I could explain it if you asked."

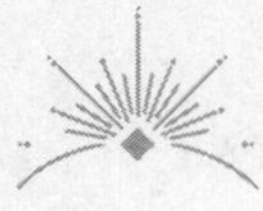

Twenty-Six

AT THE FOOTBALL game, everyone seems to know Callum Royal. Or at least, everyone wants to appear to know him. People in the stands rise and hail him with a wave. Some stop him at the bottom of the bleachers before we can find an open seat. He shakes a few hands. More than one person comments about his loss, which I find kind of rude. Callum's wife died two years ago. Why even bring it up? But Callum smiles and thanks each person for thinking of him and his family. It takes thirty minutes before we climb the bleachers to find a seat in the parents' section.

"You sure you don't want to sit with your friends?" He waves a hand toward the middle section of the bleachers, which is arranged in alternating colors of blue and gold. He squints. "All the jersey-wearing girls are down there."

My shoulders twitch under Reed's jersey. I didn't wear it to school, much to Reed's frustration, but I'm wearing it now. I figured that by sitting with Callum, the jersey looks like I'm supporting the family instead of Reed personally. Callum's wearing Easton's jersey, and he fills it out pretty well. I look like I'm swimming in mine.

"Nah, I'm good. We gotta save a seat for Val," I remind him.

But even if Val wasn't coming, I would still rather sit away from my "friends." I find the entirety of Astor Park Prep a bunch of assholes. The pranks at school have died down, but not completely. My locker was jammed the other day and I couldn't get it open in time to make it to class. Thankfully the teacher accepted my explanation for being late. In PE this week, my underwear went missing and I had to go around for the rest of the day commando.

I made the mistake of telling Reed this and he dragged me into a music practice room to "see for himself." That made me late for bio, and Easton, who's in the class with me, immediately guessed why and teased me mercilessly.

"You play football in high school, Callum?" I ask as we watch the team warm up by doing some weird leg lifts in unison.

"Yep. I played tight end."

I smirk. The football terms are so dirty.

Callum winks as if he knows exactly what I'm thinking. "And your dad played the same position that Reed plays. Defensive end."

"Did you know that my mom was sixteen when she met Steve?" I thought about the age difference the other day and was slightly horrified. Callum is in his mid-forties, and if the two of them went to high school together, that would make Steve the same age. My mom was seventeen when she had me. Sixteen when she got knocked up. So I guess Steve was a dog even back then. None of that makes me glad he's dead, though.

"Never thought of it, but you're right." Callum casts me an uncomfortable glance. "The girls around the base bars are . . . it's hard to tell how old they are."

I roll my eyes. "Callum, I was fifteen and dancing in strip

clubs. I know it's hard to tell the difference. It was just a thought that popped into my mind."

"Steve wouldn't have taken advantage of a woman. He wasn't that type."

"I never said he did. Mom didn't have a bad word to say about my sperm donor."

Callum grimaces. "I wish you could have met him. He was a good man." He snaps his fingers. "We should have a visit with some of our old SEAL buddies. You don't know a man until you've slept in a hole in a desert with him for seven days."

"That sounds legit terrible." I screw up my nose. "I think I'll take shopping trips for the win, Alex."

He laughs. "Fair enough. Oh, here's Valerie." He stands up and gestures for Val to come and join us.

She's all smiles when she takes a seat beside me. "Hey, girl, what's up?"

"Oh good, you're here to save me from Callum's literal war stories."

At Val's blank look, Callum explains, "I was telling Ella that she needs to meet some Navy buddies of her dad's."

"Ahh. I met Steve once. Did I ever tell you that?"

"No, when?" I ask curiously.

"It was at Fall Formal last year." She leans around me to look at Callum. "Remember? You brought the boys in a helicopter?"

My mouth falls open. "For real? A helicopter?"

Callum barks with laughter. "I'd forgotten. Yup. We were testing out a new prototype and Steve wanted to give it a go. We picked up the boys and their dates and flew them up and down the coast for an hour before landing on the school grounds. Beringer had a coronary over that. I had to shell out a landscaping architecture donation." He grins broadly. "Worth it."

"Sheesh. No wonder the girls climb all over themselves to date the Royals."

"Ella," Callum says with a mock-wounded look, "my sons are pictures of masculine virility. It's their character that draws the women and not their pocketbooks."

"You keep telling yourself that."

Someone grabs Callum before he can respond. As he leans away, Val nudges me. "So everyone is happy family at the Royal palace again?"

"I don't know. It seems like we're getting along?"

"This is the first time since Maria died that Callum Royal's attended one of his son's games," she says pointedly. "I can't be the only one who noticed. Everyone's kind of looking at the two of you differently, too."

"In what way?" I study the crowd, but beyond the stares that I usually get, I'm not sure what's different.

"Just that you're so easy with each other. He clearly likes you, and not in a gross way that people gossip about. But you're laughing and he's pretty talkative. It's just different. Callum's a big deal and lots of adults want his approval."

"Or access to his bank account."

She shrugs. "Same difference. Maybe it'll help at school. If these assholes' parents knew that Callum Royal's ward was being mistreated, a lot of allowances would be suspended."

"It's already dying down," I admit. "The worst thing this week was my missing underwear."

"Yeah, I heard that was a real problem for you." She rolls her eyes. "Maybe you should look closer to home for the perpetrator behind that theft."

I grin. "Reed doesn't need to steal my clothes to get his hands on me."

"You're disgusting," she says with clear affection.

"You're still the best I've had in my bed," I assure her. "How's things on the Hiro front?"

"I don't know. He's hot and all but he doesn't really get my engine running."

"What about Wade?" According to Val, they'd skipped fourth period today and fooled around in a supply closet, but she hadn't offered any more details than that.

"He's too practiced. Everything that comes out of his mouth is completely unserious. Like, I don't know what he'd do if a girl told him she loved him. That might be his worst nightmare. Like yours and mine are spiders crawling into our mouths"—I shudder—"but his are legions of girls standing up and saying, *Wade, I love you. Let's be serious.* I bet he wakes up at night, sweating in fear."

"You've given this a lot of thought."

"Better than dwelling on Tam."

"True."

The stands rise in unison as the band begins to play the national anthem, interrupting our conversation. Callum stands beside me, rigid at attention. I guess some habits die hard. Val's to my right. My man's on the field. On my back, the word *Royal* is emblazoned on my borrowed jersey.

I've never felt this accepted before. It's weird and wonderful and I can't keep the smile off my face. The game is an utter blowout, and once it's over, all anyone can talk about is the playoffs that are rolling around the corner.

On our way out, Callum stops about two bleachers from the landing and reaches across a few people to tap a small, wiry man on the shoulder.

"Mark, how are you?" Callum says politely.

A spot of tension starts spreading across my shoulders at Callum's suddenly cool tone.

"Could you step down for a minute? I wanted to have a word with you."

It's not a request, but a command. Everyone around us gets it, because the row stands as one to make way for Mark.

"That's my uncle," Val hisses in my ear.

I've never met Jordan's parents before, and Callum doesn't introduce us. Instead, he holds out his arm, almost as a barricade, forcing Mark Carrington to descend in front of us. Mark pauses at the bottom of the bleachers, but something in Callum's face has him whipping around and walking quickly toward the stairs leading to the ground.

"What's going on?" I mutter out of the side of my mouth.

Val gives me a baffled look. Since Callum hasn't told me to get lost, I follow him with Val on my heels.

"That's far enough," Callum says once we're about twenty feet away from the bleachers.

"What's this about, Royal?"

Callum reaches behind him and manages to clasp on to my wrist without even looking. He drags me forward. "I don't believe you've met my new ward. Ella Harper. She's Steve's daughter."

Mr. Carrington pales, but offers his hand. Bewildered, I shake it.

"Nice to meet you, Ella."

"Nice to meet you, too, sir. I'm friends with Val." I haul her next to me much like Callum pulled me to his side.

Val gives a weak wave. "Hey, Uncle Mark."

"Hello, Val."

"This is nice, isn't it?" Callum remarks. "My ward and yours being friends?"

Mark nods uncertainly. "Yes, good to have friends."

Val slips her hand into mine.

"Ella is very important to my family and I'm glad she's being welcomed with open arms into the Astor Park community. It would disturb me greatly to hear that she was being mistreated in any way. I'm sure you wouldn't stand for that, would you, Mark?"

"Of course I wouldn't."

"Your daughter is quite popular at Astor, isn't she?" Callum's tone is so mild he could be discussing the weather, but something about his words makes Mark's face go pale.

"Jordan has many friends."

"Good. I know that her friendliness extends to Ella, just as my goodwill extends toward your family."

Mark clears his throat. "I have no doubt that Ella is the perfect addition to my daughter's circle."

"Me, too, Carrington. Me, too. You can go and find your family now." Callum gives Mark a dismissive look and turns to me. "Why don't you girls find the boys while I have Durand bring the car around?"

"Uh, sure," I stutter, but as he starts to walk off, the urge to find out exactly what he knows comes over me and I drop Val's hand to chase after him. "Callum, wait up."

He waits for me. "Yes?"

"Why'd you do that?"

He gives me an impatient look. "I'm never the first to know things that are going on. I left that up to Maria, but I always figure it out eventually. So I know that your car was gone for a week because someone gave it a bath in honey and I know that Reed and East fight for the hell of it on the weekends and I know that you're not just wearing this for the sake of school spirit." He fingers the cuff of the Reed's jersey, then releases the fabric and, with a crooked smile, turns me toward the field. "Go find our boys, honey, and I'll see you all at home. Don't be too late and stay close to your brothers." He stops and then sighs. "Well, I guess they aren't your brothers, are they?"

God, I hope not. My mind whirling, I walk back to Val.

"Did Callum just threaten Uncle Mark?" she asks in confusion.

"I think so?"

"Did you tell him about your car?"

I shake my head. "No, I was too embarrassed. Reed took care of it for me. I just got it back today."

"Callum definitely knows something."

"Obvs. But do you think his talk with your uncle will actually change anything?"

"Sure. Uncle Mark could cut Jordan off. If he felt his business was being threatened by something she did? He'd come down on her hard."

"Hmmm. We'll have to see." I'm not entirely convinced.

Val squeezes my hand. "I guess you'll have to lose your own underwear after PE now."

I stick out my tongue. "Who says I wear them anyway?"

"Please tell me the two of you are going to kiss," Easton interrupts. He grins as we look at him.

"If we did, it wouldn't be for your benefit," I answer.

"Oh, I don't care. I just want to watch. Preferably when we're somewhere a little more private, but with a lot more light and a lot less clothing."

"You have to be eighteen or older for that show," Val teases.

"Then I know what I want for my birthday. It's in April. Start planning now. I'm partial to sexy mermaid costumes."

"Halloween is over, brother," Reed says as he comes up to us. He leans down and gives me a quick kiss on the cheek. "What're our plans?"

Easton jiggles his leg impatiently. "Whatever we're deciding, let's do it quick. I'm tired of standing around."

Reed and I exchange worried glances.

"You just got done playing football," I remind Easton.

"Exactly. I'm full of adrenaline and I need to spend it. My preferred vices are sex, alcohol, pills. You two are down on me drinking and getting high, so that leaves sex." He sends a pointed look in Val's direction.

She laughs and holds up a hand. "I'm not volunteering. I don't think my poor body could take the pounding you need to give. Let's go find someone for you, though. I'll be your spirit guide through the rocky shores of high school hookups."

"I lay my tender body into your hands." Easton slings his arm around Val's shoulders. "You two have to fend for yourself," he calls back.

I arch an eyebrow. "Leftover adrenaline?"

Reed winks. "There's some truth to that."

"I'm not really interested in any party."

A wicked smile spreads over his face. "Yeah? I have some ideas about how we can spend our post-game celebration. Wanna hear them?"

I grin back. "I think I do."

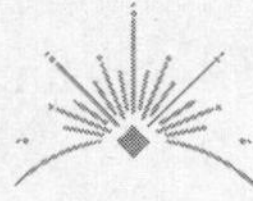

Twenty-Seven

REED

I TAKE ELLA out to the beach. One thing I've always loved about our place is how close it is to the ocean. The beach isn't big—not much more than a fifty-foot stretch that's about ten feet wide before the tide swallows up the sand on one side, while the rocky outgrowth on the other forms a natural wall from the back lawn to the shore.

But it's still ours—quiet, peaceful, and most important, private.

I lay down a heavy wool blanket, toss a down comforter on top, and drop the rest of my supplies. "Have a seat while I light us a fire."

She shucks her shoes at the edge of the blanket before sitting down. I catch a glimpse of dark-painted toes before they disappear underneath her legs.

There's always a pile of driftwood against the rocks, and in no time at all I have a small fire going, enough to provide us with a little illumination and heat. Don't want my girl to get cold.

"Watching you make a fire is weirdly sexy," she comments as I sort through the dry wood for the best pieces.

I twist around to grin at her. "Handy dudes are like porn for chicks. You like that I can do things."

"If I was a cavewoman, I'd definitely drag you back to my lair," she agrees.

"Is that how it worked back then? The men would create fire and then the women would come along and bonk the guy with the best twig from the pile and have her way with him?"

"Yup, but we let the men write the stories because their fragile egos needed the boost."

I throw one more log into the fire to keep us toasty, then join her on the blanket. She smooths the comforter over my legs as I stretch out beside her. For a while, we watch the fire dance and listen to the crackling of the tinder as it breaks under the heat. There's a simple pleasure in our closeness. The ocean is vast, the sky is endless, and Ella and I are together. Finally.

Her feet rest beside my jean-clad thighs. My arm is wrapped around her back and my hand is cupping her sweet ass. I wish she was wearing her uniform so I could slide my hand underneath until I find nothing but bare skin and heat and softness.

"Thank you for getting me my job back," she says finally.

"What makes you think I did?"

She rolls her eyes. "Who else would it have been?"

I grin sheepishly.

"I mean it, Reed. Thank you."

I pull my exploring hand back and tuck it behind my head. If she wants to talk, we'll talk. I mean, my dick is going to choke to death in my jeans, but it'd be worth it if it means she'll stick around.

"Least I could do. It's my fault you lost it in the first place."

"Not really, but I appreciate the thought." Her hand rubs briskly down my thigh.

I close my eyes. The touch is meant to be encouraging, I'm sure, but just a few more inches to the left and I'll have a little relief. I take a couple of deep, silent breaths.

"The stuff at school isn't as bad as before. Did you help with that, too?" she asks. Her hand has moved upward and she's now trailing a finger down the side seam of my long-sleeve shirt.

Is she purposely trying to drive me crazy? I swivel my head to look at her, but she's staring out at the water.

I roll back and focus my attention on finding the Big Dipper and not on how I'd like her fingers to pull up my shirt and trace a path along my abs. "Not enough," I admit. "I talked to Wade and some of the other guys. Told them I wanted to hear if anything was going on, but we both know it's Jordan behind this shit. If it was a guy, I'd take him out to the parking lot and pummel his face until he was shitting his teeth."

"That's a lovely image."

I snort. "Would you rather I take him to the mall and get friendship bracelets made?"

"I don't know. Does violence solve anything? Like, you hit Daniel, and I helped humiliate him, but he won't go away. He doesn't even appear . . . shamed." Her wandering finger has drifted lower to trace the hem of my shirt.

"It's an act," I tell her. "He's good at pretending it's all right, but he got kicked off the lacrosse squad and his run for next year's student body president is over." I frown. "It's still not enough."

"It's a start, though." Ella reaches out to stroke my arm, and that innocent touch lights a fire under my skin that's hotter than the one in the sand five feet away. "Speaking of Jordan, your dad threatened her dad at the game tonight."

"He did?" I can't hide my surprise.

She nods. "He said something like he'd hate for anything bad to happen to me and have it affect their business relationship."

"Good for the old man. I didn't realize he had it in him. Or that he even knew what goes on at Astor."

"I think he knows more than he lets on. He hinted that he knew about you and me, too."

I grin. "What about you and me?"

"That maybe wearing your jersey means something."

I use her hair as an excuse to touch her, tucking a few wayward strands behind her ear. "I know what it means to me. Wanna share what it means to you?"

She grabs my wrist and turns her lips into my palm. It feels like a brand. Her brand. I want to close my fist around it and keep it there.

"It means that all those other girls need to stand down. You're mine." She lifts her shining eyes to meet mine. "Your turn."

Again, I have to take a breath. This time it's because my heart's in my throat. "It means all those other guys need to step off. You're mine." I give up being patient and drag her onto my lap. "I want to solve all your problems for you. I want to make Jordan go away. I want to erase Brooke from our lives. I want everything perfect and shiny and beautiful for you."

"Since when are you such a romantic?" she teases.

"Since I met you." Oh man. If any of my friends were around right now, they'd start a statewide search for my balls. But I don't care. I mean every word I'm saying.

Ella cradles my head between her hands. "Well, I don't need any of that from you," she whispers, her lips inches away from mine.

"I'll do anything. Tell me what you need."

"You. Just you. It's always been you."

She kisses me. Her lips press softly against mine, sealing the promise she's made to me. That she's mine and always has been. From before we even met, she was mine and I was hers. I fought it too long, but I'm giving in now. I'm all in now.

I kiss her back, driving her down to the blanket so that I can feel the full length of her body against mine. It's innocent at first. I don't rip her jersey off or stick my hand down her pants, even though I'm dying to do both. We just kiss each other, until she starts to move restlessly underneath me.

Her legs part and I settle between them, pressing my hard-on against her welcoming softness. Her hands leave my head and fumble with the bottom of my shirt. I reach one hand behind me and whip it off.

"You're not going to get cold?" she asks, half-teasing, half-serious.

"I don't think I'd be cold if it started to snow." I grab her hand and press it to my chest. "I'm burning up."

Her fingers curl against my chest, exploring carefully. I know she doesn't have much experience, but I've never been this hot before, never been so close to the edge. Not even my first time. I could pluck her hand away and put an end to this with the excuse that my control is whisper thin, but I want her to touch me.

I brace myself over her, using my elbows for support, and let her explore. Her fingers count every rib. Her hands measure my chest and I take caveman-like pleasure in how big I am compared to her. Her palms smooth over my shoulders and spread along my back. I tremble over her, a wild animal ready to spring free, just waiting for her signal.

Fuck. This girl is wrecking me.

She uses my body as a lever and pulls downward to flick her tongue against the frantic pulse at my neck.

It's too much. I roll over and drop onto my back, my chest heaving as if I'd run a marathon.

"What's wrong?" she asks, snuggling down beside me.

I thread her fingers through mine. "Talk to me. Help me settle down."

"You sure you don't want me to help you some other way?"

That makes me smile. "Later. Right now, I want to lie here and enjoy being next to you."

"Is it always like this?"

"Like what?"

She goes quiet for a moment and then, "Like my heart is about to burst."

"You make it sound like I'm killing you."

"It feels like that sometimes. Sometimes . . . the way you make me feel scares me."

My fingers tighten on her hand. "It's the same for me, and no, it's never been like this before."

"Not even with Abby?" I can tell she regrets the question—that it slipped out before she could stop it.

I tilt my head to the side so I can look at her face. "Not even with Abby. Do you really want to talk about her?"

"Kind of." She makes a face. "But we don't have to."

I tug her closer so there's not a sliver of space between us. I don't like talking about Abby with her. Not because I have feelings for Abby but because I didn't have strong enough feelings for her and it makes me feel guilty.

"I started seeing Abby after my mom died," I admit. "I never had a steady girlfriend before that. Just the occasional hookup.

I wasn't like East, but I fooled around here and there, lost my virginity to a senior when I was fifteen. After Mom died, I was kind of . . . crazy in my head. Lots of bad shit went on upstairs . . ." I pause and then say ruefully, "Still is, I guess, but Abby came along and she reminded me of my mom. I thought being around her would be like my mom was back."

"Did that work?"

"For a while, but then . . . I didn't miss Mom as much. I mean, I still missed her, but Abby wasn't ever gonna be someone who kept my interest. She's too quiet. Too . . . passive, I guess." I was bored shitless around her, but that sounds rude and I don't want Ella to start thinking I'm an asshole again. "I broke up with her around Christmas. You realize that there's no good time in the fall to break up with someone? It's nuts. Gid always said you can't break up with a girl before Winter Formal and not right before any holidays. But I did it anyway, because delaying it wasn't good for either of us. She wasn't happy. She kept coming around even after I ended it, and the more she came after me, the more I regretted dating her in the first place."

Ella rubs her cheek against my shoulder. "Why do you sound so guilty right now?"

"Because I feel guilty," I grumble.

"Well, you shouldn't. You're not responsible for her. As long as you were up front with her, didn't make promises you didn't intend to keep, her hurt feelings are something she has to deal with."

"You're the only girl I've made promises to," I say gruffly.

"Make me a promise right now."

"Anything."

"Promise you'll always be straight with me. That if you ever regret being with me, you tell me."

I roll her over and pin her hands next to her head. "I can promise you this—I'm never gonna regret even a second that you and I spend together."

I kiss her again to silence any disagreement. That's not the promise she asked for, but it's the only one I can give, because I'm never going to be tired of her.

I break away, pressing kisses along her jaw, down the smooth column of her neck. She has no idea how beautiful she is, how the sight of her golden hair and fiery blue eyes and slender body makes every guy at school pop a boner when she walks down the hall.

"You wearing my jersey tonight was the hottest thing I've ever seen," I rasp in her ear before biting on the lobe.

"Yeah?"

"Oh yeah."

Her fingers dance hungrier and needier on my skin. I wedge my thigh between her legs and she grinds against me.

"I wanna take care of you." I rock against her. "Let me."

"Out here? Right now?" She's scandalized, but intrigued.

"No one is around for miles."

I push up the jersey and the tank she has on underneath until her creamy skin is completely exposed. I lick a slow circle around her tight nipple, and she arches upward, not satisfied with my teasing.

Chuckling, I take her into my mouth. When I flick the tip with my tongue, she gasps. Her hands tangle in my hair and urge me closer. As if I need the encouragement. The tides could rise, a hurricane could form, but I'm not letting go.

I slide down under the comforter and tug her jeans down. "You're beautiful, baby. Perfect."

Then I have other things to do with my mouth than spit out

words that don't do her justice anyway. Beside me, her heels dig into the sand. Her fingers clutch my shoulders as I kiss and tease her sweet spot until she's crazed and I can't think straight. My dick is aching, but I don't care. I'm sort of used to it. Whenever she's around, I'm hard. And now, when she's on the edge, I'm an inferno of want.

She shakes and shudders and my name passes through her lips on repeat. I crawl up her body and hold her tight until her racing heart slows. I use the time to tell my own body to settle down. It's one big hurt, but shoving my own need aside is easy to do when my girl is blissed out in my arms.

"It's getting cold out here. Want to go inside?" she asks sleepily.

Not really. I'd like to stay here with her until the next millennium. Reluctantly, I pull away. "Sure."

I help her fasten and zip, kissing her a thousand times. Then I bundle up our blankets, throw the mess over my shoulder, and grab her hand.

"Reed."

"Yeah?"

"I miss you at night."

My chest warms. Before she left, I slept in her bed nearly every night. I couldn't get enough of her.

I squeeze her hand way too tight before replying. "I miss you, too."

"Will you sleep with me again?"

"Yeah."

It's a single word, but it's the answer I'd give to anything she asked of me.

Twenty-Eight

"YOU LOOK DISGUSTING," Easton says on Monday morning as we wait for Ella to show up at school from the bakery.

I swipe the back of my hand across my face. "What? Do I have syrup on my face?" After practice, we hit the dining hall and I inhaled about ten pancakes.

"No, it's the smile, dude. You look happy."

"Asshole." I reach over to cuff him affectionately behind his head. He nimbly ducks away.

We both spot Ella at the same time, and East jogs over and pretends to hide behind her. "Save me, little sis. Big bro is picking on me."

"Reed, pick on someone your own size," she calls.

I take a moment to drink her in, all the individual parts of her that I like, from her gorgeous smile to the ponytail that swings in an arc as she walks. The plain school uniform—pleated skirt, white button-down shirt, blue blazer that everyone else wears—looks sexy as hell on her. Probably because I'm imagining what's underneath.

"You're right. East's kind of puny. I'll take it easy on him."

When she draws near, I reach out and drag her the rest of

the distance. Close enough that I can feel the straps of her backpack push against my chest. I bend down and kiss her long and hard until East starts coughing behind her back.

When she pulls away, her lips have taken on a perfect rosy hue. I want to skip school, haul her off to my car, and make her turn that color everywhere.

"Hey, little boy. Want a piece of candy?" she asks with a wicked grin.

"Absolutely," I answer immediately. "Where's the van? I'm ready to be kidnapped." I pretend to look around.

"No van, but here—" She turns around and wiggles her backpack. Right inside the top of the pack, I discover a small white box. "There's a donut for each of you," she says as I pull it out.

Easton dives for the box and has a donut halfway into his mouth before he hands the container back to me. He gives me two thumbs up. As I devour my own snack, I spot the twins crossing the lawn with Lauren. They give me a chin nod of acknowledgment when I wave them over.

"One's in there for you, too, Lauren," Ella tells her when they arrive.

Lauren ducks her head with a shy smile. "Thanks."

"No problem." Ella leans against my side as I demolish the rest of the donut. "How was practice?"

"Good. Everyone's hyped up for State. We got bounced in the semifinals last year. Guy from St. Francis Prep knocked Wade unconscious and the docs wouldn't let him back in the game. Our backup couldn't hit a target if a knife was at his throat."

Ella snorts. "Guess you don't care about winning, huh?"

"Nah, not at all." I grin. We both know I get off on winning, among other things.

Shouting over by the steps of the school draws our attention.

She squints. "What's going on?"

"Probably some playoff stuff. There's gonna be a lot of that the next few weeks. Get your spirit on," Easton warns.

Ella gives an unenthused "Woo-hoo." We'll make a fan out of her yet.

"The good thing about the four weeks of playoffs is that there will be days you don't have to wear your uniform," Lauren informs her. "Like blue days. Gold days. Crazy hat days."

"Pajama day." Easton wiggles his eyebrows up and down.

Wade and Hunter join us. "What are you grinning about?" Wade asks East.

"Pajama day."

"Favorite fucking day of the year."

Wade and East exchange a high five. "Remember Ashley M?" my brother says. "She wore the pink—"

"Baby doll dress," Wade finishes. "I remember. I had a boner every time I saw pink for a month after." He turns to Ella and asks, "What are you wearing?"

"A floor-length prairie gown and granny panties," she says with exasperation. "What about you? I assume you guys run around in boxers?"

Wade's all for it. "Dude, if it was allowed, I'd be naked all day. Free-balling twenty-four seven. That's my dream."

Before either East or I can make a crack about how we don't want to see Wade's nuts and sausage out during class, the yelling and murmuring from the front doors gets louder.

Hunter, Wade's ever-present but never-talking companion, peels away to investigate. The rest of us follow even though classes are about to begin.

The noise isn't necessarily out of place, but the mass of

students five deep is. Only football games draw this kind of crowd. Even then, for most kids the games are just an excuse to get together and socialize.

I exchange a wary look with East and Wade. Even Hunter recognizes this is out of place. As one, we press forward. Ella's hand is on my back and I reach behind to clasp her wrist. I don't want to lose her. This doesn't feel good or right.

The spectacle that greets us is about as bad as it can get. Taped up against the rough brick exterior of the main entrance is a nearly naked girl. Her head is bowed, and even from a distance, I can see a section of her hair hacked out of the back. Her arms and legs are spread wide and she seems to be supported only by tape. A shit ton of it. It crosses her body above the chest and along the thighs, emphasizing the parts covered only by her underwear and bra.

My stomach turns over.

"Jesus. What is *wrong* with you people?" Ella yells.

Before I can blink, she runs by me, dropping her backpack and ripping off her blazer at the same time. The girl is too high for Ella to fully cover, but she tries.

I reach Ella at the same time as Hunter, and we start tearing at the tape while Ella holds her blazer up. Next to me, I see Hunter pull a knife out of his boot. He starts slicing and I start peeling.

There's so much tape, it takes us five minutes before we get the girl down. East hands me a jacket and I try to place it around the girl's shoulders. She jerks away, crying so hard I'm afraid she's going to throw up. Or pass out.

Ella takes the jacket from me. "It's okay. Here. Put this on," she soothes. "What's your name? Can you tell me what your gym locker is? Do you have clothes there?"

The girl can't—or won't—respond. She continues to sob.

I clench my fists at my side in dismay. I want to kill someone.

One of the twins pipes up. "I've got shit in the car. Hold on."

A couple more jackets are tossed in our direction until Ella and the girl are covered with them. "Lauren, come here," Ella commands.

Lauren hurries to her side and crouches down. Carefully, Ella shifts the wounded girl from her arms to Lauren's. Once the transfer is done, Ella rises to her feet and stares at the assembled students.

"Who did this?" she growls at the crowd. "Someone saw something. Who did this?"

No one responds.

"I swear to God, if someone doesn't say something right now, then I'm holding you all responsible!"

"I'll find out, Ella," Wade murmurs. "I can find out anything."

"It's Jordan," I say flatly. "This reeks of her."

"It *was* Jordan," come the choked words from the girl. "She . . ." Her voice is too faint for me to make it out. Ella leans down close to the girl's mouth and listens intently. When she stands again, there's fury in her eyes.

This time I address the crowd. "Jordan Carrington. Where is she?"

"Inside," someone yells.

Another voice chimes in. "I saw her go to her locker."

Ella doesn't wait another second. She turns on her heel and jerks open a door. Easton and I are hot on her ass, while the twins stay rooted by Lauren's side.

By the time we hit the hall where the senior lockers are, Ella's running. She skids to a stop when we spot Jordan giggling with the Pastels, taking selfies in front of the locker bank.

Jordan slowly lowers the phone at Ella's approach. "What's the hurry, princess? You can't spend another second without some Royal dick in you?"

Ella doesn't respond. Instead, quick as lightning, her hand jerks out, grabs Jordan by the hair, and swings her into the locker. The phone goes flying. The Pastels back away. Gastonburg rounds the corner at Jordan's scream, but I bare my teeth at him and he disappears. Coward.

Ella's not done. She brings an elbow up to Jordan's nose. *Whack!* Blood spurts.

East winces. "Damn, that had to hurt."

"No doubt."

Jordan tears out of Ella's grip with a cry, but Ella shakes her fingers and I see that Jordan's escape wasn't without cost. A bunch of dark strands hang off Ella's hand. Yeah. That's my girl.

Claws out, Jordan lunges forward and rakes those nails down Ella's face. Easton moves to jump in for the assist, but I pull him back. "She's got this," I murmur.

I want to help, too, but I know this is Ella's match. If she takes Jordan down—no, *when* she does—no one in this school will touch Ella again. No one will say a bad word to her. They'll all fear her.

And I want that for her. She's going to need it when I'm gone next year.

As Ella surges forward, the older girl backs away, tripping and losing her balance. Ella jumps on top, straddling Jordan. She grabs Jordan's hands and pins them above her head.

"What'd she do?" Ella asks. "She look at you wrong? Wear the wrong label? What?"

"She exists," Jordan spits, wiggling under Ella's hold. "Get off me, you friggin' cow!"

Ella glances up at me. "Do you have any rope?" There's blood on her face—some of it might be Jordan's, some of it's from Ella.

She's never looked hotter.

"No. Use my shirt." I take it off and hand it to her.

She looks at the cloth and then at me with uncertainty.

"Can I help?" I ask gently.

When she nods, I whip the shirt into a long rope and tie Jordan's wrists together.

"What're you doing? Stop this! This is assault!" Jordan cries and thrashes to the side. "Get this piece of garbage off of me!"

One of the Pastels steps forward. I shake my head no, while Easton takes a menacing step in their direction. Their small show of resistance immediately dissolves.

Ella stands up and tests the knots.

"I know how to tie knots. Grew up in that yacht," I remind her.

"Let me go, bitch!" Jordan screams. "My dad will have you arrested so fast your head will spin."

"Good." Ella starts down the hall toward the exit, dragging Jordan behind her. "I look forward to getting statements from three hundred kids about what we found outside this morning."

"What do you care? I've left you alone just like your fuck buddy demanded." Jordan yanks at the cloth, but Ella's grip holds firm.

"I care because you're an entitled, spoiled rich girl who thinks she can smile out of one side of her mouth while vomiting poison out of the other. You're not untouchable. Today you're going to face the results of your awfulness." Ella marches implacably toward the front doors, pulling Jordan along.

We follow behind.

"I can't believe you guys are letting her do this!" Jordan twists around as if East and I are interested in saving her. "She's nothing. She's trash."

"Don't talk to them," Ella orders. "You don't exist for them."

My brother grins like a fool. *I love this chick,* he mouths.

Me, too.

Avenger Ella is amazing. She'll fight tooth and nail for what she wants. The key is to remain what she wants. Because she'd leave your deadweight ass behind if she didn't think you were worth it.

A few teachers poke their heads out of the classrooms, but at the sight of us they scuttle back inside. The faculty know who's in charge in this zoo, and it's not them. More than one student has gotten a teacher fired for some perceived wrong.

"What now?" Jordan snipes. "You going to show everyone that you're stronger than me? So what?"

At the front doors, I take one side and Easton the other. We bang open the doors and the sharp sound grabs the attention of the crowd.

Ella drags Jordan through and then stops. Tape still hangs on the wall, like an obscene flag. Ella jerks a strip of it off and slaps it over Jordan's mouth.

"I'm so tired of you running your mouth," Ella says.

The look of shock on Jordan's face is laughable, but when my gaze falls on the abused girl, still huddled in Lauren's arms, the humor drains away.

Ella pulls Jordan onto the landing. A collective gasp echoes in the courtyard.

The girl who was strapped to the front is sitting under a mound of coats, with Lauren's arm around her and a few other girls offering comfort. The twins, along with Wade, Hunter, and half the football team, are loitering on the steps, wondering who they should be fighting and frustrated that there isn't a target.

I empathize with them a hundred percent, but as I telegraphed to East, this is Ella's show and I'll fight anyone for her to finish it the way she wants.

"Look at her." Ella lets the makeshift rope go and grabs Jordan's hair again. With her free hand, she rips the tape off Jordan's mouth. "Tell her to her face why she deserved what you did. Explain it to all of us."

"I don't answer to you," Jordan replies, but her voice isn't as strong as it was inside.

"Tell us why we shouldn't strip you down and tape you up on the doors," Ella growls. "*Tell* us."

"She thought I was flirting with Scott," the girl says tearfully. "But I wasn't. I swear. I tripped and he caught me and I thanked him. That was it."

"That's it?" Ella turns incredulously toward Jordan. "You humiliated this poor girl because you thought she flirted with your foul-mouthed boyfriend?" She shakes Jordan in furious anger. *"That's it?"*

Jordan pulls at Ella's grip, but Ella isn't letting go. I think the apocalypse could come before she lets go.

She swings around, forcing Jordan to face the rest of the students. Ella's arms are shaking with the effort and I can see she doesn't have much strength left in her. Dragging Jordan down the hall while she was struggling couldn't have been easy, even with East and me bringing up the tail.

"She's not going to make it," Easton mutters.

"She will." I walk forward and place my body behind hers. She can lean against me if she needs to. I'm here to support her.

Beside me, I feel the presence of my brothers. All of us are behind her.

Ella's hands are shaking. Her knees are locked so she doesn't fall over, but her voice is clear and strong. "You all have so much, and instead of appreciating it, you treat each other like dirt. Your little games are disgusting. Your silence is gross. You're all pathetic, spineless cowards. Maybe no one's told you how small you are for doing it. Maybe you're all so jaded by all the money you have, you don't see how awful this is. But it's terrible. It's worse than terrible. If I have to attend school here until I graduate, this shit isn't going on anymore. If I have to, I'll come after each and every one of you and tape your asses to the school wall."

"You and what army?" some unwise asshat yells from the crowd.

Easton and I jump forward, but I push my brother behind me. "I've got this."

The crowd parts and the wiseass with the loud mouth is left standing all alone. I haul off and throw one fist at his jaw, and he drops like a stone. Damn, that felt good.

Then I smile at the crowd and ask, "Who's next?"

As they all turn away in gutless silence, I brush my hands off and walk back to my girl and my brothers. Wade throws me a spare shirt, which I quickly shrug on.

"The last bit was a nice touch," Ella murmurs.

"Thanks. I've been saving it for the right occasion." I take her bruised hand in mine. "The family that fights together, stays together."

"Is *that* the Royal motto? I thought it was something else."

The adrenaline has worn off and I can feel her trembling. I tuck her close to me, head under my chin, body wrapped in my arms. "It might have been, before you came, but I think that's what it is now."

"It's not a bad motto." With a wry look, she glances around at the scattering crowd, the remnants of tape strewn on the steps, and the droplets of blood on the limestone. "So. Is this our first date?"

"No way. Our first date was . . ." I trail off. What was our first date?

"You haven't taken me on a date, dummy." She punches me—or attempts to. It's kind of like a bird's kiss at this point given that her arms are as weak as jellyfish.

"Damn. I think you're right."

"Don't knock yourself for it. I've never been on a date before. Do people even go on dates anymore?"

I grin, because finally I can do something for her. "Oh, baby, you got a lot to learn."

✦ ✦ ✦

IT DOESN'T TAKE long for news of the morning's activities to reach the headmaster. I barely get my ass in my chair for my first class before the teacher informs me I'm wanted in Beringer's office. When I get there, I discover that Ella and Jordan were pulled out of class, too, and all the parents were called. Fuck. This isn't going to be good.

The office is crowded. Ella and I sit on one side with my father behind us. A stone-faced Jordan is next to me, and I can feel her vibrating between fear and rage.

Jordan's victim, a freshman named Rose Allyn, sits on the far side of the room. Her mom has been complaining nonstop about how she's missing an important meeting for this.

Finally, Beringer sweeps in and closes the door with a bang.

When Ella jumps at the noise, both Dad and I put a hand out to steady her—his on her shoulder and mine on her knee. Our eyes meet, and for once, I see approval in his. Whatever Beringer decides to do, it's not going to matter to Dad. What matters to him is that I stood up for our family, that I'm not the selfish prick I act like most of the time.

Beringer clears his throat, and we all turn toward him. In his thousand-dollar suit, he'd be right at home in Dad's boardroom. Idly, I wonder if he bought that hand-tailored suit using the money my dad paid him after I beat up Daniel, and what he'll buy out of the bribes he'll pocket after today's meeting.

"Violence is never the answer," he begins. "A civilized society begins and ends with spirited discourse, not fistfights."

"I thought the saying was 'an armed society is a polite society,'" Dad interjects dryly.

Ella's hand flies up to her mouth to cover a laugh.

Beringer glares at us. "I'm beginning to see why the Royals have such a difficult time getting along with their classmates."

"Wait a minute." Ella straightens indignantly. "None of the Royals taped anyone to a wall."

"Well, not this year," I murmur.

Dad cuffs me lightly across the back of my head while Ella shoots me a dirty look. "What? You think these assholes fall in line because I say so?" I mutter under my breath.

"Mr. Royal, if I may have your attention," Beringer barks out before Ella can respond.

I kick out my legs and throw an arm across the back of Ella's chair. "Sorry," I reply with absolutely zero remorse. "I was explaining to Ella that Astor really doesn't tolerate things like taping half-naked freshmen to the front of the school. She has this weird idea that public school is better."

"Callum, you need to exert better control over your son," Beringer orders.

Dad's not having any of that. "I wouldn't be here if the school actually enforced its rules."

"I agree. You interrupted a seven-figure real-estate deal because you're not capable of handling these kids," Rose's mother speaks up. "What are we paying you for?"

Ella and I exchange an amused look as Beringer turns bright red. "These aren't teenagers. They're wild animals. Look at how many fights Reed has been in."

"I'm not going to apologize for standing up for my family," I say in a bored voice. "I'll do whatever it takes to make sure me and mine are safe."

Even Mark, Jordan's dad, grows impatient. "Name-calling is hardly helpful. Clearly the students have had a disagreement about something and took care of it among themselves."

"A disagreement?" Ella echoes in outrage. "This is not a disagreement! This is—"

"It's called growing up, Ella," Jordan interrupts. "Which is what I suggest you do. And please, don't even try to tell me that if some girl looked sideways at your man, you wouldn't take her down."

"I wouldn't tape her up," Ella retorts.

"You'd just shove her face in the locker? That's so much better?" Jordan snipes.

"Don't try to compare us. We are *nothing* alike."

"You've got that right! You're from the gutter—"

"Jordan!" Mark booms. "That's enough." He looks warily at Dad, whose previously blank face is now sporting a deep frown. Mark presses his hands on his daughter's shoulders, as if to keep her in her chair, or maybe to remind her who's in charge.

"We're all sorry an event happened at school that isn't becoming of the conduct code of Astor Prep. The Carringtons are prepared to make it right for everyone."

Beringer hems and haws a bunch of bullshit about how we should all be punished, but when no one else steps up, he sniffs. "Everyone is dismissed, then."

"Finally!" Rose's mom exclaims. She darts out without even a backward glance to her daughter.

After a short silence, Ella walks over to Rose and lays a gentle hand on her shoulder. "Come on, Rose. I'll walk you to your locker."

Rose gives her a weak smile but follows her out.

"Your ward has certainly changed you," Mark Carrington says stiffly.

Dad and I exchange a mutual look of pride.

"I hope so," I answer, even though Carrington was addressing Dad. I stand up and shrug at Jordan's father. "She's the best thing to happen to the Royals in a long time."

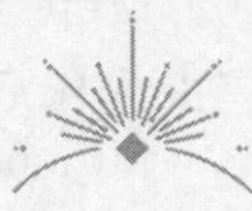

Twenty-Nine

ELLA

"THIS PLACE IS way too fancy," I hiss to Reed on Thursday evening. He insisted on taking me out tonight, but when he said *dinner* I hadn't expected such an extravagant restaurant. My black dress is much too plain compared to all the cocktail gowns I'm seeing everywhere. "I'm underdressed."

He clasps my hand tighter and practically drags me to the hostess station. "You look hot," is all he says, and then he tells the black-clad hostess that we've got reservations—Royal, table for two.

She guides us past secluded tables that are tucked away between huge planters of sweeping ferns. There's a fountain in the middle of the room with spouting arcs of water, and what looks like a waterfall behind the bar. It's the fanciest restaurant I've ever been to in my life.

Reed pulls out my chair and settles across from me at the cozy table. A waiter comes by with two leather-bound menus and a wine list, which Reed waves away. "Water's fine," he tells the guy, and I'm grateful, because I hate wine. It tastes gross.

When I flip open the menu, I'm confused to find that there

aren't any prices listed. Crap. That's never a good sign. It means everything here costs more than most people's college tuition.

"We should've just gone to the seafood place on the pier," I grumble at him.

"For your first date? No way."

I suddenly wish I'd never made that confession about how I've never been on a date. I should have known Reed would go overboard. This guy never does anything halfway.

"Why is it so important to you that I have a real first date?" I ask with a sigh.

"Because you have some shitty memories of me and I want to replace those with good ones," he says simply, and I melt right along with the wax that's sliding down the sides of the thin white candles in the center of our table.

The waiter returns with our water, and we skip the appetizers and order our main course, then sit there staring at each other for a moment. It's kind of surreal being out on a date with Reed Royal. When I told Val about our plans for tonight, she teased me about how I've done everything backward. I guess the first date is supposed to come before all the fooling around, but hey, my life has never been traditional, so why start now?

"Have you heard any updates on Rose?" he asks.

I shake my head. Poor Rose hasn't been back to school since Jordan tortured and humiliated her. "No, everyone's left me alone except for Val. I think they're scared of me."

"If you asked, someone would cough up the details."

"I kind of want to call her, but maybe she just wants to forget Astor exists."

"I think you should call," Reed encourages.

"I feel like we're always fighting some huge battle," I say

glumly. "Like, yeah, people have stopped acting like psychos at school, but everything else is still a mess."

A furrow appears in his forehead. "We're not a mess."

"Not you and me," I agree. "But . . ."

"But what?"

I draw a deep breath. "Brooke and Dinah will be back next week."

His expression clouds over. "You really want to ruin your first date by talking about those two?"

"We have to talk about them eventually," I point out. "What are we going to do about them? Dinah's blackmailing Gideon. Brooke's marrying your dad and having his baby." I bite my bottom lip in dismay. "I don't think they're ever going away, Reed."

"We'll make them go away," he says harshly.

"How?"

"I . . . have no idea."

I dig my teeth deeper into my lip. "I don't have a solution to the Dinah thing, but I might have an idea about Brooke."

He looks at me in suspicion. "What kind of idea?"

"Remember the day you overheard us talking in the kitchen? I asked her what her end game was, what she really wants, and her answer was money." I lean forward on my elbows. "That's all she's ever wanted—money. So let's give it to her."

"Trust me, I tried. I offered her cash." He makes a disgusted sound under his breath. "She wants everything, Ella. The entire Royal fortune."

"What about the O'Halloran fortune?"

There's a sharp intake of breath. Then he narrows his eyes at me. "Don't even think about it, babe."

"Why not?" I argue. "I already told you, I don't want Steve's money. I don't want a fourth of Atlantic Aviation."

"And you want *Brooke* to have it?" he says in disbelief. "We're talking hundreds of millions of dollars here."

He's right—it's an insane amount of money. But my inheritance from Steve has never felt real to me. All the paperwork is still being processed and there are still a bunch of legal hoops to jump through, so until someone hands me a check with all those zeros on it, I don't consider myself rich. I don't *want* to be rich. All I ever wanted was to live a normal life that didn't involve taking off my clothes for strangers.

"If it gets her off our backs, then I don't care if she gets the money," I answer.

"Well, I care. Steve left *you* that money, not Brooke." His hard expression says not to argue with him. "You're not giving her a cent, Ella. I mean it. I'm going to fix things, okay?"

"How?"

And once again, he looks frustrated. "I'll figure it out. Until then, I don't want you doing anything without talking to me first, all right?"

"Fine," I concede.

He reaches across the table and twines his fingers through mine. "We're not talking about this anymore," he says firmly. "Let's finish our meal and pretend, at least for one night, that Brooke Davidson doesn't exist. Sound good?"

I squeeze his hand. "Sounds awesome."

And that's what we do . . . for about ten minutes. But my earlier fear that we're always fighting some kind of battle ends up being an omen—just as our waiter delivers the chocolate mousse cake we decided to share, a familiar figure walks past our table.

Reed has his head down because he's shoving his fork into the cake slice, but he looks up sharply the moment I hiss, "Daniel's here."

We both turn toward the table that Daniel Delacorte and his date are being escorted to. I don't recognize the girl he's with, but she seems kind of young. A freshman, maybe?

"He's cradle-robbing now?" Reed mutters.

"You know that girl?"

"Cassidy Winston. Little sister of one of my teammates." His lips flatten. "She's fifteen."

Worry gnaws at me. She's only fifteen . . . and having dinner with a scumbag who likes to drug girls.

I sneak another peek across the room. Daniel and Cassidy have sat down, and she's gazing at him like he hung the stars and moon. Her cheeks are flushed pink, which makes her look even younger than she already is.

"Why is he going out with freshmen?" I push the dessert plate toward Reed. My appetite is totally gone. So is his, apparently, because he doesn't take another bite.

"Because no one in our grade will touch him," Reed says grimly. "All the older chicks at Astor know what he did to you. And after the Worthington party, Savannah made sure everyone knew he did the same thing to her cousin."

"Do you think Cassidy knows about it?"

Reed is quick to shake his head. "She wouldn't be out with him if she knew. And I don't think she told her family who she was going out with tonight, because trust me, Chuck would've broken Delacorte's face if he knew that creep was after his sister."

My gaze returns to the pretty freshman. She's giggling over something Daniel just said. Then she reaches for her glass and takes a dainty sip, and a spark of fear goes off inside me.

"What if he slipped something into her drink?" I whisper to Reed, my pulse speeding up.

"I don't think he's stupid enough to drug a girl in a place like this," Reed assures me.

"No, he's not stupid . . . but he's desperate." My heart beats even faster. "The junior and senior girls aren't touching him, and now he's asking out *freshmen.* He's definitely getting desperate." I abruptly pull my napkin off my lap and drop it on the table. "Someone needs to warn her. I'm going to talk to her."

"No—"

"Reed—"

"—let me," he finishes.

I blink in surprise. "You're really going over there?"

He's already pushing his chair back. "Of course. I'm not letting him hurt anyone else, babe." He stands up. "Wait here. I'll talk care of it."

I quickly rise to my feet. "Ha. I'm coming with you. I know how you *take care* of things, and there's no way I'm letting you cause a scene in such a fancy restaurant."

"Who says I'll cause a scene?" he protests.

"Do I need to remind you what happened at school on Monday?"

"Do I need to remind you who started it off by dragging Jordan by her hair?"

He's got me there. We grin at each other, but our humor fades when we turn in unison and march across the room.

Daniel's features darken the moment he spots us. Cassidy has her back to us, but her date's fierce eyes trigger an alarmed murmur from her.

"Evening," Reed drawls.

"What do you want, Royal?" Daniel mutters.

"Just wanted to have a word with your date."

"Me?" Cassidy squeaks, her brunette head swiveling toward Reed.

"Cassidy, right?" he says easily. "I'm Reed. Your brother and I play football together."

The freshman looks like she's about to faint over the fact that Reed knows her name. Daniel notices her awed expression, too, and his lips form an ugly scowl.

"Yeah," she says in a breathy voice. "I know who you are. I go to all of Chuck's games."

Reed nods. "Nice. Appreciate your school spirit."

"Hate to be rude," Daniel says coldly, "but we're kind of on a date here."

"Hate to be rude," Reed mimics, his blue eyes focused on Cassidy, "but your date's a rapist, Cass."

She gasps. "Wh-what?"

"Royal!" Daniel growls.

Reed ignores him. "I know he cleans up nice in his thousand-dollar suit," he tells Cassidy, "but this guy is a straight-up creep."

Two pink splotches appear on her cheeks. She glances at Daniel, then back at me and Reed. "I don't understand."

I speak up in a quiet voice. "He shot me up with Ecstasy at a party. And he would have raped me if my boyfriend"—I gesture at Reed—"hadn't shown up in time to stop him."

Cassidy swallows repeatedly. "Oh my God."

"We can drive you home," Reed says gently. "Do you want us to?"

She looks again at Daniel, whose entire face is beet-red. His fists are clenched on the linen tablecloth, and I'm pretty sure he's seconds away from launching himself at Reed.

"You're too good for him," I tell her. "Please, let us take you home."

Cassidy goes quiet for a moment. She just sits there, staring at Daniel.

Other people are staring, too, curious gazes turned in our direction even though none of us have even raised our voices.

Finally, Cassidy scrapes her chair back and stands up. "I'd love a ride home," she whispers, primly smoothing out the bottom of her floral dress.

"Cassidy," Daniel hisses, clearly embarrassed. "What the hell?"

She doesn't glance his way. Instead, she silently comes up beside me and the three of us leave the room. When we stop so Reed can hand three crisp hundreds to the hostess, I make the mistake of looking back at Daniel.

He's still at the table, stiff as a statue, his mouth set in a tight line. He doesn't look embarrassed anymore, but livid. Our eyes don't meet, because he's not looking at me. He's staring at Reed with such unconcealed rage that it sends a shiver scurrying up my spine.

Swallowing, I wrench my gaze away and follow Reed and Cassidy out the door.

Thirty

"I'M BORED. ENTERTAIN me."

Reed and I break apart breathlessly as Easton marches into my room without knocking. Great. I'm *so* glad I asked Callum to disable the scanner on my door. Reed convinced me it was pointless now that we're back together, reminding me that he can't exactly sneak in at night if he can't get through the door. But I guess we both forgot that Easton doesn't know how to knock.

"Get out," Reed mumbles from the bed.

"Why? Whatcha guys doing—" Easton stops when he notices our disheveled clothing, and legs that are still tangled together. He grins. "Oops. Were you making out?"

I glare at him. We *were* making out and it was awesome and I'm pissed at him for interrupting.

"My bad." He pauses for a beat. "Threesome?"

Reed throws a pillow at him, which Easton easily catches.

"Jeez. Chill, bro. I was joking."

"We're busy," I tell Easton. "Go away."

"And do what? It's Saturday night and there aren't any parties. I'm *bored*," Easton says plaintively.

Reed rolls his eyes. "It's almost midnight. How about you go to bed?"

"Nah. That's no fun." Easton fishes his phone out of his pocket. "Whatever. I'm texting Cunningham. I'm sure there's a fight or two tonight."

Reed disentangles his legs from mine and slides into a sitting position. "You're not going down there alone. Buddy system, remember?"

"Fine, then be my buddy. You like to fight. Let's go fight."

I don't miss the glint of excitement in Reed's eyes, but it fades the moment he notices me staring. With a sigh, I sit up, too. "If you want to go, then go," I tell him.

"See, Reed?" Easton prompts. "Your little sis slash hot girlfriend just gave you permission to kick some ass. Let's bounce."

Reed doesn't move. Instead, he studies my face. "You really don't care if I fight?"

I hesitate. His extracurricular activities don't exactly thrill me, but the one time I followed him and Easton to the wharf, I didn't see anything I considered scary or dangerous. It was just a bunch of high school and college guys pummeling each other for fun and taking bets on the action. Besides, I've seen Reed in action. He's lethal when he needs to be.

"Knock yourself out," I reply. Then I give him a wry smile. "No, wait, knock someone else out. I want you coming home looking as pretty as when you left."

Easton gags loudly.

Reed just laughs. "Wanna come with? We probably won't be long. Shit usually breaks up before two."

I think it over. Tomorrow's Sunday, so technically we can sleep in for as long as we want. "Sure. I'll come."

"Sweet. You can hold our winnings in your bra." Easton

waggles his eyebrows at me, which gets him another pillow launched toward his face courtesy of Reed.

"Anything Ella wears under her clothes—bras included—doesn't concern you," Reed tells his brother.

Easton blinks innocently. "Dude, you need me to remind you who kissed her first?"

Reed growls, and I grab his arm before he can lunge at Easton. "Save it for the docks," I chastise him.

"Fine." He jabs a finger in the air in front of Easton. "But if you make one more pervy comment, I'm dragging you into the ring."

"Can't make any promises," Easton says on our way out the door.

The drive to the docks doesn't take long, and when we arrive, a bunch of cars are already parked near the fence that blocks off the shipyard. Reed and Easton hop over with ease, while I need two tries before I can haul myself over the fence. I land not so gracefully in Reed's arms, and he pinches my butt before lowering me to my feet.

"You text Cunningham?" he asks Easton.

"Yeah, from the car. Dodson's here."

Reed's eyes light up. "Nice. He's got a wicked left."

"It's a beauty," Easton agrees. "And he doesn't telegraph it at all. It just comes out of nowhere. You took it like a champ the last time you fought him."

"It hurt like a mother," Reed admits, but he grins when he says it.

I roll my eyes. The two of them are practically skipping with delight over this Dodson guy and his manly fighting skills.

We pass rows and rows of shipping containers as we walk

through the deserted yard. I hear faint shouts in the distance, the noise getting louder and louder the closer we get to the action. The guys who come to these fights don't even try to hide their presence. I have no clue how they can get away with such an illegal activity on what's obviously private property.

I voice the question to Reed, who shrugs and says, "We pay off the dockmaster."

Of course they do. Since I moved in with the Royals, I'm learning that anything goes as long as you offer the right price.

When we reach the crowd of shirtless, rowdy boys, Reed and Easton don't waste time stripping off their own T-shirts. As usual, my breath hitches at the sight of Reed's bare chest. He's got muscles in places that I didn't even know had muscles.

"East!" someone shouts, and a sweaty guy with a shaved head comes up to us. "You buying in?"

"Damn right." Easton hands over a stack of crisp hundred-dollar bills.

It's a big enough stack that I turn to Reed and whisper in his ear, "How much do these things cost?"

"Five large to fight, plus all the side bets that go on."

Jeez. I can't believe anyone would spend that much money just to beat someone up. But maybe it's a guy thing, because every single male face I see is lit up with a feral sort of excitement.

Still, that doesn't stop Reed from murmuring, "Stay with one of us at all times, you got me?"

He doesn't kid around. For the next hour, I've got a Royal glued to my side. Easton fights two different times, winning once and losing once. Reed wins his one brawl, but not before his huge opponent—the one and only Dodson—splits Reed's lip with an uppercut that makes me gasp. But my boy just grins as he rejoins my side, completely unfazed by the blood dripping down his chin.

"You're an animal," I say accusingly.

"You love it," he answers, and then he kisses me—with tongue—and it's such a deep, drugging kiss that I don't even care that I can taste his blood in my mouth.

"Ready to go?" Easton waves around a stack of cash that's twice the size of the one we showed up with. "Not sure I want to push our luck any more."

Reed's eyebrows shoot up. "You're quitting while you're ahead? Is that"—he mock gasps—"*impulse control*?"

Easton shrugs.

"Aw, look at that, Ella, baby bro is growing up."

I laugh as Easton flips up his middle finger. "Come on," I tell the guys. "Let's go home. I'm getting kinda tired."

They put their shirts back on, slap hands with a few of their friends, and then the three of us head back in the direction we came from, with Easton trailing behind me and Reed. As we walk, Reed brings his lips close to my ear. "You're not really tired, are you? 'Cause I had plans for you when we get home."

I tilt my head up to smile at him. "What kind of plans?"

"Dirty ones."

"I heard that," Easton gripes from behind us.

Another laugh pops out of my mouth. "Didn't anyone ever tell you it's rude to eavesdro—"

Before I can finish, a hoodie-wearing figure darts out from between two shipping containers.

Reed's head whirls to the side. "What the—"

He doesn't get to finish, either.

Everything happens so fast I barely have time to register

what's going on. The hoodie guy hisses out some words I can't make out. There's a wink of silver and a blur of motion. One second Reed is standing beside me—the next, he's down on the cold ground and all I see is blood.

My entire body seizes up. My lungs burn for air. I hear someone screaming and I think it might be me, and suddenly I'm being yanked to the side as footsteps pound the pavement.

Easton. He's tearing after the guy in the hoodie. And Reed . . . Reed's lying on the ground, clutching his right side with both hands.

"Oh my God!" I scream, hurling myself at him.

His hands are red and sticky and I feel like throwing up when I realize there's blood oozing out between his fingers. I shove his hands away and instinctively apply pressure on his side. My voice sounds weak and hoarse as I shout out for help. I hear more footsteps. More shouts. More commotion. But my entire world revolves around Reed right now.

His face is almost completely white, and his eyelids flutter rapidly.

"Reed," I choke out. "Don't close your eyes, baby." I don't know why I order that, but the terrified, panicky part of me says that if he closes his eyes, they might not open again. I yell another command over my shoulder, "Someone call an ambulance, dammit!"

Someone careens to a stop beside us. It's Easton, and he drops to his knees and quickly places both his hands over mine. "Reed," he says grimly, "you okay, bro?"

"What the hell do you think?" Reed mumbles. His voice is wheezy enough to triple my panic. "Just got stabbed."

"Ambulance is on the way," a male voice announces.

I turn to find the shaved-head guy looming over us. Dodson's eyes are lined with worry.

I refocus on Reed and feel sick again. He got stabbed. Who the hell would do this to him?

"Bastard got away," Easton is saying. "Got over the fence before I could stop 'im."

"No matter," Reed wheezes again. "Y-you heard what he said, right?"

Easton nods.

"What did he say?" I demand, all the while trying not to vomit from the sight of Reed's blood pooling on the pavement.

Easton lifts his gaze from his brother and locks it with mine. "He said, 'Daniel Delacorte says hello.'"

Thirty-One

"HOW'S REED ROYAL?" I ask for the thousandth time.

The nurse brushes by as if she doesn't hear me. I want to yell, *I know you hear me, bitch,* but I don't think that would generate the response I need.

Easton sits across the room from me. He's volcano-hot and ready to explode. He wants to kill Daniel, and only the fear for Reed's life is keeping him glued to the chair.

That and the fact that the cops showed up faster than we'd expected. I'd begged Easton not to leave me, because fear was riding me hard. What if there was another knife out there with Easton's name on it?

I cannot *believe* that maniac paid someone to hurt Reed.

"The only reason I'm not making Daniel into an organ donor is because Reed would kill me the minute he got out of his hospital bed if he knew I left you alone."

I nibble on my thumbnail. "I don't know, Easton. Daniel's nuts. You could take him in a fight, but then what? He's doing shit that we wouldn't even dream of. Hiring someone to *stab* Reed? What if the knife hit something major? It's a miracle he's alive."

"Then we do something worse," Easton says, and he's serious.

"And then you and Reed get sent to prison for assault?"

He scoffs. "No one's going to prison for anything. This is between us."

"Can't you just tell the police what you heard?"

"The knifer is long gone." Easton shakes his head. "Plus, Reed would want to take care of it himself. Leave the cops out of it."

I open my mouth to object, but I don't have a good response. I didn't report Daniel for hurting me and now look at what happened. He's preying on other girls and hiring thugs to hurt the people I love.

Callum bursts through the doors, interrupting my thought process. "What do you know?" he asks us.

"Nothing. They won't tell us anything!" I wail.

"They aren't telling us shit, man," Easton agrees.

Callum gives us a brusque nod. "Stay here," he orders needlessly.

I've never been so happy to see Callum. Even if his own house is a mess, it's clear people listen to him. He leaves the waiting room to go shake down some higher-up and find out what the heck is happening to Reed.

He returns less than five minutes later. "Reed's in surgery. It looks good. They pulled him in there to see if anything vital was hit, but it was shallower than it appeared at first. The knife wound was neat and clean. There's some tissue and muscle damage but that should heal with time." He rakes a hand through his hair. "A clean knife wound. Listen to me, what am I even saying?" He levels a hard look at Easton. "I can't believe you would take Ella down to the wharf if it was this dangerous."

Easton pales. "It was never dangerous before. It was just a bunch of punks, like me, wanting to gamble and punch the shit out of each other. We knew everyone. Weapons are never allowed. This happened when we were leaving."

"This true, Ella?" Callum demands.

I nod frantically. "It's true. I never felt like I was in danger, and some of these kids were from Astor but also from other prep schools. I never saw any guns or anything."

"Then you're saying it was random?" It's clear from the disbelief on his face that Callum doesn't think this is random at all.

Easton rubs a hand across his mouth. "No, not saying that."

"Ella?"

"It was Daniel," I say in a small voice. "And it's my fault."

"How so? Did you hold the knife?"

I press my lips between my teeth to keep from crying. I don't want to break down right now, even though I feel like I'm on the edge of a real bad emotional breakdown.

"I didn't report Daniel. I should've but I didn't want to deal with the mess. My past isn't pretty and the testifying, the shit-talking at school . . . I already get enough of it." And I thought I was stronger, but apparently I'm not. I hang my head in shame.

"Oh, sweetheart." Callum comes to put his arm around me. "This isn't your fault. Even if you had reported Daniel, he would still be out. You don't go to jail just because someone fills out a police report. There's a whole trial process."

Unconvinced, I shrink away from his comfort.

Easton clears his throat. "Not your fault, Ella. I should've taught him a lesson."

Callum shakes his head. "I'm all for a fist in the face if it does good, but I don't see an end to this problem by beating the kid up. Hiring someone to stab my son is beyond the realm of an average bully. A few more inches to the left and . . ." His voice trails off, but my mind fills in the blanks.

A few more inches to the left and we'd be planning a funeral. And maybe Callum's right that Reed's stabbing would have happened even if I'd reported Daniel, but staying silent doesn't sit right with me anymore.

I can't drag Daniel down the front steps of the school and humiliate him into stopping. I tried that route once. And Reed already beat him up. Daniel's not going to stop by himself.

Someone has to stop him.

"What if I reported what happened?" I ask.

"About tonight?" Callum prompts.

Easton frowns, but I ignore him.

"No, the other night. When he drugged me. I mean, it's too late to get tests and stuff, but there were other people there in the room. Some guy named Hugh. Two girls from North. They know that Daniel drugged me."

Callum draws back so he can look at my face. There's a concerned expression on his. "I'm not going to lie to you, honey. These sort of things are really ugly for the victims, and your drugging happened a while ago. There's no way for us to take samples of your blood. If the other people don't—or won't—testify, it'll be your word against his."

I know this and it's why I never reported it in the first place. Reporting it is a big hassle that never seems to have any good results, particularly for the person who was hurt. But what's the alternative? Keep my mouth shut so that Daniel can continue to find victims?

"Maybe. But I'm not the only one he's hurt. Maybe if I come forward, other people will, too."

"All right. We'll stand behind you, of course." He says it matter-of-factly, as if there's no other path he could conceive of taking. Like my mom would do if she were alive. "We have resources. We'll hire a PR team and the best lawyers. They'll dig into Daniel's background until the Delacortes' ancestors' skeletons come popping out."

He's about to say something else, but the door to the waiting room opens and a doctor appears. There's no blood on his scrubs and he doesn't look sad.

I sigh with relief. I don't know why. I guess because if he had a lot of blood on him, it'd mean the surgery had been terrible and Reed's life would've been staining the cotton.

"Mr. Royal?" he says as he approaches. "I'm Dr. Singh. Your son is fine. The knife hit no major organs. It was largely superficial. He caught the blade in his hands and he has wounds on his palms, but those should heal within the next ten to fifteen days. He should avoid any vigorous activity."

Easton snorts beside me, and Callum throws him a glare. My cheeks turn a dark red.

"But if the Riders keep winning," the doctor adds, "he will be ready for State."

"You can't honestly be serious about the football thing!" I burst out.

This time everyone frowns at me. Dr. Singh removes his glasses and rubs them on his shirt. "Of course I'm serious. We wouldn't want one of our best defensive players out for the championship."

Dr. Singh looks at me like I'm the crazy person. I throw up my hands and stomp away as Callum and the doctor talk about the Riders' chances without Reed in the first playoff game.

"Easton, you aren't going to let your brother play again, right?" I hiss.

"Doc said it was fine. Besides, you think I have any control over what Reed does?"

"You're all insane. Reed should be at home, in bed!"

He rolls his eyes. "You heard what the doc said. Superficial wound. He'll be up and around in two weeks."

"I give up. This is completely ridiculous."

Callum comes over to us. "Ready to go home?"

"Can't I wait for Reed?" I object.

"No, he's in a private room, but there's no bed for you. Or you," he says to Easton. "Both of you are coming home with me tonight where I can keep an eye on you. Reed's sleeping and he doesn't need to be worried about the two of you."

"But . . ."

"No." Callum's not budging. "And you, Easton, are not going over to Delacorte's house to do anything."

"Fine," he says sullenly.

"I want to go to the police station and report Daniel," I announce. I need to do it tonight before I lose my nerve, and having Callum next to me would be the second-best thing to having Reed.

"We'll go there first," Callum agrees as he ushers us outside to the waiting town car. "It's all going to be fine. Durand."

Durand gives a terse nod and climbs into the driver's seat.

Once the car is moving, Callum dials a number on his phone and then lays it on his knee, face up, with the speaker on.

A groggy voice answers after the third ring. "Callum Royal? It's three in the morning!"

"Judge Delacorte. How are you?" he asks politely.

"Is something wrong? It's quite late." Daniel's father's voice is hushed, as if he's still in bed.

"I know that. I wanted to give you a courtesy call. I'm on my way to the police station with my ward and son. Your boy, Daniel, is—how do I put this—a fucking criminal asshole and we're going to see that he does some hard time."

Shocked silence greets us. Easton muffles a laugh with his hand.

"I don't know what you're talking about," Delacorte finally says.

"That's possible," Callum acknowledges. "Sometimes parents don't keep a close eye on their kids. I've been guilty of that myself. The good news is I have a team of excellent private investigators. As you know, given the government work we do, we need to be very careful about who we hire. My team is particularly good at ferreting out any secrets that could impact a person's ability to be honest. I'm sure that if there are no skeletons in Daniel's closet or . . ." He pauses for dramatic effect and it works, because the hairs on the back of my neck stand up and I'm not the one being threatened. ". . . yours, you have nothing to worry about. Have a good night, Your Honor."

"Wait, wait, don't hang up." There's a rustling. "Just a minute." A door closes and his voice is louder, more alert. "What do you propose?"

Callum remains silent.

Delacorte doesn't like that. Panicked, he pleads, "You must be agreeable to something or you wouldn't have called. Tell me what your demands are."

Still Callum doesn't answer.

The next time Delacorte speaks, he's nearly panting. "I'll have Daniel sent away. He's been invited to attend the Knightsbridge School for Gentlemen in London. I've encouraged him to go but he's been reluctant to leave his friends."

Oh great. So he's going to rape and stab kids in London? I

open my mouth, but Callum raises his hand and shakes his head no. I settle back in my seat and reach for patience.

"Try again," he says simply.

"What is it that you want?"

"I want Daniel to recognize that he's done wrong and correct that behavior in the future. I don't necessarily believe that incarceration brings about that change. In about five hours, two Naval officers will show up at your door. You will sign the waiver that allows them to take his seventeen-year-old person with them. Daniel will then attend a military academy designed to correct the behavior of troubled youths such as himself. If he passes, he will return to you. If he doesn't, we'll feed him into one of the jet combines at the plant." Callum laughs as he hangs up, but I honestly don't know if he's kidding or not.

I know my eyes are big as saucers, and I can't help but ask, "Um, are you really going to murder Daniel?"

"Damn, Dad, that was badass."

"Thank you, son." Callum smirks. "I still have my balls, no matter what you boys think. And, Ella, no, I'm not murdering Daniel. The military can save kids. It can also turn bad kids into worse ones. If my friends think he's not salvageable, then there are other options. None of which I'm discussing with either of you."

Okay, then.

When we get home, Easton gallops up the stairs to fill the twins in, while Callum disappears into his office to call Gideon and let him know what happened. I stand in the foyer, remembering the first night I stepped into this house. It was late, almost as late as tonight.

The boys were lined up against the upper railing of the split staircase, looking unhappy and unwelcoming. I was scared of them. But now? I'm scared *for* them.

Callum's changing. His actions tonight and of the past few weeks have been so much more involved than when I first came. But he's going to undo all that good if he marries Brooke. His sons will never fully trust him as long as he's with that awful woman. Why can't he see that?

If Callum was smart, he'd send Brooke away with Daniel to this special military place. But for some reason, he's so blind when it comes to Brooke.

I chew on the inside of my cheek. What if Callum knew the truth? If he knew about Reed and Brooke . . . would he still marry her?

There's only one way to find out . . .

If Reed were here, he wouldn't want me to follow Callum to his office, but I'm making an executive decision. I know he'll be furious when he discovers what I've done, but someone needs to get through to his father, and unfortunately, I think that someone has to be me.

I knock quietly. "Callum, it's Ella."

"Come in" is the gruff reply.

I walk into his study. It's very manly in here, with dark cherrywood paneling on the walls, burgundy leather seating, and forest-green drapes framing the windows.

Callum, of course, has a drink in his hand. I give him a pass. If there was ever a night for drinking, it would be tonight.

"Thank you for taking care of the Daniel thing," I say.

"I promised you when I brought you here that I would do anything for you. That includes keeping you safe from people like Delacorte. I should've had him sent away long ago."

"I really appreciate that." I wander along the rows of books. In the center of the bookcases is another big picture of Maria. "Maria was beautiful." I hesitate before adding, "The boys really miss her."

He swirls the liquid in his glass a few times before answering. "We haven't been the same since she left us."

I take a deep breath, knowing I'm about to overstep a whole lot of boundaries. "Callum . . . about Brooke . . ." I exhale in a rush. "It's the twenty-first century. You don't have to marry a girl because she's pregnant."

A sharp laugh escapes. "Yes, I do. You see . . ."

"I see what?" I'm so frustrated. I want to leap forward and knock that stupid glass out of his hand. "What aren't you telling me?"

He watches me over the brim.

"Dammit, Callum. Will you please talk to me?"

Nearly a minute passes before he heaves a massive, soul-sucking sigh. "Sit down, Ella."

My legs feel wobbly enough that I don't argue. I sink into the chair across from his and wait for him to shed any glimpse of insight about this awful compulsion he has for Brooke.

"Brooke appeared at the perfect time in my life," he admits. "I was mired in grief, and I used her body to forget. And then . . . it was simpler to keep using her." Regret is woven into his every word. "She didn't care that I slept around. She encouraged it, actually. We'd go out and she'd point to different women she thought I would enjoy. It required no emotional investment and I liked that. But at some point she wanted more than I could give. I'm never going to find another Maria. Brooke doesn't inspire anything in me but lust."

I stare at him in disbelief. "Then let her go. You can still be a dad to this kid." Hell, Brooke would sell the baby if the price was right.

Callum continues as if I'm not even there. "Maybe with Brooke as my wife, I can control her. I can bind her with contractual promises. She doesn't want to live in Bayview. She wants something bigger. A life in Paris, Milan, LA, somewhere she can rub elbows with actors, models, athletes. If I can get her away from my boys, it'll be worth it."

"You're not getting her away from your boys. You're shoving her even closer in their faces!" Why can't this man see reason?

"We'll be on the West Coast. Or abroad. The boys will be fine here on their own until they finish high school. I'll make every effort to keep her away from them. Especially Reed."

I frown. "What do you mean?"

His next words make my blood run cold. "The baby is most likely his, Ella."

I'm lucky to be sitting down. If I wasn't, I would have keeled right over.

I came in here to confess about Reed and Brooke, but Callum, the man I thought was oblivious, already knew that his son had slept with his girlfriend?

I must be revealing something on my face, because his blue eyes sharpen. "You knew," he says thoughtfully.

I give a shaky nod. It takes a moment to find my voice. "*You* knew?"

A humorless chuckle leaves his lips. "When Brooke came to me with the news she was pregnant, I said the same thing you just did. That she could have the baby and I would support her. That's when she told me she slept with Reed and that the baby could be his."

Nausea tickles my throat. "Wh-when did she say it happened? Her and Reed . . . ?"

Reed promised me that he hasn't touched Brooke since he kissed me, but he's never been specific about when they stopped sleeping together. And I haven't been brave or stupid enough to push for details.

Callum drains the rest of his glass and stands up to pour himself another. "Before you came, I assume. I know Reed. He wouldn't have laid a hand on you if he was still with Brooke."

My hand flies to my throat. "You know about us?"

"I'm not entirely blind, Ella, and you two aren't terribly careful. I thought . . . it might be good for both of you. Reed being with someone his own age and you having someone special in your life. I didn't know before you ran," he concedes. "But I figured it out after."

"Why didn't you figure out what Brooke was up to? Why didn't you protect your son from her?"

My accusatory tone brings a cloud of anger to his eyes. "I'm protecting him now! You think I want my boy to be tied to her for the rest of his life? Better that I raise this baby as my own and let Reed live the life he deserves."

"There's no way it's his, Callum. The last time he was with her was six months ago, and she's *not* six months pregnant."

Unless Reed lied to me about what happened in his bedroom last month . . .

But no. *No.* I refuse to believe it. I gave him another chance because I trust him. If he says he didn't touch her that night, then he didn't touch her.

Callum looks at me as if I'm a child, a foolish, stupid child. "It has to be his, Ella."

"How do you know it's not yours?" I challenge.

He smiles sadly. "I had a vasectomy fifteen years ago."

I swallow hard. "Oh."

"Maria desperately wanted a girl," Callum confesses. "We kept trying, but after she had the twins, her doctor told her no more. That another pregnancy might kill her. She refused to accept it, so . . . I got a vasectomy and never told her about it." He shakes his head in misery. "I can't be the father of Brooke's baby, but I can take responsibility for the child. If Reed is dragged into this, there'll be a bond between him and Brooke forever, a bond of guilt and grief and responsibility. I won't let that happen. My son might hate me enough to make a play for my girlfriend, but I love him enough to spare him a life of misery."

"How far along is she?" I ask.

"Three and a half months."

I curl my fists in frustration, wanting somehow to get it through Callum's brain that the assumptions he's made are wrong. "I believe Reed when he says he hasn't touched her in six months."

Callum just stares at me.

"I believe him," I insist. "And I wish you would, too. Just because you wouldn't cheat on Maria, and Reed wouldn't cheat on me, doesn't mean that Brooke's the same way."

"Brooke wants to be a Royal too badly to take that chance. I caught her sabotaging her birth control once."

I rub my face in my hands, because he's clearly made up his mind. "You can believe what you want, but you're wrong." I rise from my chair, shoulders slumped in defeat. At the door, I stop and give one last try. "Reed wants you to get a paternity test. He'd force it on Brooke if he could."

Callum looks startled. "He'd take the test and risk being officially named the father?"

"No, he'd take the test so the truth could come out." I meet his eyes. "She's lying to you. It's not Reed's kid, and if you trust your son even the slightest bit, you would force Brooke's hand and make this whole stupid mess go away."

I start to leave, but Callum holds up his hand. "Wait."

Frowning, I watch as he reaches for the handset and dials a number. Whoever he calls picks up right away.

"Dottie," he booms into the mouthpiece. "When you get in the office this morning, make an appointment for Ms. Davidson at the Bayview OBGYN for Friday, nine a.m. sharp. And send a car for her."

A smile spreads across my face. Maybe I did get through to him.

Callum hangs up and fixes me with a worried look. Then he sighs and says, "I hope to hell you're right about this, Ella."

Thirty-Two

REED

ELLA HAS REFUSED to leave my side since I got back from the hospital. Which is completely unnecessary. The painkillers are doing their job for the most part. As long as I don't move, the worst discomfort is that the row of stitches kind of itches. The doctors told me not to scratch them, or risk tearing them open, so I'm trying to distract myself by watching Sawyer and Sebastian toss Lauren around in the pool like she's a beach ball.

It's not really a nice enough evening for swimming, but our pool's heated and Lauren's got the twins to keep her warm, too. Ella and I are curled up together on a lounger, while Easton is texting on his phone in the chair next to us

"Wade wants to know if you're gonna have a cool scar," East says absently.

Ella grumbles loudly. "Tell Wade to stop thinking about stupid shit and just be grateful that his best friend is alive."

I snicker.

"I'm quoting you on that, sis." East types something, waits, then starts to laugh. "Wade wants to know if you yell at Reed like that when you're boning."

"Is there a middle finger emoji?" she asks sweetly. "If so, send him that."

I stroke my fingers through her soft hair, enjoying the feel of her body tucked at my side. She'll never know how fucking terrified I was last night—not for my own safety, but for hers. When that hooded guy popped out of the shadows, my first and only thought had been to protect my girl. I don't even remember the knife slicing into my gut. I just remember pushing Ella to the side and heaving myself in front of her.

Christ. What if Daniel had sent someone after her instead of me? What if she'd gotten seriously hurt?

"Reed?" she murmurs in concern.

"Mmmm?"

"You got really tense all of a sudden. Are you okay?" She sits up instantly. "Do you need another painkiller?"

"I'm fine. I was just thinking about Delacorte and what a psycho he is."

"Truth," East says darkly. "I hope he gets the shit kicked out of him in that military prison."

Ella sighs. "It's not a prison. It's an academy for troubled youths."

"Troubled youth?" East snorts. "That asshole is more than troubled. He put a *hit* out on my brother."

"You really think Hoodie Guy was trying to kill Reed? What if he comes back and tries again?" She sounds seriously upset now, and I flash Easton a hard look.

"Nobody was trying to kill me," I assure her. "Otherwise he would've just gone for my neck and slashed."

A shudder goes through Ella's body. "Oh my God, Reed! Why would you even say that?"

"Sorry. That was stupid." I pull her toward me again. "Let's not talk about this anymore. Daniel's gone. And he gave the cops Hoodie Guy's name, so they'll track him down in no time, okay?"

"Okay," she echoes, but she doesn't sound convinced.

A high-pitched shriek from the pool has us turning our heads toward the shallow end, where Seb is attempting to undo the strings of Lauren's bikini.

"Sebastian Royal! Don't you dare!" But she's sputtering with laughter as she tries to swim away from my little brother.

Sawyer swims up behind her and hauls her into his arms, and the Lauren beach-ball toss starts up again.

East leans over his chair and lowers his voice. "How do you think it works?"

Ella narrows her eyes. "What do you mean?"

"Lauren and the twins. Think it's a two-on-one sorta thing, or one at a time?"

"I honestly don't want to know," Ella says frankly.

Neither do I. I've never questioned Seb and Sawyer about their relationships. Lauren is Sawyer's girlfriend in the eyes of the outside world, but I have no clue what goes on behind closed doors.

Footsteps sound behind us, and I tense up again when my father appears on the deck. "Reed. How are you doing?"

"All good," I answer without looking at him.

An uncomfortable silence settles over the deck. I haven't been able to look my dad in the eye since Ella told me that she'd talked to him. She was shamefaced and nervous when she came to the hospital this morning, and the confession poured out of her while I sat there fighting equal doses of guilt and amazement.

My dad knows about Brooke. And me. According to Ella,

he's known for weeks—and he didn't say a word to me about it. I guess that's the Royal way, though. Avoid the tough shit. Don't talk about your feelings. And a part of me is grateful for that. I don't know how I'll react if Dad brings it up to me. He hasn't yet, but Ella told me about the paternity test he scheduled, so sooner or later he'll have to say something, right?

That's going to be one awkward conversation. I'm happy to postpone it for as long as possible.

Dad clears his throat. "You kids finishing up soon?" He glances at the pool and then the loungers. "I thought we'd all go out to dinner. The jet's all fueled up and ready when we are."

"The jet?" In the shallow end, Lauren's eyes grow larger than saucers. "Where are we going?"

Callum smiles at her. "D.C. I thought it'd be a nice treat for everyone." He turns to Ella. "Have you ever been to D.C.?"

She shakes her head. And from the pool, I hear Lauren hiss to the twins, "Who flies to another state for *dinner*?"

"The Royals," Sawyer murmurs back.

"I don't think I'm up for that," I admit. My tone is grudging because I hate revealing weakness, but the painkillers are wearing off. The thought of getting up and flying somewhere doesn't appeal to me at all. "You guys can go ahead, though. I'm cool staying behind."

"I'm staying behind, too," Ella says immediately.

I touch her knee, and I don't miss the way Dad's gaze tracks the movement of my hand. "No, go with them," I say gruffly. "You've been glued to my side since seven in the morning. You need a change of scenery."

She doesn't look happy. "I'm not leaving you alone."

"Ah, he'll be fine," East says. He's already hopping off his chair, which doesn't surprise me. I've noticed him getting stir-crazy all day. Easton's not cut out for sitting around and doing nothing.

"Go," I urge Ella. "You'll love D.C., trust me."

"Come on, little sis, we'll get to see the Washington Monument from the air," Easton says coaxingly. "It looks like a huge dick."

"Easton," Callum chides.

Eventually we manage to wear her down, and everyone scatters to get changed for dinner. I move from the lounger to the couch in the game room, which is where Ella finds me twenty minutes later.

"Are you sure you'll be okay here by yourself?" She bites her lip in dismay.

I hold up the remote. "I'm fine, babe. Just gonna watch a game and then take a nap or something."

She comes over and gives me a soft kiss on the lips. "Promise to call me if you need anything? I'll force Callum to fly us right back."

"I promise," I answer, mostly just to humor her.

After another kiss, she leaves. I hear footsteps and voices in the foyer, and then the noise dies off and the house becomes as quiet as a tomb.

I stretch out on the couch and focus on the screen, watching as Carolina scores touchdown after touchdown on the inept New Orleans defense. As much as I like seeing my team winning, it's just a reminder that I'm going to miss at least two playoff games with the Riders, and that bums me out.

Sighing, I turn the TV off and decide to take a nap, but my phone rings before I can close my eyes.

It's Brooke.

Shit.

Since I know she'll send a barrage of text messages if I don't pick up, I press the talk button and mutter, "What do you want?"

"I just got back from Paris. Can we talk?"

She sounds oddly subdued, which instantly raises my guard. "I thought you weren't back 'til next week."

"I'm home early. So sue me."

Yeah, she's definitely rattled. I sit up gingerly. "I'm not interested in hearing anything you have to say. So go bother someone else."

"Wait! Don't hang up." A shaky breath echoes over the line. "I'm ready to deal."

My shoulders stiffen. "What the hell does that mean?"

"Just come over so we can talk," Brooke begs. "You and me, Reed. Don't bring Ella or one of your brothers."

I chuckle. "If this is your way of trying to seduce me—"

"I don't want to seduce you, you little asshole!" She takes another breath, like she's trying to calm herself. "I want to make a deal. So unless you've changed your mind about wanting me gone, I suggest you get your ass over here."

My distrust only grows. She's obviously up to something, playing another game I have no interest in playing.

But . . . if there's the slightest chance she's being real right now, can I really ignore this?

I hesitate for several seconds before answering. "I'll be there in twenty."

Thirty-Three

ELLA

DINNER IN D.C. is fun, but I'm happy and relieved when the plane touches down on the private airstrip. I missed Reed, and I don't like knowing that he's been alone and in pain all night.

"Want to watch a movie with me and Reed?" I ask Easton as we climb out of the back of the town car.

He looks like he's on the verge of agreeing when his phone buzzes. One glance at the screen and he's shaking his head. "Wade's inviting me over. He's got a friend who needs an audience."

Callum walks faster to avoid hearing his son's plans. Me? I've got no choice.

"Be careful," I tell Easton. Rising on my tiptoes, I give him a kiss on the cheek.

He ruffles my hair in return. "Always. I always wrap it up." He yells after his dad, "Just like I was taught."

I can't tell in the dim light, but I think Callum flips him off without turning around.

"You be safe, too," Easton teases. "Never know if Reed's gonna try to trap you with a baby." I grimace and he winces. "Sorry, stupid mouth."

"No, it's fine. Besides, she's going to take that paternity test, so we'll know who the father of the demon spawn is in a few days, right? Or a week."

Easton hesitates. "You sure it's not Reed's?"

"He swears it isn't his."

"So it's my dad's?"

It's my turn to hesitate. I wish I wasn't keeping these secrets. I don't know why Callum doesn't tell his sons about the vasectomy. "No, I don't think it's his, either."

Easton exhales in a rush. "Good. We only have room for one more Royal in the house and you're it." Then he gives me a sweet kiss on the forehead and sprints for his truck.

Inside, the twins have taken themselves to parts unknown. Callum's light is on in his office. The upstairs hallway leading to my bedroom—and Reed's—is lit softly, and the quiet walk up the stairs is eerily similar to the night I found Brooke and Reed together. At the top, I stare down the long hall and my heart pounds a little faster.

I remind myself that things weren't what I thought they were last time and that there's no reason for anyone to be in Reed's room but him. Still, my heart's beating fast and my palms are damp with sweat when I arrive at his door.

"Reed?" I call out.

"In the bathroom," comes his muffled response.

I breathe a sigh of relief and twist the knob. The room is empty, but light spills out of the half-open door to his private bath. I stick my head in, gasping when I spot him.

His bandage is off and there are bloody gauze pads on the sink. "Oh my God! What happened?"

"I pulled a couple stitches. Just changing the bandage." He

tosses the pink-stained dressing into the wastebasket and slaps the fresh white bandage onto his side. "Help me tape it up?"

I'm beside him in a heartbeat, a frown on my face as I pick up the roll of medical tape off the vanity. "How did this happen? Were you moving around a lot?"

"Not really."

I spear him with narrowed eyes. That wasn't a denial; it was an evasion. "Liar."

"I moved a bit," he concedes. "It's no big deal."

His blue eyes are hooded and dark. Was he downstairs working the bag? Still beating himself up over Brooke? As I rip a piece of tape, I peek at his knuckles, but they don't look bruised.

"I knew I should have stayed behind," I grumble. "You needed me. What were you doing while I was gone? Lifting weights?"

Instead of answering, he leans down and kisses me, hard and brief. Pulling away, he says, "I swear it was nothing. I was reaching for something, felt my stitches pull, and here I am."

I purse my lips. "You're not telling me something. I thought we had a no-secrets rule."

"Let's not fight, baby." He grabs my wrist and tugs me out of the bathroom and over to the bed. "It was seriously nothing. I took another painkiller and now I'm feeling nice and loopy."

He gives me a lopsided grin that doesn't quite reach his eyes. But at least he's looking at me. I search his gaze for answers and notice a tightness around his mouth that I attribute to pain. Whatever happened tonight can wait until morning. He needs to get to bed.

"I don't like seeing you hurting," I admit as we get comfortable on his bed.

"I know, but I promise you it doesn't hurt that bad."

"You were supposed to rest." I slap the tape on his skin, almost not caring when he winces. "See, you're in pain."

"No shit, babe. I was stabbed, remember?" He captures my hands and pulls me tight against him.

His chest rises and falls in a steady rhythm. It could all be taken away from me—the cars, the planes, the dinners in really fancy restaurants—but I can't bear losing Reed. Anxiety churns in my stomach as the true reason that I'm so upset bubbles to the surface.

"It's my fault you got stabbed."

His lips turn down. "No, it's not. Don't even say that."

"It's true. Daniel wouldn't have come after you if it wasn't for me." Absently, I stroke the hard planes of his pectorals, down the shallow valley between his ribs, grateful the damage wasn't worse.

"Bullshit. I'm the one who beat the crap out of him and then told his date she was having dinner with a rapist. His beef was with me."

"I guess." I don't believe it, but I know I'm not going to win this argument. "I'm just glad he's gone."

"Dad took care of him. Don't worry about it." Reed rubs his hands up and down my back. "How was dinner?"

"Good. Very fancy. The menu was full of things I couldn't pronounce." Foie gras. Langoustine. Nori.

He grins. "What'd you order?"

"Lobster. It was tasty." So was the langoustine, which I learned was a smaller lobster. I skipped the foie gras (duck liver) and nori (seaweed) because they both sounded icky when explained to me.

"I'm glad you had a good time." His hands slow down,

his comforting caresses turning into something more . . . arousing.

I try to shift away, embarrassed at how easily he turns me on. I can't take advantage of him in this state. Not when he's injured.

"I missed you," I confess.

He gives me another quick peck. "Missed you, too."

"Next time, you're coming with. Obviously you can't be trusted by yourself."

He inhales deeply and then gathers me close. "Done. Next time Dad jets off somewhere, we'll go together."

"You know that sounds crazy, right?"

"Which part?"

"The jetting part." I drop a kiss on his shoulder. "The togetherness is good."

"How good?"

The only light in the room is from the partially open bathroom door. It casts interesting shadows on Reed's body. I run my nose along the column of his throat, smelling soap and shampoo. "The best."

"Baby . . ." He clears his throat. "You gotta stop doing that."

"Doing what?"

He peers down at me and I stare back, bewildered.

"Touching my chest. *Sniffing* me," he says hoarsely. "You're making me think bad thoughts."

The corners of my mouth tip up. "Bad thoughts?"

"Dirty thoughts," he amends.

My smile widens. Whether he's saying it because it's true or because he wants to distract me or both, it works. I bend down, allowing my hair to form a curtain around our faces, and press my lips to his. He glides his tongue along my lower lip, asking for silent permission to enter. I part my lips and he takes full advantage by deepening the kiss.

"We shouldn't do this," I murmur against his mouth. "You're hurt."

He pulls back with a grin. "Then make me feel better."

"Is that a challenge?"

He's laughing when I bring my lips back to his. This time it's my tongue torturing *him*, devouring his mouth until he forgets how to breathe. And my hand is in motion again, skimming down his chest toward his waistband. I slip under his boxers to find the evidence of how much better he's feeling—hot and hard and thick.

When he arches off the bed with a groan, I immediately glance up. "Are you okay?"

He growls. "Don't you dare stop."

"What part of you hurts?" I ask coyly. I love seeing Reed like this—total putty in my hands.

"Every part. Seriously, I'm wounded all over. Particularly here." He pats his crotch. "I need you to kiss it and make it better."

"You want me to kiss *that*?" I say in mock outrage.

"Oh yeah. I want you to give me a full-on, open-mouthed, lots-of-tongue kiss right *there* . . . unless you don't want to." Uncertainty colors his last words.

I hide a grin and scoot lower until I'm kneeling between his legs.

His eager hands push down his shorts until he's fully exposed. He wraps one hand around himself and looks at me with an expectant and hopeful expression.

"You poor baby," I murmur, tracing a fingertip over the back of his hand.

I duck my head and he immediately reaches down to sweep my hair away from my face. The moment my mouth closes around him, he hisses in pleasure.

"Oh shit, yes." His tone is agonized, and whatever pain he's in now, I'm causing. It's a delicious, powerful feeling. His trembling hands find their way into my hair again.

"Baby . . . Ella . . ." he chokes out, and then he doesn't have any words, only noises. Husky groans, ragged sighs, and mangled pleas. He tugs on my hair hard enough that I let him go to look up into his face, which is now loopy from lust . . . and maybe even love.

I lower myself again, taking as much of him as possible. He's big and heavy, but the weight of him on my tongue and against my lips is more of a turn-on than I ever thought was possible. Beneath me, I can feel his desperation and desire. A heady sense of power washes over me. If I stopped now, I could probably get Reed to promise me anything.

But I don't want anything. I just want him. And knowing how much he wants me in return makes me crazy hot. Using my hands and tongue and lips, I drag him to the brink.

"Stop . . . I'm gonna come," he groans and weakly tugs at my hair.

My lips curve around him. I want him to. I want him to lose control. I redouble my efforts, sucking and licking until his big frame tenses and then he explodes.

When his body finally relaxes, he pulls me upward to rest at his side.

"Reed?" I whisper.

"Yeah?" His voice sounds like gravel.

"I, ah, love you."

"I . . . love you, too." He buries his face in my neck. "You have no idea how much. I . . ." He swears softly. "You know I'd do anything for you, right? Absolutely anything to keep you safe."

Warmth unfurls in my belly. "Would you?"

"Anything," he repeats roughly, and then he kisses me until we're both breathless again.

Thirty-Four

MY PHONE SCREEN says it's two in the morning. There's no alarm going off, at least not in Reed's room, but there's an incessant dinging sound in the house somewhere. I glance over to see if Reed's awake, but he's sprawled over two-thirds of the mattress, dead to the world.

I shove the pillow over my head and close my eyes again, but the ringing doesn't stop. Not only that, but now there are footsteps running down the hallway, followed by loud banging on a door.

Reed sits up, his dark hair mussed and his expression groggy. "What the hell . . ."

An angry voice can be heard from the foyer. "Just a damn minute." It sounds like Callum, but it's hard to make out what he's saying. "I told you I'd get him."

Oh, crap. Reed and I jump out of bed. It's one thing for Callum to know about us, but he wouldn't be thrilled to find us sleeping in the same bed. My jeans are halfway up my legs and Reed's tugging on his shirt, when the noise stops outside my door.

We both freeze at Callum's incensed shout. "That's my

seventeen-year-old ward's door and you're not going in until she's decent!"

You're not going in?

"Who's out there?" I whisper to Reed.

He gives me a wide-eyed look of confusion.

"Ella," Callum barks from the hall, "we have company. I need you to get dressed and come downstairs as soon as possible."

I clear my throat. "Yeah, okay. I'll be right down." I cringe as I realize my voice is coming from Reed's room and that Callum has known I was here from the beginning. This is not his ward's room. It's his son's room.

Callum hesitates and then says, "Wake up Reed and bring him with you."

Awkward. I hastily pull my jeans up and grab a sweatshirt from Reed's dresser. He's taking his sweet time.

"Babe, it's going to be fine. You've still got your V-card. I'll tell Dad that."

I fly over and slap my hand over his mouth. "Oh my God. You will not. We're not talking about this with Callum. Ever."

Reed rolls his eyes as he moves my hand off his face. "Don't worry about it. All he's gonna do is yell at us."

"Why's he waking us up in the middle of the night to do it?" I ask.

"It's more dramatic that way. He gets to make a big point about how we need to be careful, and shit like that." He winces when I drag him toward the door.

I instantly drop his hand. "Does your side hurt?"

He winds his arm slowly, testing the wound. "Just sore. I'll be good to go in a few days, don't you worry."

Now it's my turn to give him a disgusted look. "I wasn't even thinking about that. You did do something while we were at dinner, didn't you?"

He gives a small shrug. "Nothing important. I told you, I pulled a couple of stitches, but it's no big deal."

Callum greets the two of us at the landing that bisects his wing from ours before the stairs descend to the main floor. He has a pair of trousers on and a white dress shirt that's misbuttoned.

"Dad," Reed says warily. "What's up?"

His father's wild eyes dart between us. "Where were you tonight?" An unsteady breath flies out. "No, don't tell me. The less I know right now, the better."

Reed takes a step forward. "What the fuck is going on?"

Callum rakes both hands through his hair. "The police are here. They want to talk to you about your whereabouts tonight. Don't say anything until Grier gets here."

I recognize Grier as one of the names lettered on the door in gold at the lawyer's office where Steve's will was read.

"Is it about Daniel? Did they catch the hoodie guy?" I blurt out.

Silence. The longest silence imaginable, leaving me plenty of time to conjure up the scariest, most gruesome scenarios. But none of them come close to triggering the panic I hear when Callum finally answers.

"Brooke is dead—"

What?

"—and Reed is a person of interest in her murder," he grinds out. His eyes are locked on Reed's face, which has gone completely pale.

Oh my God.

Instinctively, my gaze drops to Reed's side, where his bandage is probably turning bloody as we speak. Then I look back at Callum, my mouth opening and closing and opening and closing.

How did this happen?

I moved a bit . . . It's no big deal.

The moment the thought surfaces, I want to slap myself for even thinking it. No. No way. No matter how much he hated her, Reed would never . . . he would never . . .

Would he?

You know I'd do anything for you . . . Absolutely anything to keep you safe.

"Mr. Royal," a voice calls from the bottom of the stairs. A tired man in a rumpled suit places a hand on the banister and a foot on the first step. "The warrant's been signed. Your son will have to come with us."

"Who signed that bullshit?" Callum demands as he charges down the stairs.

The man holds a piece of paper up. "Judge Delacorte."

As Callum snatches the paper out of his hand, the man charges up the stairs followed by two police officers I hadn't noticed before. One of them grabs a silent Reed and turns him around, pushing him up against the banister.

"There's no need for that." Callum sprints back up the stairs. "He'll go with you willingly."

"Sorry, Mr. Royal. Standard procedure," the man explains, but he looks awfully smug about this.

"Do not say one word," Callum instructs his son. "Not one."

Reed's eyes burn as he stares at me.

I love you.

I love you, too.

I'll do anything.

We need to find a way to get rid of her.

I want to erase Brooke from our lives.

I love you.

"I love you," I whisper as the officer drags him away.

A fierce look passes over his face, but he doesn't say a word—and I don't know if that's because he's afraid to say anything or because he's following his dad's orders.

My entire body starts shaking. Callum slides an arm around me. "Go upstairs, get some shoes on, and I'll take you to the police station."

"The boys," I say weakly. "We should get the rest of them." I can see he's on the verge of saying no, but it's the wrong call. "We need to show Reed we support him as a family. They'd want to come."

Callum finally nods. "Get them."

I turn and run down the hall, knocking on Easton's door and then the twins'. "Wake up, you guys!" I yell. "Wake up."

The doorbell rings again. I race back, thinking for some reason that it's Reed and he's going to tell me this is all a tasteless joke. A stupid surprise. An early April Fool's Day gag.

Callum reaches the door first, flinging it open in a fast blur. He marches forward, only to freeze a second later. He stops so abruptly that I slam into his suddenly stiff back.

"Oh sweet Jesus," he breathes.

I have no idea why he stopped. I can't see past his broad shoulders.

While Callum stands there like a statue, I peer around his large frame and blink in alarm.

There's a man standing at the bottom of the limestone steps. Oily blond hair hangs down to his shoulders. A full beard devours almost his entire face. His khakis and polo shirt seem to hang off his lean body, as if they're two sizes too big.

He looks oddly familiar, but I'm pretty sure I've never seen him before in my life.

I meet his eyes. They're light blue, framed by dark blond eyelashes.

My heart speeds up, because now I'm second-guessing myself. I think I *do* know him. I think he's—

"*Steve?*" Callum exclaims.

Acknowledgments

As always, we could not have written, completed, or survived this project without the help of some pretty awesome people.

Early readers Margo, Jessica Clare, Meljean Brook, Natasha Leskiw, and Michelle Kannan, who gave us valuable insight, encouraged us to not hold back, and read the book twice!

Cindy Hwang, editor extraordinaire, who gave this series new life.

Angela Kim, associate editor, who is making sure our Ts are crossed and our Is are dotted.

Kimberly Bower, the perfect agent.

Meljean Brook, for the amazing cover concept.

Nic and Tash, for all their work behind the scenes.

Authors friends Jo, Kylie, Meghan, Rachel, Sam, Vi, and more for their support and enthusiasm for the Royals.

All the bloggers and reviewers, who continue to support this series and spread the word.

Finally, we were totally blown away by the readers who fell in love with *Paper Princess* and shouted it out to the world.

The fan art has been incredible. Readers have compiled playlists and taken the time to write and post reviews. Members of The Royal Palace on Facebook keep us entertained on a daily basis. You guys give this series life, and we cannot thank you enough!

Exclusive Bonus

PLAYLISTS OR PODCASTS?

Ella: Playlists 100 percent.

Reed: Playlists, but Easton does not get a choice in the matter.

Ella: Poor Easton, not even here to defend himself.

BEACH OR POOL?

Ella: Beach.

Reed: Pool. Wait, beach? You never swim at the beach.

Ella: That's not a beach. That's a rock formation with a sprinkle of sand. Besides, there are things in the ocean that could eat you.

Reed: There are things in the pool that could eat—

Ella: Reed!

DRIVER OR PASSENGER?

Ella: Driver.

Reed: I'm always driving. How can you choose driver?

Ella: Just wanted to see the look on your face.

DINE IN OR DINE OUT?

Reed: Dine in because—

Ella: I swear to God, if you make this dirty again—

Reed: Dine in because I like your cooking.

Ella: Oh, well, that's sweet.

RAIN OR SNOW?

Ella: Rain, but snow is beautiful in the winter. Reed is going to say snow.

Reed: Snow because a white Christmas is romantic.

SINGING OR DANCING?

Reed: Neither. Wait, for Ella, it's definitely dancing.

Ella: Dancing.

BIG OR SMALL?

Reed: I'll let Ella field that one . . .

Ella: Now you're making me blush.

Ella: . . . Big.

TATTOO OR PIERCINGS?

Ella: Tattoos. I think tattoos are so hot.

Reed: Tattoos. Ella thinks they're hot.

PUBLIC OR PRIVATE?

Reed: Both.

Ella: You can't say both! It's this or that!

Reed: Fine. Private. So I can have my way with you. What's yours?

Ella: Private. So I can have my way with *you*.

SUGAR OR SPICE?

Ella: Sugar. Because I'm sweet as pie.

Reed: Ha! It's sweet you think that. Spice, hands down.

BOOK OR MOVIE?

Reed: Is the movie X-rated?

Ella: Book. I've seen the kind of movies Reed likes to watch.

WET OR DRY?

Ella: I take the fifth.

Reed: Is this really a question?

Keep reading for an excerpt of

Twisted Palace

The next book in the Royals series
by Erin Watt

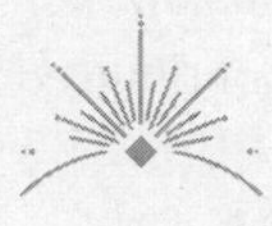

One

REED

"WHERE WERE YOU between eight p.m. and eleven p.m. tonight?"

"How long were you sleeping with your father's girlfriend?"

"Why did you kill her, Reed? Did she make you mad? Threaten to out the affair to your dad?"

I've watched enough cop shows to know that you keep your mouth shut when you're in a police interrogation room. Either that, or you just utter the four magic words—*I want my lawyer.*

Which is exactly what I've been doing for the past hour.

If I were a minor, these assholes wouldn't dream of questioning me without a parent or an attorney present. But I'm eighteen, so I guess they think I'm fair game. Or maybe that I'm stupid enough to answer their leading questions without my lawyer.

Detectives Cousins and Schmidt don't seem to care about my last name. For some reason, I find that kind of refreshing. I've gotten a free pass my entire life because I'm a Royal. If I get in trouble at school, Dad writes a check and my sins are forgotten. For as long as I can remember, girls have lined up to hop into bed with me so they can tell all their friends they bagged a Royal.

Not that I want girls lining up for me. There's only one girl I care about these days—Ella Harper. And it absolutely kills me that she had to watch me get dragged out of the house in handcuffs.

Brooke Davidson is dead.

I still can't wrap my head around it. My father's platinum-blond, gold-digging girlfriend was very much alive when I left the penthouse earlier.

But I'm not telling these detectives that. I'm not an idiot. They'll twist everything I say.

Frustrated with my silence, Cousins slams both his hands on the metal table between us.

"Answer me, you little shit!"

Under the table, my fists start to curl. I force my fingers to relax. This is the last place I should lose my temper.

His partner, a quiet woman named Teresa Schmidt, shoots him a warning look. "Reed," she says in a soft voice, "we can't help you unless you cooperate. And we want to help you here."

I arch a brow. Really? Good cop/bad cop? I guess they've watched the same TV shows that I have.

"Guys," I say carelessly, "I'm starting to wonder if you have hearing issues or something." Smirking, I cross my arms over my chest. "I've already asked for my lawyer, which means you're supposed to wait until he arrives to ask questions."

"We can ask you questions," Schmidt says, "and you can answer them. There's no law against that. You can also volunteer information. For instance, we can move this process along if you explain things like why you have blood on your shirt."

I resist the urge to clamp a hand against my side. "I'll wait until Halston Grier gets here, but thanks for your input."

Silence falls over the small room.

Cousins is visibly grinding his molars. Schmidt just sighs. Then both detectives scrape back their chairs and leave the room without another word.

Royal—1

Police—0

Except, even though they've clearly given up on me, they still take their sweet-ass time granting my request. For the next hour, I sit alone in the room, wondering how the hell my life got to this point. I'm not a saint and have never claimed to be one. I've gotten into my share of fights. I'm ruthless when I need to be.

But . . . I'm not this guy. The guy who gets dragged out of his own house in handcuffs. The guy who has to watch fear fill his girlfriend's eyes as he's hauled into the back of a police cruiser.

By the time the door swings open again, claustrophobia has set in, spurring me to be ruder than I should.

"Took you long enough," I snap at my father's lawyer.

The fifty-something gray-haired man is dressed in a suit, despite the late hour. He gives me a rueful smile. "Well. Looks like somebody is in high spirits."

"Where's Dad?" I demand, peering past Grier's shoulder.

"He's in the waiting room. He can't be in here."

"Why not?"

Grier shuts the door and walks over to the table. He sets his briefcase on it and unbuckles the gold snaps. "Because there are no restrictions against parents testifying against their children. Testimonial privilege extends only to spouses."

For the first time since I was arrested, I feel queasy. Testifying? This isn't going to go to *court*, is it? How far are these cops planning on taking this bullshit?

"Reed, take a breath."

My stomach twists. Dammit. I hate that I revealed even a trace of helplessness in front of this man. I don't show weakness. Ever. The only person I've ever been able to lower my guard around is Ella. That girl has the power to smash through my barriers and actually *see* me. The real me, and not the cold, callous ass that the rest of the world sees.

Grier pulls out a yellow legal pad and a gold fountain pen. He settles in the chair across from mine.

"I'm going to make this go away," he promises. "But first I need to know what we're dealing with here. From what I've managed to squeeze out of the officers in charge of the investigation, there's security footage of you entering the O'Halloran penthouse at eight forty-five tonight. That same footage shows you leaving about twenty minutes later."

My gaze darts around the room, searching for cameras or recording equipment. There's no mirror in here, so I don't think there's anyone watching us from some shadowy second room. Or at least I hope not.

"Everything we say in here is between us," Grier assures me when he notices my wary expression. "They can't record us. Lawyer-client privilege and all that."

I release a slow breath. "Yeah. I was at the penthouse earlier. But I didn't fucking kill her."

Grier nods. "All right." He jots something down on his notepad. "Let's go back even earlier. I want you to start from the beginning. Tell me about you and Brooke Davidson. No detail is too small. I need to know everything."

I swallow a sigh. Awesome. *This* is going to be fun.

Two

ELLA

THE ROYAL BOYS have rooms in the south wing, whereas their dad's suite is on the other side of the mansion, so I hook a right at the top of the stairs and hurry across the gleaming hardwood toward Easton's door. He doesn't answer at my soft knock. I swear, that boy could sleep through a hurricane. I knock a bit louder. When I hear nothing, I push the door open to find Easton sprawled face down on the bed.

I march over and shake his shoulder. He moans something.

I shake him again, panic bubbling in my throat. How is he still sound asleep? How had he slept through all the commotion that just happened downstairs?

"Easton!" I burst out. "Wake up!"

"What is it?" he grumbles, one eyelid slitting open. "Shit, is it time to go to practice?"

He rolls all the way over, pulling the blankets with him and revealing a lot more skin than I need to see. On the floor I find a pair of discarded sweatpants and toss them on the bed. They land on his head.

"Get up," I beg.

"Why?"

"Because the sky is falling!"

He blinks groggily. "Huh?"

"Shit's bad!" I yell, then force myself to take a deep breath, trying to calm down. It doesn't work. "Just meet me in Reed's room, okay?" I snap.

He must hear the uncontrollable anxiety in my voice, because he tumbles out of bed without delay. I see another flash of bare skin before I duck out the door.

Rather than go to Reed's room, I sprint across the wide hallway toward my own bedroom. This house is ridiculously large, ridiculously beautiful, but everyone inside of it is so messed up. Including me.

I guess I really am a Royal.

But no, I'm really not. The man downstairs is a glaring reminder of that. Steve O'Halloran. My not-so-dead father.

A wave of emotion sweeps over me, threatening to buckle my knees and send me into a bout of hysterics. I feel terrible about just leaving him down there. I didn't even introduce myself before spinning on my heel and running upstairs. Granted, Callum Royal did the same thing. He was so racked with concern for Reed that he simply blurted out, "I can't deal with this right now. Steve, wait here for me." Despite my guilt, I push Steve into a tiny box in the back of my mind and slap a steel lid on top. I can't think about him right now. My focus needs to be on Reed.

In my room, I waste no time sliding my backpack out from under my huge bed. I always keep it in a place where I can easily access it. I unzip the pack and sigh in relief when I see the leather wallet that holds the monthly cash payments I've been getting from Callum.

When I first moved here, Callum promised to pay me ten

thousand dollars a month as long as I didn't try to run. As much as I hated the Royal mansion at the beginning, it wasn't long before I grew to love it. These days, I can't imagine living anywhere else—I'd stay even if I didn't have the cash incentive. But because of my years of living without any cash—and my generally suspicious nature—I never told Callum to stop.

Now I'm eternally grateful for that incentive. There's enough money in my bag to sustain me for months, probably longer.

I shoulder the backpack and then hurry toward Reed's door at the same time Easton emerges into the hall. His dark hair is sticking up in a hundred different directions, but at least he's got pants on now.

"What the fuck is going on?" he demands as he follows me into his older brother's bedroom.

I throw open the doors of Reed's walk in closet, my gaze frantically darting around the large space. I find what I'm looking for on a low shelf in the back.

"Ella?" Easton prompts.

I don't answer him. He frowns as he watches me drag a navy blue suitcase across the cream-colored carpet.

"Ella! Dammit, will you just talk to me?"

The frown turns into wide-eyed gawking when I start throwing stuff into the suitcase. Some T-shirts, Reed's favorite green hoodie, jeans, a couple of tanks. What else would he need . . . um, boxers, socks, a belt—

"Why are you packing Reed's clothes?" Easton is practically shouting at me now, and his sharp tone snaps me out of my panic.

The worn gray T-shirt in my hands falls to the carpet. My heartbeat accelerates as the gravity of the situation hits me again.

"Reed was arrested for killing Brooke," I blurt out. "Your dad's at the police station with him."

Easton's jaw drops. "What the hell?" he exclaims. And then, "The cops came when we were at dinner?"

"No, after we got back from D.C."

Everyone minus Reed had gone to D.C. for dinner earlier. That's how the Royals roll. They're so loaded that Callum has multiple private planes at his disposal. It probably helps that he owns a company that designs airplanes, but it's still ridiculously surreal. The fact that we took a plane from North Carolina to D.C. tonight—to go for *dinner*—is crazy-rich. Reed stayed behind because his side hurt.

He'd been stabbed at the docks the other night and claimed that his pain meds made him too woozy to go with us.

But he hadn't been too woozy to go see Brooke . . .

God. What had he *done* tonight?

"It happened about ten minutes ago," I add weakly. "Didn't you hear your dad screaming at the detective?"

"I didn't hear a goddamn thing. I . . . ah . . ." Shame flickers in his blue eyes. "I kinda pounded a mickey of vodka when I was at Wade's tonight. Came home and crashed right afterward."

I don't even have the energy to lecture him about his drinking. Easton's addiction issues are serious, but Reed's *murder* issues are a million times more urgent at the moment.

I curl my fingers into a fist. If Reed were here right now, I'd punch him—both for lying to me and for getting hauled away by the police.

Easton finally breaks the stunned silence. "Do you think he did it?"

"No." But as confident as I sound, inwardly I'm shaken up.

When I got back from dinner, I saw that Reed's stitches were pulled and he had blood on his stomach. I keep those incriminating tidbits from Easton, though. I trust him, but he's hardly ever sober. I need to protect Reed first and foremost, and who knows what might come out of Easton's mouth when he's drunk or high.

Swallowing hard, I refocus on that task—protecting Reed. I hurriedly toss a few more items of clothing into the suitcase and zip it up.

"You haven't told me why you're packing," Easton says in frustration.

"In case we need to run."

"We?"

"Me and Reed." I bolt to my feet and race over to Reed's dresser to raid his sock drawer. "I want to be prepared just in case, okay?"

That's the one thing I excel at—being prepared to run. I don't know if it'll come down to that. Maybe Reed and Callum will stroll through the front doors and announce, *All fixed! Charges were dropped!* Maybe Reed will be denied bail or bond or whatever the hell it's called, and won't come home at all.

But in the event that neither of those things happen, I want to be ready to skip town in a heartbeat. My backpack is always stocked with everything I need, but Reed's not a planner like I am. He's impulsive. Doesn't always think before he acts—

Before he kills?

I shove the horrible thought aside. No. Reed couldn't have done what they're accusing him of.

"What are you guys yelling about?" a sleepy voice comes from Reed's doorway. "We can hear you all the way down the hall."

The sixteen-year-old Royal twins step into the room. Each one is wearing a blanket around his waist. Does no one in this family believe in pajamas?

"Reed offed Brooke," Easton tells his brothers.

"Easton!" I say in outrage.

"What? I'm not supposed to tell my brothers that our other brother just got arrested for murder?"

Sawyer and Sebastian both hiss out a breath.

"Are you serious?" Sawyer demands.

"The cops just took him away," I whisper.

Easton looks a bit queasy. "And I'm just saying, they wouldn't have done that if they didn't have some kind of evidence against him. Maybe it's about the . . ." He draws a circle in front of his stomach.

The twins blink in bewilderment.

"What? The baby?" Seb asks. "Why would Reed care about Brooke's demon spawn?"

Crap. I forgot that the twins weren't in the loop. They know that Brooke was pregnant—we were all there for that horrible announcement—but they're in the dark about Brooke's other claim.

"Brooke was threatening to say that Reed was the father of the kid," I admit.

Two sets of identical blue eyes widen.

"He wasn't," I say firmly. "He only slept with her a couple times, and that was more than six months ago. She wasn't that far along."

"Whatever." Seb shrugs. "So you're saying Reed knocked up Dad's child bride and then offed her because he doesn't want to have a little Reed running around?"

"It wasn't his!" I yell.

"Then it's really Dad's?" Sawyer says slowly.

I hesitate. "I don't think so."

"Why not?"

"Because . . ."

Ugh. The secrets in this house could fill half the ocean. But I'm done with holding any of them back. It hasn't done us any good.

"He had a vasectomy."

Seb narrows his eyes. "Dad told you this?"

I nod. "He said he did it after you guys were born because your mom wanted more kids and couldn't have them because of some medical condition."

The twins look at each other again, communicating silently.

Easton rubs his chin. "Mom always wanted a girl. She talked about it a lot, said a girl would've softened us up." His lips twitch. "But I don't think girls make me soft in any way."

Frustration jams in my throat. Of course Easton's going somewhere sexual. He always does.

Sawyer smothers a laugh behind his hand while Seb grins openly. "So let's assume that Reed and Dad are both telling the truth—who's the baby daddy, then?"

"Maybe there isn't one?" Easton suggests.

"There has to be," I say. Both Reed and Callum never doubted Brooke's pregnancy claim, so it had to be true.

"Not necessarily," Easton counters. "She could've been lying. Maybe her plan was to fake a miscarriage after Dad married her."

"Sick, but possible." Seb is nodding, clearly on board with this idea.

"Why don't you think Reed killed her?" Easton asks me, his blue eyes flickering with curiosity.

"Why do you believe he's capable of that?" I shoot back.

He shrugs and looks at the twins instead of me. "If she was threatening the family, maybe he is. Maybe they got into an argument and there was an accident. There're lots of explanations."

The sick feeling in my stomach threatens to erupt. The image Easton is casually painting is . . . possible. Reed's stitches were ripped out. He had blood on him. What if he . . .

"No," I choke out. "He didn't do it. And I don't want us to even talk about it anymore. He's innocent. End of story."

"Then why are you getting ready to skip town?"

Easton's quiet question hangs in the bedroom. I swallow a moan of agony and rub my eyes with both hands. He's right. A part of me has already decided that Reed could be guilty. Isn't that why I have his suitcase and my backpack all ready to go?

The silence drags on, until it's finally broken by the unmistakable sound of footsteps somewhere below us. Since the Royals don't have live-in staff, the boys instantly tense up at the signs of life downstairs.

"Was that the front door?" Seb asks.

"Are they back?" Sawyer demands.

I bite my lip. "No, that wasn't the front door. That was . . ." My throat closes up again. God. I forgot about Steve. How could I forget about him, dammit?

"That was what?" Easton pushes.

"Steve," I confess.

They all stare at me.

"Steve's downstairs. He showed up at the door just as Reed was taken away."

"Steve," Easton echoes, slightly dazed. "Uncle Steve?"

Sebastian makes a croaky sound. "*Dead* Uncle Steve?"

I grit my teeth. "He's not dead. He looks like Tom Hanks from *Cast Away*, though. Minus the volleyball."

"Holy shit."

When Easton starts for the door, I grab his wrist and try to haul him back. I don't have the strength for that, but the contact gives him pause.

He tilts his head to study me for a second. "You don't want to go down there and talk to him? This is your *dad*, Ella."

My panic returns in full force. "No. He's just a guy who knocked up my mom. I can't deal with him right now. I . . ." I gulp again. "I don't think he realizes I'm his daughter."

"You didn't tell him?" Sawyer exclaims.

I slowly shake my head. "Can one of you go downstairs and . . . I don't know . . . take him to a guest room or something?"

"I'll do it," Seb instantly replies.

"I'm coming with you," his brother pipes up. "I've gotta see this."

As the twins race for the door, I quickly call out to them. "Guys, don't say anything about me. Seriously, I'm not ready for that. Let's wait until Callum gets home."

The twins exchange another one of those glances where a whole conversation takes place in a second.

"Sure," says Seb, and then they're gone, galloping down the stairs to greet their not-dead uncle.

Easton steps closer to me. His gaze lands on the suitcase near the closet, then locks onto my face. In a heartbeat, he grabs my hand and laces his fingers through mine. "You're not running, little sis. You have to know it's a stupid idea."

I stare at our entwined fingers. "I'm a runner, East."

"No. You're a fighter."

"I can fight for other people. Like my mom or Reed or you, but . . . I'm not good with conflict at my door." I chew harder on my bottom lip. "Why is Steve here? He's supposed to be *dead*. And how could they arrest Reed?" My voice trembles wildly. "What if he actually goes to jail for this?"

"He won't." His hand tightens on mine. "Reed's going to be back, Ella. Dad will take care of everything."

"What if he can't?"

"He will."

But what if he can't?

About the Authors

PHOTO BY AMANDA NICOLE WHITE

PHOTO BY TIME OUT LLC

A *New York Times*, *USA Today*, and *Wall Street Journal* bestselling author, ELLE KENNEDY grew up in the suburbs of Toronto, Ontario, and holds a BA in English from York University. She is the author of more than forty titles of contemporary romance and romantic suspense, including the international bestselling Off-Campus series.

JEN FREDERICK is a Korean adoptee living in the Midwest with her husband, daughter, and rambunctious dog. Under the pseudonym Erin Watt, Frederick has cowritten two #1 *New York Times* bestselling novels.